...geme.

LISA HALL

...ged but engaging central character, sharp dialogue, tw...ty p
...pay-off – *The Syndicate* has all the ingredients of an excellent thri...e.

SIMON BRETT

'*The Syndicate* is a gripping story that builds to a stunning conclusion.
Kavanagh is a complex and original creation; a man haunted by his past and
living on borrowed time'

HOWARD LINSKEY

'Captivating, cleverly written, unputdownable. I devoured *The Syndicate* in
one night. Minett and crime at its finest'

REBECCA THORNTON

'I raced through this book. A beautifully written, character-focused novel that
reminded me of George Pelecanos at his best. Definitely one of my reads of
the year so far'

DAVID JACKSON

'Pacey, heart-stopping and poignant'

JULIE CORBIN

'This is G.J. Minett's best yet. Absorbing, nuanced and emotive. A superior
thriller with a real sucker punch of a twist'

CHRIS WHITAKER

'With Kavanagh, Minett has created the ultimate hero – dark, dangerous, but with
a depth of heart. *The Syndicate* is a truly sinuous suspense that when you think
you've got it worked out, has a resolution that snaps back and bites. More please'

KATE BRADLEY

'That rare type of novel that manages to be subtle, compassionate and with a
real moral heart, but at the same time packed with enough twists and turns
to the point you can't put it down. A really entertaining read, but made
exceptional by the emotional punch it carries'

ROD REYNOLDS

'A compelling, intricately plotted novel peopled with fascinating characters,
particularly the brilliantly drawn Jon Kavanagh, in whose outcome I was
completely invested throughout. The writing is superb, the story intriguing
and what an ending. Wow!'

GILL THOMPSON

'A master of language and character, *The Syndicate* is dark and treacherous
with a real sting in its tail'

'Wha...   ...rprises, this
particul...   ...usly satisfying.

G.J. Minett studied at Cambridge and then spent many years as a teacher of foreign languages. He studied for an MA in Creative Writing at the University of Chichester, and won the 2010 Chapter One Prize for unpublished novels with the opening chapter of *The Hidden Legacy*.

Also by G.J. Minett

The Hidden Legacy
Lie In Wait
Anything For Her

THE
SYNDICATE

G.J. MINETT

ZAFFRE

First published in Great Britain in 2020 by
ZAFFRE
80–81 Wimpole St, London W1G 9RE

A CIP catalogue record for this book is
available from the British Library.

ISBN: 978-1-78576-536-0

Also available as an ebook

1 3 5 7 9 10 8 6 4 2

Typeset by IDSUK (Data Connection) Ltd
Printed and bound in Great Britain by Clays Ltd, Elcograf S.p.A.

Zaffre is an imprint of Bonnier Books UK
www.bonnierbooks.co.uk

For Gemma, Alex and Leah
Constant source of pride

Prologue

6th July 2018
Praia D'El Rey, Portugal

There's a moment during the seemingly interminable mono-logue coming his way when Kavanagh simply tunes out. Gives up. Wishes this could just be over and done with. He allows the smug, self-satisfied voice to wash over him, finds himself focus-ing instead on the digital clock on the unit against the far wall. He squints, struggling to make out the digits. From here it looks like 21.43 and in a moment of weakness he wonders whether he'll get to see them click over to ten o'clock. It doesn't seem likely somehow . . . not the way things are going. The expression *living on borrowed time* was made for moments such as this.

Not so long ago he was standing at the window, watching the sun slide beneath the waves, a red glow bleeding out across the water as it sliced through the horizon. It did occur to him at the time that this might well be the last chance he'd have to do some-thing like this. There was a momentary surge of regret, a reawak-ening of his old defiant instincts urging him to run – find a way to survive for as long as those tiny fragments of shrapnel in his frontal lobe might permit. It was no more than a reflex though, the shadow of a fighter's mentality. He's looked at this mess from every conceivable angle and all roads seem to lead here. To this moment. His only shot at redemption.

He's no stranger to the prospect of death. Years ago, in what feels like another lifetime, it was a constant companion, squatting on his shoulder, forever whispering in his ear. He's speculated often enough as to what guise it might take when his own time comes around. An IED maybe, at the end of a hot, dusty patrol as concentration levels go down with the sun. A sniper's bullet from a ruined building. Maybe a double tap to the back of the head in an Irish wood or some dark London basement. The last place his imagination would have come up with was a rented villa on a Portuguese golf resort. Under different circumstances he might even find a touch of dark humour in this. He's never played a round of golf in his life. What was it Mark Twain had said – waste of a good walk?

They say it's the hope that kills you . . . and even though he suspects he's about to prove just how figurative a statement that is, right now he gets it. He really does. There *was* hope – there *was* a potential way through this impasse as long as both sides were prepared to put longstanding grievances and egos to one side and focus on essentials. Now it feels more like wishful thinking, embarrassingly naïve. Petty vindictiveness is just too powerful a force to resist. He's been hoping for reconciliation but the two men opposite him have only ever had one outcome in mind and don't understand the meaning of compromise.

Another thing they say: *You don't hear the bullet with your name on it.*

He's never been sure how anyone can possibly know something like that.

He suspects he's about to find out.

1

March 1999
Weybridge

It doesn't take much to throw a person's life out of kilter. If the slightest twitch of a butterfly's wings in New Mexico can cause a hurricane in China, there's no telling what havoc might be wrought by something as violent as a cough on a cold March night in Weybridge.

Or even a simple sneeze.

Kavanagh had just opened the door which gave onto the hallway when he heard it – an indeterminate noise, half yelp, half squeak. It might easily have been dismissed as the sort of background noise to be expected in an old house, nothing more threatening than a gurgling radiator or floorboards bedding in for the night. But his senses were on heightened alert and if he needed confirmation that he was not alone in the building, it wasn't long in coming. Three soft bumps. No way he'd imagined those.

He ducked swiftly and silently back into the lounge, casting a quick glance over his shoulder. Even as he did so, he knew this went against all prevailing logic. *Funny the tricks the mind can play,* he thought. In the long list of things dead men don't do, sneezing is right up there, and he was pretty sure Leon Murphy was not about to defy the laws of nature . . . or do anything else for that matter. He was precisely where he'd left him moments earlier, slumped over the desk, droplets of blood slipping from his earlobe and soaking into the rectangular green blotter which was rapidly losing its original colour. One arm was dangling at his side, his fingers somehow still clinging on to the small unregistered handgun that Kavanagh had placed there post-mortem, more in hope than realistic expectation. It wasn't going to fool any pathology team worth its salt but that wasn't the point – anything that might wrongfoot the authorities and mislead them into thinking they were dealing with a rank amateur was always worth a shot.

So – if the source of the disturbance wasn't Leon Murphy . . .

Kavanagh rested his head against the door frame and listened, heart rate steady, mind sifting through the possibilities. This, he told himself, was what Maurice would euphemistically refer to as *a major snafu*. He was not going to be happy when he heard about it. Murphy had supposedly been under surveillance and nothing in the feedback suggested that tonight would be any-thing other than a slam dunk – in and out. Murphy was a loner by all accounts, wife and kid long out of the picture – Dunedin, the last anyone had heard. No meaningful other in his life since they'd left and nothing to suggest he was the sort to go out and bring someone back for the night. In short, there was no way anyone else should be there at that late hour, sneezing or other-wise. Someone was going to have a lot of explaining to do later.

First things first, though.

He risked the quickest of glances around the door frame. Nothing. His best guess, not one he'd want to stake his life on, was that the noise had come from upstairs and already a tiny, recusant voice was whispering in his ear, telling him to play the percentages, get the hell out of there. Just slide open the patio door and leave the way he'd come in. Job done. Home free. But he knew he couldn't listen to it. If there was someone else in the house who might later be able to identify him, he needed to know . . . and the thought sickened him.

Fear had no part to play in this. He knew fear intimately – had faced it down several times in the past. Fear was patrolling the Bogside. Fear was clearing a suspected sniper post. He'd proved himself over and over, trained himself to accept that churning sensation in his gut as a positive, as clear an indication as you can get that you're thinking straight, because anyone who goes into situations of that sort with no realistic appreciation of the risks involved is living on borrowed time. You give yourself the best possible chance by embracing it, using it to your own advantage and allowing your survival instincts and basic training to kick in and do the rest.

No, this wasn't fear. His reluctance owed more to regret than anything else. It had its roots in the knowledge that if there was someone else in the house, the victim count for the night wasn't going to stop at one. One he could handle – it's why he was there in the first place. He knew what he was buying into and had no qualms about Murphy. From what Maurice and Vic had told him, the life he led was only ever going to end one way and the world was already a better place than it had been a few minutes ago. But anything else came under a different heading, that of collateral damage, and that was a different beast altogether. That, as he knew from personal experience, was literally the stuff of nightmares.

He'd heard nothing since those initial three bumps, so he risked another quick look. Satisfied that no one was directly on the other side of the door, he crept stealthily over to the desk and retrieved the gun from Murphy's hand. Then he wrapped himself round the partially opened door and eased his way into the hallway, hugging the wall opposite. The three bumps, his instincts were telling him, had definitely come from the staircase at the end of the corridor which disappeared out of sight behind the wall on its way up to the first floor. From his present position, he could see only the bottom two steps, but that was enough to make his heart sink . . . because on the penultimate one was a child's plastic drinking cup with a screw top, lying on its side. He tilted his head to get a better view of the picture emblazoned on it. It looked like a purple dinosaur as far as he could make out, and some sort of coloured liquid was dripping from the lid and soaking into the stair carpet.

He moved forward, slinking his way along the wall, using it to shield him from view and hoping to God it was anything but a child hovering at the top of the stairs. There was nothing worse for muddying the waters. A child usually meant a mother or nanny wouldn't be far away and there was a clear, agreed protocol in situations such as this that Maurice and Vic would expect him to follow.

No witnesses, no matter who they might be.

At the end of the corridor, he took a deep breath, gave a silent count of three and risked the briefest of checks around the wall before jerking his head back out of any possible line of fire. Another short count, then he reached out, grabbed the plastic drinking cup and threw it up the stairs. He was already back behind the wall before he heard it hit the stair gate and start rolling back down again. No other sound though, which meant one of two things. Best case scenario: whoever was lurking up there was unarmed and not in any position to respond. Worst case: that *someone* was no rookie.

Or maybe a third possibility?

He thought again about the cup on the stairs. The stair gate. Risked a second quick look.

Still no one there . . . as far as he could see.

Easing his way out from behind the wall, he crouched at the foot of the stairs, both arms outstretched, weapon swinging in an arc, right to left and back again, ready to respond to the slightest sign of movement. This was almost home territory, but he was aware of the dangers inherent in that word *almost*. It was one thing to enter situations such as this in protective clothing and helmet, with an SA80 at the ready and professional back-up primed to cover all the angles. Here he was on his own – and the small handgun with its suppressor, however handy for discreet work up close, now felt inadequate somehow.

He started to climb the stairs, as light on his feet as possible, grateful for the carpet to muffle the squeak of any loose boards. He was no more than a third of the way up when he heard a door creak and then the unmistakable pitter-patter of tiny feet making their way across the landing, heading towards him. Seconds later a small figure appeared at the stair gate, barefoot in a pink nightdress. She was up on tiptoe to peer over the barrier, gazing down either at him, as he continued to crouch on the stairs, or the drinking cup lying there next to him. He wasn't very good with children's ages but placed her at two, maybe three years old, no more than that. Far too young to be fazed by his presence or the gun which he'd instinctively trained on her. One hand went to her eyes and started rubbing the sleep from them, the other clung on to a large cuddly toy. It looked like the same purple dinosaur as the one on the drinking cup.

He climbed a few more stairs, bringing more and more of the landing into view – the girl remained the only visible presence. She watched him for a moment, then without saying a word she took the toy in both hands, lifted it above the top bar of the gate and dropped it onto the stairs. It bounced twice and came to rest against his feet.

Focus, he reminded himself, because he was now aware of another distraction, an image swimming into view . . . another girl, a little older than this one maybe, standing at a bedroom window, waving down to him as he stepped into the moonlight in their back yard in Spencer Street. Their home in Bristol – a lifetime ago. The same sleepy expression, face pressed up against the glass.

Katy.

In her hand a battered old teddy bear which had been his for a while until a burgeoning sense of street cred had got the better of him.

He shook his head, then stooped and picked up the dinosaur and drinking mug. At the top of the stairs he handed both to this other girl, stepping over the gate rather than opening it, his eyes still making sure his initial assessment was correct – no one was lurking on the landing.

The girl toddled off towards the only room with an open door, which automatically made that the first on his checklist. In the dimmed light from a bedside lamp, he could make out an unmade bed. Picture books dotted around the floor. Lots of open spaces – nowhere for anyone to hide. The gap under the bed was too small even for the girl herself to wriggle underneath. He pushed the door flat against the wall to make sure no one was behind it, then slipped inside the room. No one here. Just the girl, sitting on the bed. Watching him.

He checked the other three rooms upstairs, the girl following him onto the landing, silent and curious but apparently unconcerned. Finally satisfied that no one was there, he stepped back over the stair gate and made a point of searching the downstairs rooms for a second time, even the lounge where Murphy was as motionless as before. He told himself he was being professional but knew his real purpose was to delay the inevitable. At some point he was going to have to focus on the problem presented by a two-year-old girl in a pink nightdress.

He knew what was expected of him. It had been drummed into him at every opportunity by Vic, who never knew the glass to be anything other than half empty and had a dark, cautionary tale for every deviation from the party line. His take on a situation like this was unambiguous. *No witnesses. You play the percentages*. He wouldn't waste a second calculating the likelihood of a girl this small being able to identify anyone. *Is it lower than zero? No . . . so clear the decks and get out.*

But Spencer Street drifted back to him. Katy at the window, reaching out across the years of grief and self-recrimination. Waving and turning slowly away, heading back to the bottom rung of the bunk bed they'd shared. Probably tucking into the Maltesers before her head even hit the pillow. The past was calling, tugging at his shirt collar . . . and he knew instinctively he couldn't go through with this.

Vic wouldn't like it. He'd be spitting bullets, squeezing every last drop of emotional capital out of such an irrefutable dereliction of duty. He'd be in Maurice's ear for weeks to come, hissing I-told-you-sos and offering insidious reminders about the absurdity of placing quite so much trust in the hands of a novice, an outsider whose every instinct was not steeped in the ways of the Syndicate. *Too much, too soon. Accident waiting to happen.*

He wasn't the problem, though. Vic he could handle. Maurice on the other hand ... that was a different prospect altogether. Disappointing Maurice would hurt. He was a rock, a fixed point of reference for every decision Kavanagh had taken since he first came to London. He'd found in him the father figure the army had failed to provide – someone who had faith in him, trusted him to do the right thing. Maurice provided a moral compass on permanent call while Kavanagh worked on developing one of his own, and he would have trusted him with his life if it came to it. In eight years he couldn't remember a single occasion when he'd strayed from clearly defined protocols and allowed his own conscience to dictate his actions. If Maurice said it was OK, who was he to argue?

But this? This felt wrong ... simple as that.

He made his way back upstairs. The girl was sitting on the landing outside her room, so he scooped her up in one arm and carried her inside. He smiled to try to get some sort of response from her, but she just stared back at him sleepily. At least she didn't flinch, which was what he'd come to expect from anyone seeing the scar for the first time. Instead she gazed vacantly at it, looking for one moment as if she was going to reach out and touch it. Then she sneezed and the spell was broken.

He laid her head gently on the pillow and pulled the quilt back over her as he knelt beside her, lifting the tangle of curls from her face. Tried not to think about the body downstairs and the impact tonight would have on the rest of her life. He ran his fingers over her eyes, telling her to go to sleep. Then he placed her drinking mug on the bedside table and tiptoed from the room, noticing for the first time the plaque on the door as he pulled it to behind him.

JESSICA.

He checked the house one last time, just to make sure he hadn't missed anything that might be a problem later. Then he took the gun from his pocket and slipped it back into Murphy's hand, resolutely trying to persuade himself as he did so that there was no need for remorse on his part. Murphy had signed his own death warrant. Anyone prepared to wipe out a young family in an arson attack deserved whatever came his way. Any ambivalence he might be feeling was reserved exclusively for the little girl upstairs. He still had no idea why she was there but hopefully she'd be reunited with her mother before long. She had to be better off there . . . anywhere but here.

He picked up a VHS video cassette from the table where he'd left it earlier, looked round for one last time and quietly opened the patio door. As he did so, he heard the same three bumps again on the staircase and paused on the threshold.

And realised he couldn't leave things like this.

He just couldn't.

Stepping back inside, he slid the door back into place.

2

April 2018
Dorset

When the early morning fog comes sweeping in from the Channel over the Dorset coast, it tends to be anything but equivocal. There's no flirtatious chink of sunlight to suggest this will be merely a fleeting visit. Instead it makes its intentions crystal clear from the outset, taking Lulworth Cove and Durdle Door unawares, wrapping the cliff walks in a swirling, shape-shifting, sound-muffling shroud. One minute the air is suffused with birdsong and the less-than-melodious cries from the occasional scavenging gull; the next both are mysteriously absent, as if the choristers have fled the scene or, more likely, been swept up in this rolling blanket and spirited away, leaving only the occasional shout from anxious dog walkers and the eerie sound of invisible waves washing over the shoreline below. Visibility, which on a sunny morning can stretch to several miles in any direction, is reduced to a minimum, familiar landmarks no longer handy reference points but transformed instead into unrecognisable shapes that loom suddenly out of the murk.

If the mist offends by stealing from the senses, it compounds the felony for clifftop walkers by giving free rein to the imagination. Even the most experienced among them begin to doubt themselves. They know to the nearest metre how far each footpath is from the edge – provided they keep the compacted soil and shingle of the well-worn track beneath their boots, they're unlikely to come to any harm. Even so, the swirling mists and general sense of disorientation are enough to persuade the strongest of minds that mysterious forces are at work here. Experienced or not, they find themselves treading more cautiously than usual, doubting themselves, seduced into imagining against all logic that paths have been re-routed and disaster is only an ill-considered step away.

Kavanagh knows this landscape like the back of his hand. He's been running here four or five mornings a week for nearly twenty years, ever since he left London and moved back into his grandparents' cottage just outside Wareham. The routine lends a measure of shape and structure to the start of the day – rise at six, fifteen-minute drive to Lulworth in his ten-year-old runaround, which he invariably leaves in the same lay-by just up from the church. Then he sets out on foot, using these next few minutes to shake any stiffness out of his legs, until he reaches the car park at the entrance to Lulworth Cove, which is almost deserted at this early hour. Here he breaks into a gentle trot, easing himself into what is always an arduous ascent over the cliffs to Durdle Door and beyond. He's been known to run as far as Osmington Mills and back, the best part of thirteen miles of lung-bursting, muscle-bruising effort, taking in a series of climbs and descents which verge on the brutal, but that level of ambition has been tempered lately by a touch of pragmatism. At sixty-three he defers to the ageing process, settling for more appropriate targets.

He's reached the top of a climb that marks his customary turning point and is well into the latter stages of the return journey when he first becomes aware of the change in atmosphere as the mists swarm in from offshore. He's not overly concerned. He's run here in all seasons: blinked through torrential rain that plastered his running vest to his skin within seconds, battled against fierce winds as they revelled in the liberating absence of any features to break up their momentum, shielded his eyes against sunshine glaring enough to make him regret having left his Ray-Bans at the cottage. Admittedly the early starts mean he hasn't often run in the full heat of the day, but he's coped often enough with the opposite extreme. Only a few weeks ago he was skidding down icy slopes that had been rendered even more treacherous than usual by a layer of snow and ice. These mists have never worried him unduly. He's been here often enough to feel his instincts will always stand him in good stead.

So maybe it's a touch of complacency that's his undoing. He's more surprised than alarmed when, halfway down the last of the really challenging descents before reaching Durdle Door once more, his trailing leg catches his front heel on its way through and sends him hurtling into a series of somersaults down the steep, well-worn path. He thrusts his arms out, just too late to break his fall, and rolls head first . . . arms flailing, trying to grab anything which might halt his momentum. He's not inclined to panic – there's a fence and a fair bit of land between himself and the edge of the cliffs. He can even laugh to himself at the absurdity of it all as clumps of grass and vegetation are uprooted by his desperate fingers. Then, just as he thinks it's over, he's flipped into the air and lands on his back, his head taking the worst of the impact.

The next few seconds, as he lies there with his eyes closed, are a confusing swirl of sensations. Later he'll wonder why it took him so long to realise there was a problem but so many messages are clamouring for his attention in these first few moments that the obvious eludes him. *Breathe . . . slowly,* is the first thought to peep through the veil. *Lie still, just for a second or two. Quick inventory . . . head sore, shoulder too. Left hip burning, certainly grazed, maybe cut. Better check it out.*

That's when he decides to open his eyes.

And realises they've been open the whole time.

The walkers who come to check he's OK tell him it can only have been a matter of seconds before their two-year-old Alsatian led them to him. They didn't see him fall because of the poor visibility but they were close enough to hear the commotion. If their estimate is reliable, those must have been the longest few seconds he's ever experienced. Longer even than that afternoon on the outskirts of Dunloughraine, which feels like a lifetime ago now. The border checkpoint. The Toyota pick-up truck slowing for what looked like a routine stop. Then the squealing of tyres and revving of the engine as it suddenly picked up speed, heading directly towards the barriers. Over the years he's met with some success in shutting out the past but every so often it comes creeping back with a sickening inevitability and he's forced to remember, the events replayed in slow motion on his own private screen. A very individualised waterboarding.

It's long been his unspoken belief that if he could survive that, he can survive anything.

Now he has a new yardstick against which to measure that conviction.

A total loss of vision has been a shadow lurking in the background for almost thirty years now – never more than a possibility but there nonetheless. He's always given it what he considers to be due consideration but for those first few seconds after the initial impact, during which he lay there, eyes wide open and absolutely nothing registering, he realised for the first time that he'd never come close to comprehending the enormity of it all. He remembers closing his eyes again, squeezing tight and then reopening them in case some irrational attempt at a reboot might do the trick. Then he tried rubbing them, which is what he was doing when everything gradually began to swim slowly back into focus . . . or at least as much as the mists permitted. The relief that overwhelmed him in that moment was indescribable.

But as he sits here now with his rescuers still fussing over him, he's amazed at just how much the brain can process in such a short space of time. For those first few seconds when he couldn't see anything at all, you'd have thought he had enough to worry about and yet somehow other images managed to elbow their way in, each feeding off its predecessor:

Sean freezing as the truck flashes past.
People scrambling. Screaming.
Maurice at Musgrave Park.
Blood dripping from Leon Murphy's fingers.
The girl at the top of the stairs.
Katy. God . . . Katy.
The girl at the top of the stairs.

All of them in quick succession, crowding him, seeking an audience.

He needs to think. For one thing, these attacks *are* becoming more frequent and that's disconcerting to say the least. *And* there's no getting around the fact that this is the first time since the explosion all those years ago that the loss of vision has been total, however momentary this lapse turned out to be. Until now these sporadic aberrations have taken the form of blurred central vision, sometimes causing straight lines to appear wavy, at others causing words on the page to look as if someone has dragged his thumb across and smudged the text. The peripheral vision, though . . . that's always been unaffected and what's happened just now feels like a worrying escalation, as if stakes are being raised at a table to which he is denied access. He doesn't much care for what that might signify.

He pats the Alsatian on the head, thanks his rescuers and takes great care on his way back to the car park. His head is throbbing and his vision is still a little hazier than he's prepared to admit. The last thing he wants is to put it under any more stress than necessary . . . at least, until he's had a chance to arrange another appointment with his specialist. And above all else, he needs time and a quiet room to make sense of the chain of thoughts that came flooding in as he lay on the ground.

It's difficult to escape the feeling that the events of the past are calling out to him, demanding to be heard.

And he's not sure he has it in him to resist them.

3

1990
Royal Army Medical Corps Unit
Recovery Ward
Musgrave Park Hospital, Belfast

When the visitor first arrived, Kavanagh was lying on top of the sheets in a raised position, dressing gown wrapped loosely around him, head and shoulders supported by enough pillows for three patients.

Wishing the hours away.

He listened as the footsteps approached, picked up on a momentary hesitation followed by the scraping of a chair as it was pulled up alongside his bed. He turned his head slightly towards the sound to make it clear he was awake.

There was a thud as something substantial was deposited on the bedside cabinet. Then came a deep sigh, the product of aching limbs and a tired mind, as the visitor took his seat.

'Corporal Kavanagh, I presume?'

'Sir.'

'Jon, right? Mind if I call you that?'

'No, sir. That's fine.'

'Not disturbing you, I hope?'

'No, sir. I've been awake for a while.'

'That's good.'

He listened as the visitor shifted around in his seat, removing an outer garment by the sound of it.

'Know who I am, son?'

'Yes, sir,' he confirmed, using the voice to build a mental picture of the man from behind the bandages. Deep, gruff, the clipped sentences conveying an aversion to wasted words. Kavanagh was surprised by the Scottish accent hovering near the surface – Sean's had been as South London as Peckham. 'Colonel Holman said to expect you sometime this afternoon.'

'A favour, son . . . before we go any further?'

'Sir?'

'You think mebbe, given it's just the two of us, you could give all the sir business a rest? I had more than my fill of the military when I did my National Service. To be honest, it sticks in the craw just a tad. What say we pretend we're normal members of society, eh . . . for a few minutes or so?'

'I'll try to remember, sir.'

'Maurice.'

'Yes, sir.'

Maurice gave a low chuckle as if remembering from his own experience just how tight a grip the ingrained habit can exert.

'How are you feeling . . . if that's not a stupid question?'

'I'm fine.'

'And if you were to skip the bravado and give an honest answer?'

Kavanagh took a deep breath. He was, in fact, far from fine. Hopelessly conflicted would be more accurate – desperate to have the bandages removed and to be given the answers to questions that had been shredding his nerves for the past forty-eight hours, but only as long as they were the right ones.

He wasn't sure though how his own concerns stacked up against those of a father whose son had just been blown to bits – decided they were almost certainly some way down the pecking order. He scrambled around for a neutral reply that wouldn't sound insensitive.

'I'll be glad when they've taken the bandages off,' he managed eventually.

'Too right. They given you any idea yet as to when that might be?'

'Tomorrow, maybe the day after. They keep pushing it back, which is a bit—'

He broke off, struggling for an adjective which might apply here.

'Have your family been able to visit you at all?'

'My grandparents fly out tomorrow.'

'And do they have far to come?'

'They live near Wareham. In Dorset. They've booked a B&B for a couple of days.'

'That's good – times like this, you need family around you.'

Nanna Belle had been in touch the day before to say they'd both be travelling. He'd urged them to stay where they were, promised them he was fine. He was sure his grandfather wasn't fit enough to make the journey and Nanna Belle herself was no spring chicken – he knew she was due for a hip operation in a month or so. She'd insisted nonetheless and deep down he had to admit to a touch of relief that there would be someone there to support him through the next few days. If anyone ever embodied down-to-earth common sense and positivity, it was his grandparents.

He wondered what Maurice made of the absence of any reference to his parents – braced himself for the usual follow-up. Seeking a possible diversion he remembered the item Maurice had presumably placed on the bedside cabinet. He groped for it, exploring the package with his fingers before removing what felt like a hefty paperback.

'They tell me you like your books. I thought . . .'

There was a brief pause.

'No idea what your reading preferences are, so I took a punt on this – it's my old copy of *A Scots Quair*. You ever heard of Lewis Grassic Gibbon, son?'

'No, sir.'

'Well, that's something you should put right as soon as possible. What are you, early thirties?'

'Thirty-five.'

'I must've been about your age when I first read this. You'll have to let me know what you think of it.'

'I will. Thank you, sir.'

'Maurice.'

'Thank you . . . Maurice.'

Head back on the pillow, he flicked through the pages and felt the weight to get a sense of the size of the book. Its spine was intact although the cover itself felt creased. The smell brought back memories of Saturday morning trips to the library with Nanna Belle, leaving with a bagful of novels – Buchan, Rider Haggard, Stevenson, Dickens. They'd filled the empty hours, offering a welcome distraction from the oppressive sense of loss that had dominated his childhood and early teenage years. Through them, his eyes had been opened to a world of possibilities and adventure beyond rural Dorset.

'Should last you a wee while at any rate,' said Maurice. 'Let's hope it's tomorrow they whip those bandages off, eh?'

He took the book from Kavanagh's hands and there was the same clunk as he replaced it on the bedside cabinet.

'I'll be thinking of you. I'd offer to say a prayer on your behalf, but you might nae welcome that, given my track record of late.'

There was an awkward silence as each sought a way to steer the conversation into less troubled waters. Kavanagh wondered whether Maurice was a religious man and, if so, whether his faith in the power of prayer had been fatally undermined by recent events, crippled below decks. He wasn't sure any belief system could survive what this man must be going through.

'Look,' said Maurice, as if reverse paddling. 'I've no wish to take up too much of your time. You've probably been told why I'm here and, if not, then I'm sure you'll have guessed.'

'I was told you wanted to talk about Sean, sir.'

'Aye . . . I do. But I also wanted to thank you first of all – for what you did for him. Tried to do.'

A trolley trundled past the door and a couple of nurses exchanged greetings as they passed in the corridor, one of them breaking into an uncontrollable fit of giggles. The green shoots of normality.

'There's really no need, sir.'

'On the contrary. Colonel Holman tells me you acted with a bravery and compassion that . . . *went well beyond the call of duty*, is how I think he put it.'

Kavanagh hung his head.

'I don't remember much about it, to tell the honest truth.'

Which was in fact anything but. He remembered enough to know it had been a total bloody shambles. The events of that afternoon, some of them at least, were branded on the inside of his eyelids with a frightening intensity that wouldn't allow him to sleep in anything more than snatches and caused him to scream himself awake. He'd been assured this was perfectly normal and would fade over time. Even so, he felt instinctively this was not something to share with Sean's father.

'Your modesty does you credit. Do you mind if I ask ... how well did you know Sean?'

'Well enough, sir – as well as I knew anyone in my section, that is. He was respected and liked by everyone.'

Even now the past tense took some adjusting to. The lie, he suspected, would take even longer. It felt as if with every sentence he was closing another door between this man and his son.

'Would you describe yourself as a friend of his?'

'That would have been difficult under the circumstances,' said Kavanagh, trying to disguise the hesitation. 'I mean, I was older than him and then there was the difference in rank – you'll know how that works. But I spent enough time around Sean to sense I could trust him. He was a good man.'

'Boy.' Maurice was on it like a flash, almost as if he'd been searching for the opening.

'Sir?'

'Let's be accurate about this, shall we? He was a good boy. It would be nice to think he had the potential to develop into something ... something more than mere cannon fodder,' he added after a momentary pause. 'But I guess we'll never get to find out for sure, will we?'

There was an awkward silence again, the conversation seemingly littered with them. Kavanagh wondered whether some entirely fabricated suggestion of Sean's bravery under fire might help them move past this, but Maurice didn't strike him as someone to be soft-soaped that easily.

'I'm sorry for your loss, sir.'

'Aye. Aren't we all, son – aren't we all?'

Kavanagh felt acutely aware of the vulnerability of his present position. Unable to see Maurice's features or pick up on any other visual clues, he was forced to rely on instinct to gauge the man's reaction to every twist and turn in the conversation. The world of nuance was closed off to him for now.

'You know he only joined the army to teach me a lesson?' said Maurice eventually. It came across as a digression of sorts.

'I don't think it ever came up in conversation.'

'Aye, he did, right enough. Wanted to prove a point, although God knows what that might have been. He was meant to come and work for me in London once he'd finished school. I was happy for him to have a crack at university if he fancied it – Law or Business, something that might have come in handy, you know? Transferable skills they call it, right? But he decided he wanted to take a couple of years out to travel – *find himself* was the term he used, whatever that's supposed to mean. Seems to be all the rage these days – everyone wants to go halfway round the world to find out what exactly? That they're the same numpty who left in the first place?'

There was a slight tremor in his voice, the first indication that he was in anything short of total control of his emotions.

'Anyway, I kicked against it, like he must have known I would, but the apple did nae fall far from the tree with that lad. If I'd agreed to back him, he'd never have seen it through. He'd have been phoning me from Bangkok before the month was out, asking for money for the flight home, ready to start work on Monday morning.

'But no ... I had to dig my heels in, didn't I? Told him there was no way he was prolonging his adolescence at my expense – I was doing National Service at his age. If he wanted to go on some trek to the back of beyond, good luck to him but he'd be stumping up for it himself. Next thing I know he's only made an appointment at the recruiting office without telling me or his mother. Just about broke her heart, him signing his life away like that. Literally, the daft wee ...'

Kavanagh nodded, recalling his own decision years earlier to enlist and the way his grandparents had responded on hearing the news. Both had made their thoughts crystal clear without saying a word. Nanna Belle had continued peeling potatoes in the kitchen sink, pausing every now and then to blow her nose. Grampy Joe had shaken his head and spent the rest of the evening in his shed.

He waited for Maurice to continue. When he did so, it was with another sigh, the product of an unforgiving world and lessons not learnt.

'I'm sorry – I did nae come here to embarrass you,' he said, suddenly less reflective, as if mentally rolling up his shirt sleeves. 'Like I said, I just wanted to thank you in person for putting your own life at risk in trying to save him. He'd have wanted me to do that much for him.'

'If our roles had been reversed, I'm sure he'd have done the same for me, sir.'

'Aye – it would be nice to think so.'

The regret in his voice was unmistakable but it was alloyed with a touch of something else – scepticism maybe? Kavanagh wished again that he could see this man, take his true measure. If he had doubts about his own son in circumstances such as these, it suggested a great many things but above all else it demonstrated that he was no fool. When all was said and done, he knew Sean Hayes.

'Listen,' Maurice continued, leaning far enough forward for Kavanagh to catch a whiff of cheese and onion on his breath. 'The reason I made this journey . . . I have to ask you something . . . before I head off. I've no wish to make things any worse for you, but there's something that keeps eating away at me and I need to do something about it.'

Wary all of a sudden, Kavanagh wondered where this was going. It felt during the ensuing pause as if Maurice was looking around to make sure they couldn't be overheard. When he spoke again, his voice was not much above a whisper.

'Your Colonel Holman says that investigations are still underway and there are things he won't be allowed to divulge for operational and tactical reasons, blah blah blah.'

'Yes, sir.'

'Well, I know military blether when I hear it. I'm not exactly wet behind the ears, nor am I without a modicum of influence myself. I made a few calls before I came out here and I think I have a serviceable notion of what went down. Correct me if I'm wrong but, as I understand it, some poor soul was grabbed off the street and told he was a dead man walking anyway but could still save his wife and children if he did exactly as he was told. Best guess is they strapped him in a vest packed with explosives and ordered him to drive straight at the checkpoint barrier. I've picked up that much but even that was more than he was prepared to confirm.'

Kavanagh thought carefully before offering a considered response. 'That's not so surprising, sir. These things are delicate – they're always kept strictly under wraps while the investigation is ongoing.'

'I understand the need for discretion, son. I don't have a problem with the concept of need to know, just their assessment of who should make the list. It seems to me any parent who's lost his son in the line of duty has as much right as anyone to be included . . . if not more. All he's prepared to tell me about Sean's last moments is that he was on guard at the barrier, the first line of defence, and that was where the blast would have been at its most destructive. Tells me he was killed outright, along with the other lad standing there. Wouldn't have felt a thing.'

He paused. Kavanagh waited him out.

'And you know what? That's not good enough,' he continued, a touch of anger creeping into his voice for the first time. 'I deserve better than that. This is my boy we're talking about. If I could nae be with him when he died, the least I'm entitled to is an accurate account of how it came about and what he went through, not some diluted version of events they've cooked up to make things as easy for me as possible. Send the poor old fossil on his way with something he can live with, eh? You think that's any way to treat a man who's lost his eldest son?'

No, Kavanagh thought to himself. *No – I do not.*

'That version of events – you think it makes any sort of sense?'

'I'm not with you, sir,' he said, hating himself.

'Oh, I suspect you are, son. I don't mean to be disrespectful, but you don't strike me as some sort of dimwit and my guess is you know exactly where I'm going with this. You see, I found myself thinking, a truck hits a barrier with Sean standing next to it and the bomb goes off . . . Sean's gone, right? History. So the obvious question I've been asking myself is this – what exactly is there for you to rescue? I mean, everyone who's ever put on a uniform knows a bomb that size is going to wipe out anyone in the vicinity. Yet in the same breath they're telling me you came racing across and were seriously wounded, trying to get Sean to safety.'

Another pause, during which it felt as if he was being invited to respond . . . an invitation he couldn't bring himself to accept.

'So that begs the question,' continued Maurice. 'Safety from what exactly? From a blast that had already blown him to smithereens?'

He pressed on, his mouth now against Kavanagh's ear, voice almost a hiss.

'What exactly was there for you to rescue, eh?'

Kavanagh shifted his weight in the bed and turned onto his side, plumping up the pillow. He felt very exposed all of a sudden, hating the position in which he'd been placed. These questions should have been dealt with at a higher level, not left festering in the mind of a grieving father who had clearly been seriously underestimated. This mess was not of his making, yet guess who was picking up the tab?

'*And*,' continued Maurice, 'how were you managing to do this when you yourself were presumably a victim of the same blast, carrying around half a ton of shrapnel in your head from what I can gather? A blast which, forgive me for mentioning it, had also taken your sight from you – temporarily at least, let's hope to God.'

'I'm sorry, sir,' he mumbled, gripping the edge of the bed with both hands and squeezing the hell out of it. 'I wish I could help you but, as I said earlier, I don't remember much of anything, either before or after the explosion.'

'Yes . . . a point your Colonel Holman was keen to emphasise several times before he let me see you. A bit of a mystery, isn't it? We had a few of those when I was doing my National Service and you know what? Nine times out of ten they came down to some snafu or other, left hand not sure what the right hand is doing, garbled versions of the same story released too soon, none of them standing up to close examination.'

Kavanagh felt him back off and heard the sigh of the cushion as he flopped back down in his chair.

A telephone rang in the corridor and one of the nurses answered it which was unusual. Usually they were so busy there was no one at the desk and the phones would keep ringing for ages, often starting up again immediately. Kavanagh listened to the nurse's voice, the accent so familiar after his time here in Belfast.

Maurice seemed to have used the diversion to bring his emotions back under control.

'Listen, son. I'm not getting at you. I understand the difficult position you're in and under different circumstances I'd probably admire your loyalty, even if I think you're backing the wrong horse. But you were there and I wasn't. I know where they're coming from, but they've got the wrong man, son. I've never taken too kindly to being patronised and if there's something they're not telling me, I will get to the bottom of it, I can assure you of that much. I came here to speak with you because I was hoping maybe I could persuade you to save me some time and trouble by filling in some of the gaps, but with or without your help . . . I *will* get there.'

The ensuing silence was excruciating. Kavanagh knew he was being put to the test. Maurice didn't actually know anything for certain, but he was never going to be satisfied with some half-arsed story that had been cobbled together with no real attempt to think it through. But the line had been drawn in the sand. Respect for grieving relatives could only go so far. There were security implications to consider, investigations to be carried out, lessons to be learnt. They couldn't be compromised by any loose cannon such as an angry father who might go off at any moment. Maurice, as an ex-serviceman, knew this . . . and yet still he sat there.

There was a snap as something was placed on the cabinet.

'I've left you my card,' he continued. 'It has all my contact details. You'll come to the funeral, I hope? My wife would love to meet you. My younger boy Jimmy, too.'

'I'm sure that can be arranged, sir. Always assuming . . .'

He touched the bandages with one hand, crossed his fingers on the other.

'Och, you'll probably be leaping around like a newborn lamb by the time they release what's left of Sean. It's going to be a while yet, so they tell me. If you do decide to come, you'll let me know of any difficulties you face in getting there? I'd be happy to arrange any transport you need. My way of saying thank you.'

'I'm sure that will be taken care of at this end—'

'Mebbe not, son. Perhaps I should have made it clear. This is going to be a private funeral.'

'Sir?'

'I've told them I'll do whatever I can to make sure the army plays no part in it. They can fly the body home if they like but that's it. No flag, no draped drums or military music, no photo opportunities for brass monkeys to parade around and show off their medals. They've done their bit. They can say their own goodbyes to Sean if they like, but I'll have no truck with any official ceremony. His funeral will be private – just family and friends. I'd like to think you come into that category.'

The chair scraped across the floor and there was an audible groan as he hauled himself to his feet.

'Good luck, son,' he said, wrestling with his overcoat by the sound of things. 'I'll pray for you when the bandages come off, if it's not tempting fate. And who knows – when you get your sight back, maybe it'll bring your memory with it. Funnier things have happened.'

A hand rested briefly on his shoulder.

'That wee card on your cabinet – the moment you decide you'd like to try something different, just call that number, OK? Look upon it as your own personal get-out-of-jail-free card.'

He listened to the slow, weary footsteps as he headed for the door.

Felt the memories returning.

Tried not to remember.

Failed.

Watches again now as he steps out of the accommodation block, just beyond the defensive sangars. Sees the pick-up truck at the end of the road as it slows to a crawl and is immediately on the alert. Sean thirty yards or so beyond the barrier – playing the fool as usual, stalking a wounded fox in the undergrowth while the others egg him on. Then the sudden acceleration of the truck, shouts from other members of the unit. Sean whirling round, alert far too late to the danger, freezing instead of challenging the truck while it is still a good way off and his actions might be of some use. Response from behind the barrier taking out the tyres and windshield of the truck, which veers off to the left before crashing into a ditch just a few yards short of the first barrier. Sean still motionless at the side of the road like a rabbit in headlights, then flying through the air as the first explosion rips through the truck. Pandemonium. People running everywhere. Shouts, muffled and indecipherable. Burning debris littering the tarmac. And he's scrambling to his feet, instinct more than bravery sending him through the smoke and debris and beyond the barrier to where Sean is lying in the middle of the road, the deafening roar still in his ears, mutating to a shrill, whistling sound, which only partially obliterates Sean's screams that seem to be everywhere. He scoops him up and throws him over his shoulder, leaving the lower part of the right leg in the road as he stumbles back towards the barrier.

Then nothing . . . a blank, a dark curtain he's since tried to draw back without success. Just vague memories of lying in a chopper, drifting in and out of consciousness, on his way to Belfast and Musgrave Park.

It was only later he was told about the armoured dumper truck which appeared out of a side road the moment the pickup truck exploded, adding grenades and bursts from AK-47s to the chaotic scene up ahead before scuttling away through the network of country lanes that always seemed designed specifically to foil the best efforts of intruders and protect the locals. It was a miracle there were only two fatalities at the end of it all.

Total bloody disaster all the same. They'd all been briefed on the simultaneous attacks just a couple of months earlier, the so-called *human proxy bombs* at Coshquin, Cloghoge and Omagh. The possibility of similar attacks in future led to a review of security measures, precautions that had proved completely ineffectual when push came to shove.

In the rarefied atmosphere of High Command, there would be hell to pay for this and given that shit on a shovel held by a senior officer tends to travel in one direction only, no one was in any doubt as to where the blame was going to lie once the spotlight had moved on. In the meantime, however, in the full glare of publicity, it was all about containment.

Colonel Holman had been quite clear. It was in no one's best interests for the truth to be made public. How would it serve anyone's interests, other than those of the aggressors, to portray the events of that afternoon as a shambles? And what about the families of Sean Hayes and Philip Craine, the other soldier killed at the barrier? Wouldn't they rather believe their son had shown bravery under fire in the service of his country than been needlessly sacrificed in a fiasco that should have been avoided?

Kavanagh understood this. Until he'd met Maurice Hayes in person, he could appreciate the logic underpinning the strategy, even give a grudging nod in its direction. But things were different now. He had not met Craine's parents, had no idea whether they would be likely to take consolation from the cover story and accept what they were told at face value. But he *had* met Maurice Hayes. And even on the basis of such a short meeting, he knew with absolute certainty that he would not want to be fobbed off in that way. Nor would he allow it to happen. He could live with his son having failed. He could live

with his son having suffered. He was probably half expecting
it. But he couldn't live with a fictional narrative conceived with
the sole intention of evading responsibility.

'I will get to the bottom of it,' he'd said moments ago. 'One
way or another, you can take that as gospel.'

Kavanagh sank his head into his pillow. He didn't doubt it
for one moment. He also knew where his own sympathies lay.

And if he wasn't aware of having come to a decision, it was
because the decision had already made itself.

4

April 2018
The Ascot Lounge, Soho

Anna closes her eyes as the fingers of her right hand trip softly over the keys, using the high notes to tease every last drop of emotion out of the song. She's aiming for a soothing, almost mesmeric effect, raindrops in a forest. Head tilted back, she sways involuntarily, the sensation of stardust dripping from her fingers as they give expression to a sense of longing somewhere deep inside and seek to draw a similar response from the audience.

It's her own arrangement of 'Ain't No Sunshine' which she's been tinkering with recently. She's gone for haunting rather than soulful, hoping that slowing it right down will avoid unflattering comparisons with Bill Withers and that golden voice of his. She thinks it works, knows it does for her anyway. And as she allows the final notes to drift away, she keeps her eyes closed for a second or two longer, savouring that moment when the audience will slowly emerge from the trance in which she's held them for the past few minutes and burst into rapturous applause.

The spell is broken even before she opens her eyes and takes in the usual Saturday night crowd. There is barely organised chaos at the bar where staff are under mounting pressure from the sheer volume of customers trying to get their attention. Couples – the Tinder Brigade, she used to call them, a little disparagingly, although she herself has done more than her fair share of left-swiping recently – are dotted around the room in comfortable chairs, spruced up and mentally polishing cover stories before they're put to the test over dinner. The obligatory lounge lizard at the end of the bar appears to be the only person actually applauding her efforts with any enthusiasm and his motives are suspect anyway. He hit on her the moment she finished her set two nights ago and was summarily blown off but apparently subscribes to some optimistic equation between persistence and reward. He may be in for a reality check before long.

At least he's been listening. Her performance seems to have gone pretty much unnoticed by everyone else and, not for the first time, she wonders if she's ever going to break free from this never-ending cycle of one-nighters in bars where the music doesn't even reach the heights of incidental – it's just there, buzzing in the background. When Ches first told her about The Ascot Lounge, it felt like a step in the right direction. Then again, what's new? Everything he comes up with is parcelled up as another foot in the door, the next step on the ladder. Problem is, steps go both ways and doors are only worth opening if they lead to something worthwhile. In this business, she's discovered, you get a lot of bruised toes.

Ches sold this gig to her in his usual theatrical way – made three nights in Soho sound like a season at La Scala. Told her The Ascot Lounge were making quite a thing of it. Posters on the windows. Fliers distributed outside. Big social media push and every chance of an extension if she smashes it. So much hot air as usual – as far as she can see, not even the posters have materialised. Instead there's a white board on an easel near the entrance and someone with no spatial awareness whatsoever has scribbled her name in an untidy scrawl which is getting smaller and smaller as it nears the edge of the board. It's beyond depressing.

She's been wondering for a few months now whether this might be the time to move on from Ches. She wouldn't be the first. Although his company lists a number of artistes on its website, she knows for a fact that several have long since graduated to bigger and better things. Of the half dozen acts still on his books, she's only ever met two – a Corrs tribute band from Barnet who can at least hold a tune, and a 63-year-old supposedly Italian crooner from Hillingdon who palpably cannot. She's expressed disappointment before now at the fragmented and funereal progress she seems to be making. Ches always falls back on the same stock answers, all revolving around the need for patience.

'In this business you have to build slowly, sweetheart,' he tells her. 'Two steps forward, one step back. Let the word get around. Slowly, slowly, catchy monkey.'

She's told him that if she goes any more slowly she's going to be the most protracted overnight sensation in history. Humour seems to be lost on him.

And then there's this bee he's got in his bonnet about her material. He's forever asking her to spice it up a little, give the punters songs they know and love so they can all join in if they feel so inclined.

'No one wants to sit there and listen to songs they've never heard before. Success in this business depends on some sort of connection between you and your audience.'

What he wants apparently is some sort of upmarket karaoke event – maybe not even upmarket. She has a feeling she'd be doing 'Agadoo' and 'The Birdie Song' every night if he had his way. She's not prepared to compromise on this. She's an accomplished jazz pianist and vocalist, fortunate enough to inherit her mother's voice and timing – about the only worthwhile things Colette passed on before walking out on her family and starting a new life for herself somewhere on the Costa Brava.

Anna has been brought up on her father's CD collection of Big Band vocalists – Ella, Sarah, Billie, Dinah, Peggy. With friends at school she made a point of swearing allegiance to Katy Perry and Pink but that was no more than an attempt to blend in. To the same end she also professed undying love for Chris Martin, which was less of a stretch, but as soon as she arrived home each evening she cast off these allegiances and turned to her father's CDs for genuine inspiration. They were a focal point for their relationship, if not exactly a warm fire then at least one of those three-bar heaters they could huddle in front of and pretend they were still a family, irrespective of where Colette might have disappeared to. She wonders if he still listens to these CDs, now that he's settled in Thailand with wife number two. And whether he even thinks of her now. He always encouraged her to come up with songs of her own and she's been working at this of late, slipping one or two into her routine. What she needs though is a discerning audience – one that actually knows she's there would be a step up. In bleaker moments it feels as if she's no further forward now than when she met Ches five years ago, and the echoes of her mother's experience are as eerie as they are unnerving.

Colette, her father used to say, always wore her martyrdom like a favourite coat, ready at the drop of a hat to remind everyone of just how much she'd sacrificed. She tried for a while to keep alive the illusion that her singing career was still a viable option, merely on temporary hold, but there can't have been anywhere near as many opportunities for her in Kettering as there are in London and eventually something had to give. The temptation to walk away from a husband she didn't love and two young girls who embodied every obstacle life had put in her way ... well, sometimes it seems to Anna like nothing short of miraculous that she stayed around for as long as seven years before pissing off to Spain and relaunching herself. In more charitable moments, she can maybe understand the frustrations to which she fell prey. Forgiving her, though ... that's something else.

Her younger sister is even more hawkish on the subject. Emmie hates Colette with a vengeance, refers to her as *TB* or *The Bitch*. The mere mention of her name will spark her into citing a list of grievances as long as her arm. She claims to remember any number of injustices as if they were yesterday, even though she was only four when the break-up occurred. Anna herself has only the haziest memory of those few years when Colette was around.

The earliest incident she can recall with any real clarity is a trip to Hamerton Zoo Park to celebrate her fifth birthday when Colette insisted on driving and managed to slam into another car at a roundabout. Emmie claims to remember the whole thing – the force of the impact; her mother screaming hysteri-cally because she had a small cut above her eye *which didn't even need stitches, for fuck's sake*; their father trying to placate the driver of the other vehicle who seemed hell-bent on taking his rage out on someone, anyone; the long wait for the tow truck and the taxi ride back home in silence. Thing is, Emmie was still a couple of months short of her second birthday at the time and these so-called memories can surely be no more than piece-meal reconstruction based on accounts she's listened to over the years, yet she swears she remembers it all like yesterday.

Anna remembers little of the detail ... other than the fact that she never did get to see the animals in Hamerton Zoo. And two years later her mother was gone for good.

5

April 2018
Bournemouth

Kavanagh closes the door behind him and steps out into Poole Road. At some stage during the past half hour or so, it's started to rain quite heavily, so he breaks into a trot, dodging pedestrians as he heads for the side street where he left his Polo earlier. Once inside and out of the rain, he peels off his jacket and drapes it over the passenger seat, adjusting the rear-view mirror until his features swim into view.

He sees the scar first. In twenty-eight years it's faded to some extent, the burning, livid disfigurement gradually morphing into a paler, puckered blemish which still conveys an air of menace. He's not a man naturally predisposed to smiling, which is just as well given that any such attempts more closely resemble a scowl than anything else. If he catches sight of the scar unexpectedly, it no longer takes his breath away but it's still conspicuous enough to draw double-takes from passersby, who invariably avert their gaze, keen to suggest they haven't really noticed anything untoward.

He remembers once – years ago, soon after he left the army and started working for Maurice – he went home with one of the girls who used to hang around the Tin Tack club. He can't remember her name . . . Lola, maybe? She'd been fascinated by the scar, tracing it as they lay in bed, running her finger in a four-inch arc from his forehead, down through the left eyebrow and coming to rest just below his cheekbone. She said it gave definition and character to his face, told him she found it attractive. No one had ever suggested anything like this before – or since, for that matter – and he'd been taken by surprise, almost touched by the intimacy of the moment. It hadn't stopped her asking for her money and leaving before the night was out, though.

He grabs a towel from his sports bag on the back seat and rubs his hair until it's dry – still as thick as ever, he's pleased to note, but with pepper losing out to salt with every passing year. Then he throws the towel into the footwell and flops back in his seat, eyes closed, neck supported by the headrest, as he replays the appointment he's just had with Judith Weimann.

He understands where she's coming from – she's an experienced ophthalmologist who presumably takes the view that there's not much point in consulting her if you're not prepared to act on her advice. His loss of vision, however momentary it may have been, has clearly raised the stakes as far as she's concerned. She wants to refer him to a specialist in London, has already outlined a timetable for what needs to be done and is surprised by his reaction. What she was saying makes perfect sense, but that's not enough for him. Not any longer. What he wants from her are certainties and it appears she has none to offer – at least, none he's prepared to consider just yet.

If he takes her up on the offer and it's decided his only option is a high-risk operation to remove those tiny fragments of shrapnel he's lived with for nearly thirty years now, he knows what that will entail. He's done his research, knows there are no guarantees. Knows also what sort of time scale he's looking at if he does go down that road. It will mean a series of tests, followed by a major operation and a lengthy spell in hospital with an indeterminate recovery period.

He's reached a stage in his life when that sort of decision should be easy. There are few demands on his time. The book-shop would be in safe hands with Conor, his assistant. There are no major commitments that should prevent him from agreeing to surgery that might significantly improve his quality of life for however many years he has left in him. He can see why Judith Weimann might find his reluctance so bewildering. To her it must seem like a no-brainer and not so long ago, in all prob-ability, he would have felt the same way.

But that was then ... and now his priorities have changed and time is no longer immaterial. For the past few days – ever since he lost his footing on the grassy downslope and took that blow to the back of his head – his waking thoughts have been consumed by that flash of insight that came flooding in to fill the vacuum left by his departing vision. It feels almost predes-tined ... like nature compensating for his loss.

He should have died in Dunloughraine.

Sean Hayes did. So did Philip Craine.

And yet he was spared – why? All through the recovery process, people were queuing up – surgeons, nurses and comrades alike – to tell him that, for all his injuries and however ridiculous it might sound, he was a very lucky man. It was a miracle he came out of that carnage as unscathed as he did. Sean's body, draped across his shoulders, had almost certainly taken some of the shrapnel that should have come his way and the ditch into which they'd been blown offered more protection than the open road where he could so easily have ended up, an open and helpless target. All prevailing logic suggests he should have died on December 3rd 1990, a month before his thirty-sixth birthday.

Instead he survived.

He's never thought of himself as a religious man – not even mildly superstitious. But something has changed since that run over Durdle Door ... or maybe it's always been there, and the change lies in his acceptance of what he needs to do. He senses a pattern to his existence, a sequence of grace and spurned opportunity, repeated down the years. It's a cycle he'd like to break. All these years, his vision has been 20/20 or as near as makes no difference, yet he's been able to see nothing at all that matters. That flash of insight that came with his temporary loss of vision has changed everything.

Time to move forward, he tells himself. He has a list of people he'll have to talk with as soon as possible. There are journeys to plan, difficult negotiations ahead, financial arrangements to set up. There's the immediate future of the bookshop to sort out. Maybe even the cottage, depending on how things pan out. Legal advice too, in all probability. These will all take time. Even if everything goes smoothly – a prospect in which he would be unwise to invest too much faith – he's still looking at something in the region of four to six months, assuming his calculations are correct. The moment any obstacles are factored in, it could stretch out to a lot longer than that. It will demand focus, every scintilla of concentration he's able to call upon, and the last thing he can afford is distractions on the scale of major eye surgery and indeterminate recovery periods.

Not yet, he tells himself. He's told Judith Weimann he'll give serious consideration to what she's said and get back to her. He didn't say anything about when. If the gamble fails and this delay causes irreparable damage to his sight, so be it. He'll cope. Others are forced to make similar adjustments every day of the week. If he has to, he can do the same. But deep inside him there's a growing conviction, which he can't explain, that it won't come to that. After years of drifting, he feels as if he's stumbled – literally – onto something that could give some sort of meaning to his life and maybe even a touch of redemption for all the wrong paths he's taken in the past, inadvertently or otherwise. It would take a particularly malignant deity, he tells himself, to give up on him after all this time.

He opens his eyes and turns the key in the ignition. Pulls away from the kerb, driven by a sense of purpose he's still struggling to assimilate.

And wondering how best to go about finding the girl at the top of the stairs.

6

1999
Twickenham

When he was shown into the drawing room and realised Vic was sitting at one end of the expensive-looking sofa, leafing through a motoring magazine, Kavanagh's early warning systems were instantly on the alert. He'd been hoping for a one-to-one chat with Maurice, the chance to put his side across as part of a calm, rational exchange of views. The odds on that happening now had just lengthened considerably.

It wasn't so much that Maurice was anyone's idea of a soft touch. The avuncular smile and measured delivery disguised a steely core and, in that quiet way of his, he knew how to impose himself whenever the need arose. After all, you didn't get to stay in control of the sprawling criminal enterprise he'd built from scratch without knowing a thing or two about asserting yourself. He was undemonstrative though, in control of his emotions, as if sticking to a script that might not be of his choosing, but which he was required to follow to the letter.

Vic, by way of contrast, was a ticking bomb whose involvement in any dispute automatically upped the ante by several points. Kavanagh had come across his fair share of hard men in the army and was not easily intimidated. What made him wary of Vic was his sheer unpredictability. He was a volatile, seething pot just waiting for the slightest excuse to boil over. On the one hand, Kavanagh had seen him maintain remarkable self-control when under real pressure in a crisis, yet he'd also seen him fly off the handle at the flimsiest provocation, responding with a lack of proportion which at times bordered on the savage. Some misguided souls, on first acquaintance, made the mistake of assuming that the tales they'd heard about Maurice's right-hand man must be apocryphal, that it was all an act with no substance to back it up, merely Vic's allotted role in the good cop/bad cop routine. That was a miscalculation which invariably came back to bite them.

Urban myth had it that they'd first met outside a pub in Deptford one night when Vic had waded in to rescue Maurice from a group of drunken navvies who were intent on beating the crap out of him. They'd been working together ever since, had even become brothers-in-law, raiding the same well-to-do family for their wives, a step up in class and social aspiration which Maurice had negotiated rather more easily of the two. So when Vic and Angie were unable to have children of their own, it was only natural that he should form an attachment to Sean and young Jimmy that was tighter than the one most uncles traditionally enjoyed with their nephews.

In the eight years Kavanagh had known Vic, their relationship had been uneasy at best. He was acutely aware of a coldness in the man's attitude towards him. In quieter moments, he was able to rationalise it. After all, for as long as anyone could remember, it had been the Maurice and Vic show: Maurice the schemer, spending much of the time directing strategy in the background, and Vic his trusted lieutenant, who did all the dirty work and made sure the machine ticked over nicely on a day-to-day basis. He was the go-to person, the one who had not only Maurice's back but his ear as well, and when he spoke, it was understood that he did so with absolute authority.

When it came to Vic, Kavanagh felt as if he was a victim of circumstances. The alacrity with which he'd been welcomed into the fold by Maurice on leaving the army eight years ago would have taken most people by surprise, making an element of resentment and mistrust almost inevitable. To make things worse, Vic had lost a nephew he worshipped. In his place now was an interloper who, just to rub salt in the wound, had somehow managed to survive the same blast that had taken Sean. It didn't take a degree in psychology to understand the warmth of the welcome Maurice was extending, the tide of transferred affection that was responsible for fast-tracking Kavanagh through the ranks. Equally Vic's inability to muster the same enthusiasm for this unwelcome foundling was only to be expected.

So while there had been no outbreak of hostilities as such, it had always felt like the most fragile of truces, as if the pair of them were circling each other warily, waiting for the right pretext to present itself.

And he might have just handed it to Vic on a plate.

Maurice was in the far corner of the room, replenishing glasses from the drinks bar – vodka and orange for Vic, single malt Laphroaig for himself. He nodded to acknowledge Kavanagh's arrival and held up a can of Diet Sprite which he'd already taken from the fridge.

'Know better than to offer you a real drink,' he said. 'You want ice with this?'

Kavanagh shook his head and took the armchair he'd been offered. It was facing the sofa, where he knew Maurice would sit as soon as he'd handed out the drinks. It was a well-established routine which others often joked about, although the laughter rang hollow for anyone who'd already had his turn in what they euphemistically called the *naughty chair*. The arrangement reminded him of those occasions when he had managed to upset his grandparents – choice of university, failure to stick with his English degree beyond the end of his second year, pre-emptive decision to enlist with no prior discussion. He understood however that the stakes associated with upsetting Maurice and Vic were on another level altogether.

Vic took his drink from Maurice and stayed at one end of the sofa without taking his eyes off Kavanagh. If it amounted to a challenge of some sort, an invitation to engage in a staring contest, it was never going to be met. It was not in Kavanagh's nature to back down from anything, but he saw no mileage in thrusting his hand into an open fire for the sake of it.

Maurice dropped into his own armchair next to the sofa and stretched his legs, resting his feet on the glass coffee table. He took a sip from his drink and stared thoughtfully at the tumbler for a moment, as if surprised by its contents.

'I had a phone call from our favourite local councillor this morning,' he said eventually. 'It seems he's had a change of heart, may be voting our way after all.'

Kavanagh nodded.

'Care to tell me how you managed to bring about that minor miracle?'

'I showed him a photo.'

Maurice raised an eyebrow.

'A photo?'

'Yes.'

'And that's all?'

'It was a photo of his son's room. He's just started a Business degree at Portsmouth. I told him his son had lectures all morning and I was sorry I missed him. Maybe next time.'

Maurice smiled. Wagged a finger at him.

'And that shipment from Eindhoven ... did you remind Lennie to have a word with them about the twenty grand that's due at the end of the month?'

Kavanagh nodded again.

'He's been getting a wee bit forgetful of late,' Maurice continued. 'Probably ought to think about replacing him before long but it's what to move him on to that's the problem. Can't just chuck him onto the scrapheap at his time of life.'

He leant forward and rested the cut-glass tumbler on the table.

'No way to reward loyalty, is it?'

He looked at Vic, in a way that somehow italicised the words, then sank back into the sofa, arms folded across his chest and lips pursed.

'So how are things with you, son? You're looking a bit off-colour, if you don't mind me saying. Everything OK?'

'I'm fine,' he lied, wondering where this was leading. When he was first told that Maurice wanted to see him, he knew immediately that it would have something to do with the way he'd left things at Murphy's house the previous week. He'd given Vic a selective and somewhat sanitised version of events and hoped that would be enough. Sitting there facing them both, he realised he'd have been better off if he'd come clean from the outset. The atmosphere in the room was only partially explained by Vic's brooding presence.

'Good to hear, good to hear.'

The ormolu clock on the mantelpiece chimed twice to signal the half hour. Kavanagh waited, still avoiding Vic's glare which was threatening to burn a hole in his temple.

'I gather our little business in Weybridge last week wasn't without its problems, though,' Maurice said, picking his words carefully. He was very particular about his choice of vocabulary. Everything was always *business* or *deals* or *negotiations* – financial jargon seemingly designed to disguise the harsher reality of the world in which they operated. The words covered a multitude of sins.

'The intel could have been better,' said Kavanagh with deliberate understatement. He looked around for a coaster he could use before deciding to hold onto his glass instead, rather than risk leaving a mark.

'Yes. So I understand. I swear I don't know what the world's coming to. Two-man team, one on, one off for three days, and yet still they managed to make a complete gorroch of it, as my dear old grandad used to say. I can only apologise. You shouldn't have been put in that position.'

Kavanagh shrugged his shoulders to convey the impression that it hadn't been that much of an issue. He'd spent several minutes in front of a mirror rehearsing this reaction and wasn't sure he'd quite nailed it – maybe there was something about the scar that automatically militated against the innocent look.

'Vic has had a few words in the ears of those responsible and pointed out the error of their ways. Needless to say, there will be a marked improvement in their performance in future . . . not that that's much consolation to you, I'd imagine.'

Kavanagh felt that to ignore Vic any longer would be a mistake. A certain amount of apprehension was only to be expected, but if he avoided eye contact for too long he was going to look shifty. That was the last thing he needed right now.

'Not that it makes a lot of difference now,' he said, eyes flitting between the two of them, 'but do we know how the girl came to be there?'

'We're still looking into that. Should have a clearer picture in a day or two. From what we've pieced together so far, it seems the mother did indeed go back to Dunedin, so they got that much right. Bringing up a daughter on her own though – that was never part of the plan apparently. Bit of a flake by all accounts. Rumours of a serious drug habit too. You wouldn't say Murphy was father of the year exactly, but word has it she makes him look like a paragon of virtue. Anyway – bottom line, the girl was in his care and somehow our eagle-eyed surveillance team managed to miss it. As I said, I can only apologise.'

Maurice cleared his throat.

'Having said that, though . . .'

There was an extended silence during which Kavanagh became increasingly aware of Vic's left foot which was beating out a tattoo on the parquet floor.

Maurice cupped his chin in one hand and took a deep breath, exhaling through his nose.

'There was another reason for asking you to come here. I understand from Vic that you've put us in a wee spot of bother.'

So . . . his suspicions were well founded then. Kavanagh tried for a disingenuous frown.

'The girl, you mean?'

'Let's start there, shall we?'

'I wouldn't call her a problem.'

'Well, if that's supposed to reassure me, I'm not sure I share your optimism, son. I appreciate it wasn't your fault Murphy had company, but the bottom line is you left behind a potential *witness*.'

'I left behind a two-year-old girl.'

'Three actually,' said Maurice, correcting him with a raised finger. 'A three-year-old *witness*. I'm reliably informed her fourth birthday is only a few months away but we're splitting hairs here. What matters is the word witness. And whether or not she saw you.'

'She was half asleep,' said Kavanagh, seeking to make his point without appearing too complacent.

'But she did see you?'

'Well . . . yes. Briefly.'

'And you don't think that poses a problem?'

'I'm not sure how. It's not like she's going to be able to offer a description.'

'And you know that for a fact, I suppose?'

Kavanagh sighed, running a hand through his hair.

'I've no idea how many words she can put together, but I seriously doubt it goes much beyond *dada*. How's that going to hurt us?'

'Well . . . you say that,' said Maurice, using his free hand to rummage in his trouser pocket. 'I can't say with hand on heart that I remember from my own experience of Sean and Jimmy, but Mary tells me they had plenty to say for themselves at that age, so why wouldn't this girl . . . especially if she has experts there to help her?'

Kavanagh gave a decisive shake of the head.

'She didn't say a single word all the time I was there.'

Maurice produced a large chequered handkerchief and blew into it before refolding it carefully. He was a past master at creating pauses that might allow space for any taut nerves to twang a little.

'As you said . . . she was half asleep. For all you know, she might talk the hind legs off a donkey on a good day. And if she did get a good look at you . . .'

Kavanagh took a sip from his drink and rested the glass on the floor next to his feet.

'You think scar is one of those words she'll have picked up?' he asked.

'I haven't the faintest idea what strategies the authorities might have developed for coaxing a workable description from a child of that age. More to the point, neither do you, which is why we have certain protocols in place. We take the time and trouble to explain them in detail, so that everyone knows where he stands. You weren't in any doubt about this, were you?'

Kavanagh shook his head.

'And yet you decided to act on your own initiative.'

Kavanagh allowed himself time to come up with an answer that might be acceptable.

'I made a judgement call.'

'And what the fuck gives you the right to make one of those?'

When Vic decided to contribute to a discussion, he knew how to make an entrance. Its impact was further enhanced by the use of the f-word. Maurice's hatred of gratuitous swearing was legendary. He regarded it as not just offensive but indicative of lazy thinking and a lack of imagination, and anyone foolish enough to use it within his hearing could expect to be challenged. The worst excesses to which he himself might be driven were the words damn and blast and his much-loved acronym snafu slipped through the net only because he chose to interpret the last two letters as standing for *fouled up*.

Despite this, his only response to Vic's outburst was to raise one hand and shake his head, as if to indicate that this particular contribution was less than helpful.

'You say you made a judgement call. I'd say from where I'm sitting your judgement looks seriously flawed.'

'With respect,' said Kavanagh, his increasing frustration coming to the fore. 'I was the person in that house, having to react to whatever was in front of me. I didn't have the luxury of taking my time and weighing up the pros and cons of every possible course of action. The one thought in my mind when I saw the girl was damage limitation.'

'So tell me how that works.'

'It's simple. Scumbag gets killed – OK, that's news for a day or two, then it's history. Baby daughter gets taken out as well? That's different. Now you've got a human-interest story on your hands. The media will be all over it like a rash. Stack that up against the remote possibility that they might – just might – get some sort of description out of her and it seemed to me I was doing the right thing in leaving the girl alone and getting out of there.'

There was a pause, during which Maurice appeared to be considering the merits of his argument. The expression on Vic's face suggested strongly that there was no room at all for debate.

'And is that what you did?' Maurice said at length.

Kavanagh frowned.

'I'm not with you.'

'Just leave the girl on her own. Is that all you did?'

He thought he understood now. Knew what this was really all about – why he was here. He hoped he was wrong.

'Well ... I checked the house first to make sure no one else was there, if that's what you mean.'

Maurice shook his head.

'Have another go. You're sure there's nothing else?'

'Like what?'

'Seems to me you're missing the point of the question, son. It's not for me to tell you what to say. What I'm asking is whether there's anything you left out of your feedback to Vic here, either because you forgot or because you felt it might be better to hold back that particular snippet of information for some reason.'

Kavanagh found himself shaking his head, even before he'd had a chance to work out what the best answer to that question might be.

'Not that I can think of, no.'

A cloud swept across Maurice's face, as if the answer disappointed him, and Kavanagh sensed he'd stumbled through the wrong door.

'You see, I was having a wee chinwag with an acquaintance of mine just last night,' Maurice continued. 'Handy lad, one of my contacts at the press agency. He gets in touch from time to time if he thinks there's something I might be interested in knowing. Seems to me you can never have too much information. Anyway, he tells me there's a ... what did you call it? A human-interest story? My contact tells me there's one about to

break in the next day or so. He tried the headline out on me –
KILLER WITH A CONSCIENCE. Has quite a ring to it, don't
you think?'

Kavanagh kept his own counsel. This was nowhere he wanted
to go.

'It's all about the killing of some lowlife in Weybridge,'
Maurice continued, in a jaunty fashion which fooled no one in
the room. 'Shot in the head. The killer did his best to make it
look like a suicide but they're not buying that for one moment,
not least because – and here's the good bit – someone phoned
the emergency services to tell them there was a toddler on
her own in the house and asked for the relevant authorities to
come and make sure she was OK.'

'Maurice—'

'Not now, son. Your turn was a few moments ago when I
asked if there was anything you wanted to add. Now you just sit
there and listen, OK?'

Kavanagh didn't even bother to nod.

'So the police arrive and are amazed to find a body in the
lounge – the caller hadn't said anything about that. As for the
wee girl, she's upstairs right enough, fast asleep. On her own,
just like the caller had said. And they can't believe their luck
because it turns out the call came from the phone in the very
same house where the murder had taken place and they can't
come up with any explanation as to who could have phoned
it in if not the killer. If anyone else had been present, it's not
very likely that they'd have been spared, so they now have a
pretty good idea as to the time frame they're dealing with . . .
all of which means they're in a much stronger starting position
when it comes to questioning neighbours and trawling through

any camera footage they can find that might help identify cars entering and leaving the area. And just to top it all off nicely, they have a voice on tape that may prove useful for comparison purposes at some stage. All because the killer, it seems, had a conscience.'

He broke off to toss back the rest of his drink, resting the glass on the arm of the sofa. 'Which is why we make our expectations clear,' growled Vic, recognising a tacit invitation to throw his hat into the ring at this point. 'Because, if we don't, there's always a chance some wet-behind-the-ears dickhead will think his poxy education means he knows better than we do and balls everything up.'

'Why the phone call?' asked Maurice.

Kavanagh said nothing for a moment. He'd been naïve in underestimating the extent of Maurice's reach. He was always going to find out about the call and trying to hide it from him only made him look unreliable.

'I'm sorry,' he said eventually. 'Sorry for not coming clean. But I don't regret making the call because if I'm honest I'd do the same again if I found myself in that situation.'

'You arrogant prick—'

'Let him finish,' said Maurice, flashing a look in Vic's direction. Vic looked less than happy at being cut off before he'd had a chance to say his piece but gave way. Maurice turned back to Kavanagh and nodded to let him know he should continue.

'I'm sorry. I know I should have been straight with you from the outset, but the call's not going to bounce back on us in any way – I guarantee it. I kept to a handful of one-syllable words. Sounded like some sort of robot. And when I left, I kept to the shadows, covered up at all times, so there's no way I'm going to show up on any camera. I know what I'm doing, right? And OK, I'll admit it would have been handy if Murphy had been discovered a few days later, but that wasn't an option.'

'Because?'

Kavanagh paused before answering, looking Maurice in the eye.

'Because of the girl,' he said. 'Just that. I couldn't leave her on her own with her father's body downstairs. She'd done nothing wrong. She didn't get to choose her parents and wouldn't have been anywhere near the place with a fair shake of the dice. I couldn't do it.'

'So the army didn't teach you how to follow orders?' growled Vic.

Kavanagh sighed. It had taught him little else. He'd had years of doing exactly what he was told, irrespective of whether he saw the point of it. He'd left when his contract was up because it had reached the point where he was worried about becoming institutionalised, unable to decide anything for himself any longer. He'd then headed for London at the first opportunity because there was something about that afternoon in Musgrave Park that had stayed with him all through the recovery process. He'd seen how much it had mattered to Maurice to get to the truth about his son's death, sensed an integrity there that he felt he could work with.

He was anything but a wide-eyed innocent. He knew from very early on what he was getting into. Money laundering and counterfeiting, extortion, prostitution, weapon and drug trafficking, shady property development deals – if there was money to be squeezed out of any activity in London's seamier districts, the Syndicate had a hand in there somewhere. But everything he'd been asked to do so far had made sense – was something he felt he could live with. It didn't mean his actions hadn't caused him any sleepless nights. Munir Sirhan, Max Judd, Eddie Larner – the names and faces came back to him far too easily for that. But when it came to it he hadn't hesitated for one second to take on the job because at least he could tell himself that every one of them had brought it on himself. The world was a safer and better place without them.

He could add Leon Murphy to the list now. He wasn't going to be agonising over him either. A three-year-old girl, though? That would make him no better than the people he was punishing. The problem was, he wasn't sure this was what Maurice wanted to hear right then. As for Vic, he sure as hell would have a view on it.

'I can only tell you what I know,' he said. 'I was there. I've seen the girl. She's no threat at all, not in a million years.'

'And if she was ten years older?'

'You want an honest answer?'

Maurice raised one eyebrow to make his feelings clear – stupid question.

'I won't know until that happens.'

Kavanagh paused to allow the words and their implications to sink in.

'I know that's not what you want to hear,' he added by way of damage limitation, 'but I promise you this much. Nothing I do will ever lead back to you. Never. The only person who will ever pay for my mistakes is me.'

'Well, you'd better be right about that, Sean.'

There was a moment when time seemed to stand still.

Kavanagh had heard it. So too, judging by the look on his face, had Vic.

'Son,' Maurice said, quickly correcting himself and colouring slightly as he did so.

A simple slip of the tongue, easy enough. Sean, son . . . Probably happened several times a day. His use of the word son was a reflex, a term he employed with everyone younger than himself. *Sean* however was different. In the context of Vic's suspicions about possible nepotism, the slip was more than unfortunate.

And for the first time it occurred to Kavanagh that his time here might be drifting towards a natural conclusion. Vic's hostility, the disparity between Maurice's actions and the qualities he thought he'd seen in him . . . it was all getting a bit too much to handle. Somewhere, not too far down the road, there would be a major confrontation and he couldn't be sure how that would work out. Maybe it was time to start living a simpler life where morality was easier to define and questions of right and wrong would no longer carry such grave consequences. Time to start looking for a possible exit strategy.

That, he knew, would be anything but straightforward. If there was one certainty in the path he'd chosen that was non-negotiable and understood by everyone, it was that there was no turning back.

He might have found a way out of the army.

The Syndicate though was supposed to be for life.

7

April 2018
Peckham

He steps out of the taxi, handing a couple of notes to the cab driver and instinctively tapping the roof as it drives off. His choice of a black cab from Waterloo station was a matter of habit. They're a part of London that he can recall with a degree of nostalgia and affection. A cabbie once told him that many of his customers tap the roof as he pulls away in the hope that it will bring them good luck – interesting that the reflex should still be there after all this time.

He turns to take a closer look at the building he used to visit often enough back in the day, but which is almost unrecognisable now. It's much larger for one thing, taking up half the block, albeit on one level. He remembers it used to be bordered by a small fabric shop on one side and a Greek barber on the other, but these have now been swallowed up by Excelsior Print Services or Lowes (irritatingly minus apostrophe) as it used to be known.

It's clear that the business has plotted a more profitable course than most through the various financial crises at the start of the century. What was once essentially a one-man operation back in the 1990s has embraced the age of technology and looks as if it could cater for even the most esoteric printing requests. Adrian Lowe always impressed Kavanagh back in the day with his enthusiasm and his eye for the main chance. He can see now his judgement was spot on.

He steps through doors which open automatically for him and makes for the nearest available employee. Like everyone else on the shop floor, the lad is dressed in black trousers, a dazzling white shirt bearing a rectangular name badge, and an olive-green tie with the letters EPS intertwined in a small crest. Kavanagh asks for Lowe by name, and declines to give his own, suggesting instead that 'JEZ' might like to give his employer a small paper bag which he takes from his pocket and presses into the young man's hand. Jez peers doubtfully at it and disappears for a minute or so, unable to resist peering inside as he turns the corner. Kavanagh smiles to himself and wonders what he must be thinking.

When he returns, Jez escorts him down a series of aisles and stops outside a glass-fronted office at the rear of the building. He knocks and steps back to make room for Kavanagh to enter. As he does so, a large, shambling figure hauls himself to his feet at the second attempt, two meaty hands pressing against the edge of the desk to lever him into an upright position.

In the twenty years since leaving London, Kavanagh has returned on only a couple of occasions, preferring to keep the break as clean as possible. If, on either occasion, he'd happened to chance upon the figure now standing in front of him, he very much doubts he would have recognised him. The eyes, perhaps – they always used to twinkle with merriment and there are still traces of that, although much of their former lustre is lost in folds of flesh that have stripped any real definition from the cheekbones. For the rest, there's next to no resemblance. If the years have been kind to him financially, they've surely found other ways to redress the balance. He looks as if he is carrying at least an extra three or four pounds for each one of those twenty years, none of it in any of the right places. His hair, which used to be tied back from his face in a fashionably short ponytail, now hangs loose, a small island immediately above the forehead fighting a losing battle to maintain contact with the rest. He looks a shambles.

'Jon Kavanagh – as I live and breathe,' he cackles, holding up the small paper bag in one hand. 'I knew it had to be you the moment Jez showed me these little beauties.' He helps himself to a couple of jelly babies which he waggles in front of his face before dropping them into his mouth. Then he offers his free hand for Kavanagh to shake and beckons to him to take a seat.

'Damn, you haven't changed a bit,' he adds. 'Whatever deal you struck with the devil, it was worth it, let me tell you. You're putting me to shame.'

'You look well,' Kavanagh lies.

'Bullshit,' Lowe says, flopping back into his chair and patting his stomach, which quivers under the momentum. 'I've let it get away from me a bit lately. Big bones, that's my problem. I was thinking of getting one of those personal trainers, you know? Someone who'll draw up a fitness programme I can follow. I could do with losing a stone or two.'

Or six. Kavanagh watches as he pops another couple of jelly babies into his mouth, then opens a drawer and drops the bag inside.

'That's my lot for the morning,' he says. 'I'm watching what I eat. I've got this slow-burning metabolism. Means I pile the weight on the moment I even look at food. I've joined a gym not far from here. First day there, I had a go on the treadmill for a bit, did a few weights, you know the drill. Weighed myself the next morning and found I'd put on two pounds. Well, sod that. I still go to the gym, but I just use the spa now. Life's too short, if you ask me.'

Kavanagh decides to keep his thoughts to himself. If Lowe prefers to hide behind excuses and gorge himself into an early grave, that's his funeral – literally, in all likelihood. He reminds himself this is not a social visit.

'What d'you think of the place?' Lowe asks, waving an arm to take in the enhanced premises. 'Pretty bloody impressive, eh?'

Kavanagh nods.

'I take it business has been good.'

'Business can only ever be good,' chortles Lowe. 'It's lack of business you should worry about. How about you – still got that bookshop in . . . Wareham, wasn't it?'

Kavanagh nods, slightly taken aback by this, then reminds himself he shouldn't really be surprised. Of course Lowe would know. Information is his lifeblood. It's probably been as instrumental as any business acumen he might possess in financing the expansion of this enterprise of his. It's the reason Kavanagh is here after all. Even so, he feels a little uncomfortable at the thought that, after all this time, his own personal circumstances are so familiar to this man that he doesn't need to drag them up from some dusty corner of his memory.

'I ought to try Dorset again sometime,' Lowe continues, wheezing in a way that makes Kavanagh feel uncomfortable. 'Went there once with some mates when I was a teenager. Lulworth Cove? Did a bit of youth-hostelling, went up over

Durdle Door, is it? Christ, what a schlepp that is. I'd need a bus to get up there now. Chair lift.'

Kavanagh remembers that self-deprecating humour was always part of the Adrian Lowe schtick. It was as if he wanted to highlight his own failings and trivialise them before anyone else had a chance to wade in.

'God, it's good to see you,' Lowe says now. 'How long's it been . . . must be ten years at least?'

'Nearer twenty.'

'Bloody hell – is it really?' he gasps. 'So how come you haven't been to see me before now? Should I be taking this personally?'

'I don't visit London that much. Only been back a couple of times.'

Lowe nods as if able to make sense of this. Kavanagh wonders just how much he knows about the circumstances surrounding his abrupt departure. More than most, he decides. But not everything, that's for sure.

'Thought I might see you at the funeral last summer, but I guess you weren't able to make it.'

Kavanagh explains that he was out of the country at the time and didn't hear about it until too late. A more truthful answer would be that he sat the whole thing out in Dorset and travelled up the following day to visit Maurice's grave and pay his respects in private, but that would only invite further speculation he doesn't need. Anything that hints at a reluctance on his part to associate with certain individuals is best kept to himself.

'Something else, that was,' says Lowe. 'So many people there, they had to set up a PA system to allow the people outside to follow the service. They had the wake afterwards at The

Grosvenor – you remember that place? Shut the tables down for the day and used it as a spillover from the main bar area. It was that crowded, you could hardly breathe. They reckon Jimmy put fifteen grand behind the bar. Likes his big gestures, does Jimmy.'

Kavanagh picks at a piece of fluff that has attached itself to his trousers and brushes it onto the floor, a gesture that is not lost on Lowe.

'Small talk, eh?' he laughs. 'Never did have much time for that, did you? Nice social chat with you was like getting blood out of a stone. So what brings you here then? I take it you didn't come all this way just to bring me my favourite sweets.'

Kavanagh says nothing for a few moments. He's learnt from the best the value of leaving significant gaps in the conversation to put the other person on edge and emphasise the importance of what comes next.

'I have a job for you,' he says.

'Always good to hear.'

'A few ground rules first, though.'

'Of course.'

'I'm not looking for any favours. I'll pay the going rate, but I need to be sure this stays strictly between the two of us. I'm taking something of a risk coming here.'

Lowe grins, then draws an imaginary zip across as if to seal his lips, turns a non-existent key and pretends to throw it over his shoulder. There is something too casual and light-hearted about the gesture for Kavanagh's liking.

'I'm serious about this,' he says, leaning forward. 'One hundred per cent confidential. You tell no one.'

Lowe flinches and gives an unconvincing chuckle.

'For Christ's sake, Jon – lighten up, will you? This is me you're talking to. Discretion's not just my middle name. It's my calling card.'

'I'm not doubting you – just making myself clear. If this gets out, and the wrong people hear about it, it won't be because I've been shouting my mouth off. That will leave you as the only person I'll be coming to for explanations. You understand what I'm saying, right?'

'OK, OK – I get the message. Schtum. Jesus, how many times have we worked together, eh? And how many times have I let you down?'

'You haven't. But there's a first time for most things and I don't want you to get the wrong idea. This is very, *very* important to me.'

'Got it.' He realises Kavanagh's stare hasn't left him. 'I've *got* it, OK?' he repeats. With something approaching a pout, he opens the desk drawer again and takes from it a notepad. As an afterthought, he dives back inside and removes a handful of jelly babies from the bag, lining them head to toe along the edge of the desk before picking them off one by one.

'Your fault,' he says when he senses disapproval in Kavanagh's expression. 'Stressing me out like that for no good reason.'

He opens the notepad and takes a biro from the tray in front of him.

'So what is it you want me to do exactly?'

'I want you to find someone.'

'Well, I guessed that much,' says Lowe, apparently still determined to make clear his resentment at Kavanagh's lack of faith in him. 'Who are we talking about?'

'It's a girl.'

'Ah, *cherchez la femme*. Name?'

'Can't say for sure.'

Lowe puts the pen down for a moment and looks at Kavanagh as if to reassure himself that he's being serious.

'No name?'

'Start with Jessica Murphy, although she might conceivably have taken her mother's surname after her father died. And whether she did or not, there's every chance she ended up in the system and was fostered afterwards which could mean her name has been changed since then. As I say, I've no way of knowing what it is now.'

Lowe scribbles furiously, then sits back to look at what he has on the sheet in front of him.

'So . . . we'll assume Jessica for now. Date of birth?'

'Don't have one.'

'Of course you don't.'

'I do know she was three in early 1999. Had a birthday coming up soon,' he adds, remembering what Maurice said at the time. 'So if we say sometime in the summer of 1995, that's about as close as I can get.'

'Better than nothing, I suppose. Name of parents?'

'Father was Leon. I never knew the mother's name. All I know about her is that she might have had a bit of a drug habit and went back to New Zealand when she and Murphy split up. Dunedin, as far as I know. Your guess is as good as mine where she went from there.'

Lowe scribbles down the meagre details. The next three or four minutes are taken up with other questions to which Kavanagh has few definite answers.

'So,' Lowe says eventually. 'To summarise, you'd like me to track down a girl whose name is possibly Jessica Murphy but who may now be Jessica Something Else or not even Jessica at all, who lived in Weybridge nineteen years ago but might also have been brought up on the other side of the world and who may have been adopted, either in this country or in New Zealand and given a completely different name and whose movements and whereabouts are a complete mystery since the end of the last century. Have I missed anything?'

'If it was easy I'd do it myself. I'm paying for your services.'

'Jesus,' says Lowe, shaking his head and deciding now is as good a time as any to polish off the remaining jelly babies. 'This is going to take a while, you know that.'

'How long?'

'Hard to say. We're talking needles and haystacks here and you can't even tell me which haystack.'

'You're good at what you do. And it's urgent.'

Lowe shrugs his shoulders.

'I get that. I've got a lot on my plate, though. You're not my only customer – there are others ahead of you in the queue, expecting results from me in the next couple of weeks.'

'So bump them.'

'*Bump* them? Christ, Jon. You know the sort of people who come to me for this kind of service. You don't even smile at them in case they think you're taking the piss. They're not used to coming second to anyone. And you sure as hell don't *bump* them.'

Kavanagh says nothing, waiting for the storm of protests to blow over. Lowe is the first to break the silence.

'Look, you know me. I'll do what I can, but at a conservative estimate you're looking at a couple of weeks minimum for this. I don't suppose you can tell me what's got you so fired up about this girl and why she needs to be found yesterday?'

Kavanagh narrows his eyes.

'No – course not,' says Lowe. 'Stupid question. Forget I asked. It's just . . . there's so little to go on here. You know me – I'm not shy when it comes to shouting my mouth off about how good I am at this sort of thing but there *are* limits. I can't offer any guarantees I'll be able to track this girl down at all . . . not with the little you've given me.'

'I'm sure you'll find a way. Just let me know how much this is going to cost and I'll forward the money. In the meantime I'll be waiting to hear from you. I take it you know how to contact me?'

'Funny.'

'And remember what I said. Our little secret.'

'Yeah, yeah. *Omerta* – I get it.'

They shake hands as Kavanagh gets ready to leave, and Lowe can't shake the feeling there's something artificial about it, as if much of the warmth that was present earlier has gone. It's been replaced by more than a touch of awkwardness. Kavanagh, it seems to him, has been uncharacteristically prickly, almost unapproach-able throughout the meeting. Or maybe *uncharacteristically* is the wrong word because, now he comes to think of it, there was always this slightly unnerving distance he wore about him like a scruffy overcoat. The scar didn't help, of course – it's always made Lowe feel uncomfortable, undecided as to whether he should look away or whether that in itself would be more offensive than gawping at it. It goes beyond that though, as if the external wound is only a pale reflection of significant scarring within.

There's certainly *something* damaged about Kavanagh. Lowe remembers now that however hard he tried in the past to draw him out of himself, get him to *chill, for Christ's sake*, he never quite managed to do it. There was always this reserve, a barrier he could never get past. He's always had respect for the guy but there's this slight frisson of fear somewhere in the mix which means they've never been as close as they might have been. All the same, they've at least enjoyed a solid, professional relationship until now and he certainly deserves a little more respect than has been shown to him in the past few minutes.

He escorts Kavanagh as far as the front entrance, struggling with the aches and pains in his knees and aware of the exaggerated roll in his gait, a subconscious attempt to redistribute the weight. Heaven only knows what all this exercise is doing to his hips. The only reason he's volunteered to see him out is to make sure he actually leaves the premises. He offers to call a taxi for him, but Kavanagh says he fancies a walk. He's been cooped up all morning, wants to stretch his legs for a bit, then get a Tube back to Waterloo. As they walk through the store, Lowe considers telling him to have a little flutter on a horse named Monkscroft Lad which is running at Newton Abbot tomorrow but decides he doesn't deserve it if he can't treat an old friend with appropriate respect.

They shake hands again, Kavanagh nodding, Lowe grinning as if the awkwardness of the past few minutes never happened – *just business*. But the smile disappears from his face the moment Kavanagh turns his back and sets off down the street. He stays where he is, watching surreptitiously from the doorway, causing the automatic doors to open and close repeatedly. Once he's sure it's safe to do so, he goes back inside and snaps at one of his young employees in passing for sitting casually on the corner of one of the desks. Or maybe for no better reason than that he's there.

He blames Kavanagh. *That's what he does to people*, he thinks. *Unnerves you. Leaves you with all this pent-up anxiety that has to come out somehow.*

When he gets back to his office, he opens the blinds so that he'll see if anyone is coming. He knows what he's going to do but takes a minute or so just to weigh the relative merits of alternative courses of action. It doesn't take long. This, a seductive voice is telling him, this could be the answer to all his problems. It could also be extremely dangerous, of course, but if he turns his nose up at such an obvious opportunity, he's finished anyway . . . as good as. It doesn't feel as if he has much choice in the matter.

He opens the drawer again and checks on the off-chance that another jelly baby might be lurking there. Then he screws the empty bag into a ball and lobs it at the bin in the far corner of the office. It hits the rim and falls in first time, a success he's happy to interpret as a good omen.

Then he picks his mobile up from the desk and flicks through his list of contacts.

8

1999
The Grosvenor Snooker Club, Bromley

If Kavanagh was anywhere within striking distance, The Grosvenor was where he preferred to spend odd breaks during the day. The bar section had a few lunchtime regulars who'd never been near a snooker cue in their lives. He'd had dealings with one or two of them in the past – nothing serious, just a gentle reminder that everyone has his place and stepping out of line inevitably invites consequences. He might exchange nods with them while he bought his drink and one of Lennie's rolls, but their attempts to ingratiate themselves through casual conversation never kept him from his table in the far corner where he would read his book without fear of being disturbed. Lennie might come over now and again to wipe the table and check whether he wanted another drink, but otherwise his desire for privacy was understood and respected.

The regular crash of snooker balls next door competed with the beeps from a couple of gambling machines and the medley of 1960s pop songs that Lennie played on a loop throughout the day, but Kavanagh was always able to tune it all out. He never went anywhere without a book. Doctor's appointments, chauffeuring duties, Tube journeys – there weren't many everyday activities that didn't offer up pockets of dead time, twenty minutes or so that could profitably be filled by reading a few more pages. Vic clearly regarded him as some sort of alien, accused him of preferring the world of make-believe to the one everyone else lived in. It probably never occurred to him for one moment that he wasn't far wrong.

Kavanagh had been given an extended break for lunch. He was due to drive Vic to Balham at some stage that afternoon, a decision on Maurice's part which he interpreted as an attempt to thaw out some of the atmosphere that had been distinctly chilly since that meeting a week earlier. The two of them had been tasked with breathing a touch of realism into a local journalist whose enthusiastic pursuit of a story was in danger of making waves for Maurice, but Vic had phoned The Grosvenor to say he was held up and wouldn't be there for another hour and a half at least. Kavanagh had given a silent cheer. This was shaping up to be a better than average day.

He was about three-quarters of the way through *Waterland*, completely lost in the tortured world of Tom and Mary Crick, when he heard the first shouts coming from next door. Whatever noise there might be in the bar, there was an unwritten rule that, in the snooker suite itself, voices should be lowered and used sparingly. Lennie was something of a traditionalist when it came to snooker. Atmosphere was everything. Silence was a given, to be broken only by the collision of the cue ball with its target, the swish of the brass pointer as it slid across the runner on the scoreboard, and the occasional squeak as players chalked their cue. These unwritten house rules were clear and understood by everyone.

Except Jimmy Hayes.

When he heard the shouts, Kavanagh glanced across at Lennie and nodded to let him know he had this. The tables were rarely busy at that time of day, so it was more out of curiosity than serious concern that he left his book open on the table alongside his unfinished drink and walked over to the door leading to the snooker suite.

He arrived just in time to see four young lads advancing on the occupants of the only other table in use. He was surprised to discover that the person making all the noise was Jimmy, not because this was in any way atypical of him but because he was meant to be revising at home on study leave. If he wanted to sneak off and not draw attention to himself, choosing to go somewhere his father owned and then getting involved in a fracas didn't seem like the smartest of moves. Then again, that made it par for the course where Jimmy was concerned.

'Who the fuck do you think you're talking to?' He was yelling, his back to Kavanagh as he sauntered over to the other table where two men had broken off from their game. His three mates were happy to hang back slightly, intrigued to see where Jimmy might choose to take this.

'Away back to your own table,' said the older of the two men, who seemed relatively unconcerned. 'And keep the noise down. There are rules in here.'

'You have any idea who I am?'

'Dunno, lad. That kid from *Home Alone*, maybe?'

'Jimmy,' barked Kavanagh, aware that the boy was holding the narrow end of his cue. He knew what was coming, knew also that he wasn't going to get there in time unless his voice created enough of a distraction to buy the extra three seconds he needed. But even as he spoke, Jimmy swung the cue with as much force as his sixteen-year-old frame could muster and although the man threw up his left hand to take some of the force from the blow, the follow-through caught him somewhere near the temple, sending him to the floor. Standing over him, Jimmy gripped the cue in both hands above his head and was about to take another free shot when he was suddenly yanked off his feet as Kavanagh flung himself across one corner of the table, grabbing him by the collar and sending them both to the floor. Jimmy was on his feet again almost immediately, eyes blazing, stance wide, arms swinging wildly until Kavanagh spun him round and grabbed him in a bear hug from behind.

For most people this would have been enough of a deterrent. Instead Jimmy slammed his heel into Kavanagh's shins with enough force to do serious damage if it had caught him flush on the bone. Angry with himself for having let his guard slip, Kavanagh swept Jimmy's feet out from under him and turned him onto his stomach, pushing his face into the floor. He knelt on him, twisting one arm behind his back and clamping it firmly in place while his victim squirmed and yelled beneath him.

'Are you going to calm down?' he asked, striving for the quietest voice he could conjure up in an attempt to draw the heat out of Jimmy's protests.

'Get the fuck off me.'

'When you've calmed down.'

'You're breaking my arm, you freak!'

'Then I suggest you stop struggling. You're embarrassing yourself.'

'What the fuck are you doing, just standing there?' Jimmy yelled, twisting his head round to glare over his shoulder at his three mates. 'GET HIM OFF ME.'

Two of the three clearly presented no threat at all, more than happy to stay on the other side of the table. The third took an instinctive step forward as if to wade in on Jimmy's behalf.

'Could be the worst decision you've made all week,' panted Kavanagh, pinning the have-a-go hero in place with a stare that left no room for ambiguity. The boy took half a step back, having thought better of it. Sometimes the scar had its uses.

'My dad will fucking DESTROY you for this,' grunted Jimmy, who was clearly in a lot of discomfort from the grip Kavanagh was exerting on him. 'You got any idea what he's going to say when I tell him what you did?'

'I don't know,' said Kavanagh. 'How about I phone him and we find out?'

'Fuck . . . you.'

Kavanagh could sense Jimmy was weakening. The boy had made two or three sudden surges in an attempt to take him by surprise. Each time Kavanagh had responded by pushing his face firmly into the floor and tightening his hold.

The man who had been assaulted by Jimmy was now sitting upright. There were already signs of a swelling over his left eye and his playing partner was stooping to attend to him, assisted by Lennie who had come through to offer help.

Kavanagh nodded and Lennie helped the man to his feet, taking him through to the toilet area with the aid of his playing partner, who was clearly shaken by the sudden outbreak of violence. Then Kavanagh turned his attention back to Jimmy, who seemed to have given up at last on the idea of anyone coming to his rescue.

'OK, here's what we're going to do,' he said, gradually easing the grip but maintaining enough control to be in a position to tighten it if necessary. 'I'm going to let you go and you're going to get to your feet and behave yourself. I need you to understand that if you don't – if you start acting up in any way – I'll put you on the floor again, only this time I won't be quite so gentle about it. You with me?'

Jimmy lay there, mouth clamped shut, stubbornly refusing to give him the satisfaction. The word quit had never been part of his vocabulary. Kavanagh debated for a moment whether it was worth insisting on an answer. He remembered the seething rage he used to carry around with him when he was Jimmy's age, the bitter sting of humiliation on those occasions when his body wasn't able to cash the cheques his mouth had written. Pushing more buttons wasn't going to achieve anything positive. With some people you just had to redefine where to draw the line between success and failure and live with it.

He let go of Jimmy's wrist and removed his knee from the small of his back. Then he got to his feet and stepped back slightly, not just to the give the boy some space but also because he'd learnt from his earlier loss of concentration and wouldn't be making any more careless mistakes. He picked the cue up from the floor and placed it on the table as Jimmy clambered to his feet, trying to manipulate the discomfort from his shoulder without making it obvious.

'Go home,' Kavanagh said. 'You're meant to be revising for your exams, not pissing your life away in snooker halls.'

'Fuck you, you freak,' said Jimmy, spitting blood from his mouth onto the floor. 'You don't get to tell me what I can and can't do.'

Kavanagh ignored the personal insult but kept a close eye on the cue, which was still within Jimmy's reach. If he made a move for it, he knew he'd have to react quickly and come up with a response that was measured rather than extreme. This was a sixteen-year-old boy, he reminded himself. Maurice's only remaining son. He knew from past experience that the only lessons people like Jimmy would ever learn from being humiliated were ones that led to major problems later. His instincts told him that allowing Maurice to deal with it would be the right option here.

Jimmy pushed himself away from the table, barging his way through his chastened friends who hurried meekly after him. They looked as if they knew what was in store for them once they'd left the building and were already mentally preparing their excuses. Kavanagh followed them out of the snooker suite and watched as Jimmy paused in the doorway leading to the stairs. He turned to face Kavanagh, dragging his sleeve across his mouth to wipe away the blood that was seeping from a cut on the inside of his lip.

'If I looked like you, I'd fucking shoot myself,' he said. Then, without averting his eyes for one second, defiance blazing in his expression, he caught hold of the end of the nearest table and turned it over before disappearing through the doorway.

9

May 2018
The Ascot Lounge, Soho

Anna takes a break after the next song and walks over to a table that has been reserved for her by the bar staff. Lounge Lizard is smiling and waggling his glass, presumably offering to buy her a drink. She's sure he's going to get up and walk over any minute now and is searching for a put-down that will dampen his enthusiasm when she sees a familiar figure emerging from the crowd at the bar and heading in her direction. Lounge Lizard promptly swivels on his stool in search of alternative prey.

Ches Headley looks like a fifty-year-old eccentric on his way to a fancy-dress party. His style is singular to say the least, somewhere between cowboy chic and rockabilly retro. Tonight his outfit consists of a studded white shirt, buttoned at the wrist; obligatory bootlace tie; black waistcoat; skinny black jeans and grey suede creepers. He's not wearing his black Stetson for once, presumably because he wants to show off the pompadour hairstyle, which is new and would probably look better on someone thirty years younger. *Have to applaud him for effort, though*, she thinks. *You can say what you like but he's never going to go unnoticed.*

He's carrying a tray bearing two glasses and what looks encouragingly like a bottle of champagne, which is an interesting development to say the least. She can count on the fingers of one hand the number of times he's been in contact in recent weeks, let alone put his hand in his pocket. When she first signed with him he came along to a number of her appearances to offer moral support. He was phoning and emailing on a regular basis yet, in the past eighteen months or so, any contact has been initiated by her and he's been difficult to pin down. She understands she's not the only client he has to worry about but is worried that Ches once thought he saw something in her that hasn't actually materialised and is otherwise occupied, scouring the clubs and bars for *the next big thing*.

All of which makes his presence here tonight and the bottle of champagne all the more intriguing.

'Go on then,' she says. 'To what do I owe the pleasure?'

He's beaming, not quite from ear to ear but clearly feeling very pleased with himself.

'What – a man can't come and buy his favourite lady a drink from time to time?'

'You hear me complaining?'

She waits patiently for an explanation while he wrestles with the foil and the wire cage protecting the cork. *Veuve Clicquot*, she notes. *Pushing the boat out a bit. What is this?* There's a satisfying pop as the cork finally comes free. Ches picks up a glass and fills it carefully to the brim, pausing at intervals to allow the bubbles to drop to their natural level. He hands it to her and fills his own before putting the bottle down on the tray. Then he raises his glass to tap it against hers.

'So . . . what are we celebrating exactly?' she asks.

He sits back in his chair, smugness personified.

'Go on, then – how much do you love your Uncle Ches?'

'Depends on how long he's going to keep ducking my questions.'

He looks around, as if to make sure he's not likely to be overheard. *Always the showman,* she thinks. She watches as he fingers the bootlace tie, grin still fixed in place.

'You got any plans for the next few months?'

'Depends what you mean by *a few.*'

'How about . . . start of June through to the start of September?'

She raises an appreciative eyebrow at this, taking a sip from her drink and half choking as some of it goes down the wrong way. She puts the glass down and reaches into her bag for a tissue.

'You're kidding me – three months?'

She's never had a contract anywhere near that length.

'Near enough.'

'OK . . . so where's the catch? How many nights a week are we talking about?'

'Five,' he says, clearly enjoying the way he's keeping her dangling, feeding it to her piece by piece. 'You get two days clear each week, one in midweek plus Sundays. Maybe the chance for some lunchtime sessions to top it up if you fancy it.'

She shakes her head.

'You know I can't do anything during the day.'

'Ah well,' he says, raising a finger to stop her right there. 'You haven't heard where it is yet.'

'It doesn't matter where it is. I'll never get time off work for lunchtime gigs.'

'Well, let's see how you feel when you've heard the rest of it, shall we?' he says, apparently not troubled in the slightest by this setback. 'Start by having a guess at where you'll be singing.'

'Ches,' she sighs, her impatience getting the better of her. 'You know how many bars and clubs there are in London? Just tell me.'

'A clue then. Forget London.'

Now she knows he's losing it, and she can feel the sense of anticipation that has been building ever since he arrived starting to drain away. This is just typical Ches bullshit.

'Forget Lon— how can I forget London? I can't travel any distance, you know that. There's no way I can get away from work before five. Where is this place anyway?'

Ches chuckles. This is clearly the best thing that's happened to him all week.

'You got a bikini?'

'Excuse me?'

'OK – how would you prefer to spend your summer?' he asks with the conviction of a man who knows the question is all but rhetorical. 'Option one, you traipse around London day after day for peanuts, trying to keep groups of tourists in line, churning out the same old pre-rehearsed material till you're sick of it, either dodging downpours or sweating like a pig every time the sun comes out and swearing you'd give your right arm for a breeze to take the edge off it.'

He pauses to allow her to join the dots and accept that this is pretty much her average working day.

'Or . . .' he continues, dragging the word out until it stretches way beyond two letters, '. . . there's this.'

He takes his Samsung from his pocket, taps away for a few seconds, then passes it across to her.

'No brainer,' he says, leaning back in his chair to take in her reaction.

Bognor, she's been thinking. *Weston.* He's got her a summer season on some end-of-the-pier show. She's preparing herself for a difficult decision because the idea appeals to her and will certainly be the best opportunity she's had so far to get herself out there in front of a wider audience and make a name for herself. The fabric of the business is stitched together with tales of struggling singer/songwriters who've dragged themselves from one gig to the next in the hope of being discovered and who finally get that lucky break. A summer season would certainly be a step in the right direction – and after all her complaints about the lack of opportunities coming her way, she can expect a shedload of grief from Ches if she rains on this plan he's put together, but . . .

But.

It took her eight months to find a house share she can afford in London, *house share* being a bit of a euphemism but at least it's *her* small bedroom for as long as she has a guaranteed income and can pay the rent. The fact that it took her so long to find somewhere within her limited budget and in an area where she felt reasonably safe makes her feel very edgy about the prospect of having to give it up. Any summer season outside a manageable radius is going to be out of the question. If it means walking away from her job, there's no guarantee it will still be there for her when the three months are up. Dreams are one thing but pursuing them is a lottery and at twenty-three, with nothing and no one to fall back on, she's not sure she can afford to gamble away a hard-earned and secure base that easily.

Then she sees the photos.

And realises it's neither Bognor nor Weston he's talking about. It's not even England.

When she goes back to the piano for her second set of the night, she's still in something of a daze. Ches has apologised, saying he can't stay – *so many details still to tie up, you know what it's like, sweetheart. Busy busy.* She's not remotely bothered, has enough to think about as it is. She'll need to switch on in a minute, put her game face back on and focus on the music but first she could do with a moment or two to compose herself.

Portugal, she thinks, trying not to drum her fingers on the piano in her excitement.

Praia D'El Rey.

She's never actually heard of it. In fact, ridiculous as it might seem, she had this momentary surge of disappointment when Ches corrected her immediate assumption that it must be some-where in the Algarve. The moment he mentioned Portugal, her thoughts automatically turned to places like Albufeira and Praia da Rocha, which have been on her wishlist for some time. Praia D'El Rey, it turns out, is further north on the Silver Coast, well away from the buzz and energy of the Algarve, but the photos are stunning nevertheless. It's described as a golf and beach resort and although the golf course does nothing for her, the rest looks irresistible – golden beaches stretching into the distance at the foot of dramatic cliffs and hemmed in on the other side by the Atlantic. According to Ches, the accommodation clause in her contract won't extend to anything like the top end of the range but, as guest performer for the summer, she will at least have her own rent-free apartment just up from the beach. And she'll be performing there five nights a week!

Will be, she notes with a smile to herself, because *would be . . . if* has been taken off the table. Despite any reservations she may have, she knows she can't turn this offer down – not if she's serious about making a name for herself in this business. She tried for a while to go down the pragmatic route, the adult one maybe. Beat herself up for being so irresponsible as to give this proposal even the time of day. The reality would never match up to whatever Ches was pitching – if she knows anything at all from her dealings with him, it's that nothing he promises ever bears more than a passing resemblance to what he delivers. It was just too big a gamble with too many unknowns.

But a season in Portugal . . . fourteen weeks' work guaranteed and a new audience. Accommodation provided. Travel covered for her. It's like all her Christmases coming at once. And she's not stupid. Even if it *does* sound too good to be true, how is that any different from dreams that eventually materialise? How is she supposed to know the difference unless she takes a chance for once in her life and goes for it?

There's a lot she'll need to think about, like her job with IC Tours for starters. They're not going to be happy to let her go at such short notice and may not be prepared to take her back when the summer's over. There's her house share too which she'll have to sublet if she doesn't want to lose it . . . and she definitely doesn't.

On top of all that, there's the small matter of her sister who is meant to be coming to stay with her in London for a couple of weeks once she finishes her second year at the Dance Academy at the end of next month. She and Emmie don't see each other as often as she'd like and they were wondering about disappearing off to Cornwall for a week if she could get time off work.

Now she's wondering about the possibility of Emmie flying out to Praia D'El Rey to stay with her. Maybe she can give her a ring later tonight and see how she feels about it all. Surely they'll be able to work something out between them.

Problems . . . but none of them insurmountable, because she knows this much: if she walks away from this opportunity, and it turns out to be the only chance she'll ever have, she'll spend the rest of her life regretting it.

And there are enough echoes in her life of her mother's fate without adding to them unnecessarily.

Gamble or not – she's in.

10

1999
Twickenham

Two months since he was last here . . . and no Diet Sprite on offer this time, he was quick to note. Maurice had poured himself a glass of Laphroaig, but his customary hospitality was conspicuous by its absence in ways that went beyond the simple failure to offer his guest a drink. There was no trace of warmth in his welcome. No hand on Kavanagh's elbow as he ushered him into the room. No small talk about the weather or the ache in his joints as he made his way across to his favourite armchair. Everything felt more formal and business-like, as stiff as Maurice's movements. It didn't necessarily amount to much in itself, but when the stakes are high it's easy to read into the tiniest of gestures a level of significance that is entirely disproportionate.

At least there was no Vic to contend with this time, which could only be a good thing. In asking for Maurice's lifelong friend and trusted partner to be excluded from the meeting, Kavanagh understood he'd been pushing his luck more than a little, but anything that shifted the odds even marginally in his favour had to be worth the gamble. The next hour or so was going to be hard enough without unnecessary distractions, most of them the product of macho posturing. There was no reason why this shouldn't be a civilised conversation between adults . . . if he could just keep a lid on things.

This wasn't the most encouraging of starts, though. Maurice nodded at the naughty chair and Kavanagh dropped into it, making himself as comfortable as the circumstances permitted. Through the open French windows the sound of a motor mower drifted up from the lawns at the rear of the house. He wondered whether Maurice might decide to close them, if not to shut out the disturbance then at least to ensure a modicum of privacy, but instead he chose to ignore the stiff breeze that was rippling the curtains and took his customary seat directly opposite.

Game face on.

Kavanagh knew better than to waste time trying to pick up any clues from his expression.

'Thank you for agreeing to see me,' he began, aiming to get things off on the right footing. Businesslike. Assertive without the arrogance. Resolute but not insensitive. Grateful, yes . . . but totally unambiguous.

Almost immediately the phone on the rustic oak sideboard started to ring. Maurice stayed where he was, tapping his fingers on the arm of his chair while he waited for it to fall silent. When it did so after half a dozen rings, he crossed the room and lifted the receiver, leaving it off the hook to ensure there would be no further interruptions before resuming his seat. Kavanagh wondered if he'd engineered this call as a tactical ploy. He wouldn't have put it past him.

'Before we get started,' Maurice said, the moment he was finally ready, 'there's something I'd like to clear up. Just so you know where we stand.'

He loved his ground rules. Kavanagh nodded. Waited.

'You know how many times someone's asked me for a face-to-face chat and specifically requested that Vic be excluded from said meeting?'

The question was almost certainly rhetorical but Kavanagh decided to cover himself with a brief shake of the head.

'Never,' came the reply. 'You know why? I'll tell you, even though I'm pretty sure you're smart enough to work it out for yourself. No one's ever asked because they have a healthy regard for their own personal wellbeing and prospects within the company.'

He reached down to straighten his socks. Any part of his apparel was ripe for exploitation when it came to factoring in pauses. A conversation with Maurice was a symphony in clothing adjustment, each movement conceived with a specific purpose in mind.

'Vic and I may go way, way back,' he continued, 'but he's accountable the same as everyone else. If anyone has concerns regarding the way he goes about his work, they're more than welcome to raise them with me. The least I expect though is that they'll have the decency to include him in the conversation so that he can face his accusers and defend himself. If they haven't the—'

He paused, presumably seeking an expression that would keep his language out of the gutter.

'—the *intestinal fortitude* to be open about things and discuss matters of this sort like adults, they can keep their comments to themselves. This is a business, not a school playground.'

Kavanagh knew exactly why no one had ever come forward. Criticising Vic to his face, even with Maurice there to keep the peace, would be nobody's idea of fun. As for what they might be letting themselves in for once the meeting was over . . . well, that didn't bear thinking about.

'I have to confess, I was a wee bit surprised that you of all people should ask for him to be excluded from this discussion. I've always thought you were the one person who wasn't intimidated by him.'

'I'm not intimidated.'

'And yet you'd rather not speak in front of him?'

Kavanagh thought for a moment, choosing his words carefully.

'This has nothing to do with Vic.'

'Is it to do with the Syndicate?'

'Yes.'

'Then it has everything to do with Vic.'

Kavanagh took a deep breath.

'I'm not trying to go behind his back,' he said, not entirely sure that was true. 'I'm not complaining about how he does his job but there are things I need to discuss with you on a personal level. Vic's presence tends to complicate matters.'

'Complicate in what way?'

'He . . . tends to spice things up unnecessarily.'

Maurice took a few seconds to weigh this up. Then, for the first time since Kavanagh entered the room, he thought he detected traces of amusement in his expression.

'He does, doesn't he?' said Maurice . . . and Kavanagh persuaded himself that the ice was starting to crack just a little. 'I can assure you he's a lot less impulsive than was once the case.'

If this latest incarnation was a significant improvement on the old model, Kavanagh could only imagine what the unreconstructed version of Vic must have been like. Again he opted to keep his thoughts to himself. Cheap shots at Maurice's lifelong friend when he wasn't there to defend himself could only be counter-productive.

'We'll call him a work in progress,' said Maurice. He chuckled, pleased with himself, and swirled the liquid around in his glass before taking a sip and replacing it on the table.

'So,' he continued, leaning back and tugging thoughtfully at his lower lip with thumb and forefinger. 'If it's not about Vic, what's this burning issue you wanted to raise with me? Please don't tell me Jimmy's been up to his tricks again.'

Kavanagh shook his head.

'I trust he's apologised to you for that business in The Grosvenor?'

This time he thought before nodding. Swallowed. Hoped Maurice hadn't picked up on the slight hesitation.

'I haven't thanked you yet for the way you dealt with that,' Maurice continued. 'Just as well you were there. Jimmy's not a bad lad but he's at that age, you know? A sense of entitlement and the absolute conviction that he's invulnerable – not to mention a mischievous streak.'

He paused briefly and Kavanagh wondered for a moment whether something in his own expression was betraying his thoughts.

'He's a handful, I'll be the first to admit it,' Maurice added quickly, 'but I'm convinced that once he's worked his way out of this phase he's going through, there's a fine young man in there waiting for his day in the sun. The more exposure he has to the sort of example you yourself can provide, the sooner he'll grow out of it.'

Kavanagh didn't see it as a phase, more a serious character defect, stimulated by too little discipline and too much time on his hands – pretty much the way he'd felt about Sean, in fact. The apology Jimmy had offered under duress was a joke, no other word for it. He'd barely been able to keep the smirk off his face or the yawn out of his voice. And if there was any doubt at all about the lack of sincerity in the gesture, that was wiped out two weeks later when Kavanagh returned home one evening to find a police car outside his building and his flat ransacked – drawers emptied, the contents smashed and strewn across the floor. A neighbour had seen two lads climbing out of a window and called the police. They hadn't even bothered with balaclavas or masks and his description of Jimmy was almost as good as a photo.

Kavanagh had told the police he didn't want to pursue the matter, dismissing it as a practical joke that had gone too far, an explanation they hadn't believed for one minute but were more than happy to accept. He'd said nothing to Maurice and made a point of avoiding Jimmy, preferring instead to focus on the bigger picture.

'OK,' said Maurice. 'It's not Vic or Jimmy, so what was it you wanted to discuss?'

Kavanagh paused and allowed the moment to breathe with him. He'd spent his time here learning from the best.

'I came to see you about six months ago . . . about my grand-father,' he said. 'I don't know how much of it you remember.'

Maurice frowned, trying to recall the details.

'Dementia, wasn't it?'

Kavanagh nodded.

'Things have got worse since then. Problem is, he's a very stubborn man – doesn't trust doctors, refuses to see anyone.'

'How old is he?'

'Ninety-two.'

Maurice smiled. 'It's tough getting old,' he said. 'People have their pride, especially your grandfather's generation.'

'My grandmother phoned yesterday,' Kavanagh continued, anxious to keep the agenda moving forward. 'She was in tears – I don't remember hearing her cry before. The other night he got out of bed without waking her and wandered off, wearing just his pyjamas and slippers. A patrol car picked him up at 3 a.m. in an unlit country lane. He was three miles from home. No idea what he was doing there.'

Maurice's face fell.

'I'm sorry to hear that, son,' he said, leaning forward and patting him on the knee. It was an awkward gesture but that seemed to matter less than the need to establish some sort of contact. 'I know how much they both mean to you.'

'They brought me up. Took me in when they didn't have to. It can't have been easy for them, both in their fifties. I owe them a lot.'

'I understand,' said Maurice, shifting back in his chair. 'And now you want to do your bit for them, I suppose.'

'I need to,' said Kavanagh, encouraged by the way this was going. 'He won't go into a home. She can't get him to shift on that. It's their cottage – he's lived there all his life and he says that's where he's going to die, not in some institution. And my grandmother accepts that and wants to make whatever time he has left as comfortable for him as possible, but she can't cope. It's a full-time job and she's pushing ninety herself. She's more or less permanently on the front line and would never have rung me if she wasn't desperate.'

'Of course she wouldn't,' said Maurice. 'And you should be there. You did the right thing in coming to me. So . . . bottom line. How long do you think you'll need?'

And here, Kavanagh thought to himself, is where things might just get a little sticky. Maurice has missed the point – possibly inadvertently, more likely anything but. Subtexts rarely escaped him.

'I said I owe my grandparents a lot,' he said, studying his own hands as they struggled to find something with which to occupy themselves. A can or glass would have been so useful. Instead he found himself threading his fingers through the lace pattern on the antimacassar on each arm of the chair. 'The same goes for you these past nine years.'

'You want to take a couple of weeks?' suggested Maurice, brushing off the compliment. 'A month maybe?'

'I don't want you to think I'm ungrateful. I appreciate everything you've done for me.'

'It'll take some rescheduling but we can probably stretch to that.'

Kavanagh paused before answering, knowing he needed to break up the parallel lines the conversation was taking.

'A month's not going to do it.'

Maurice pursed his lips.

'A month's a long time, son. You don't think that will give you long enough to get the lie of the land, check out what your grandmother needs and put it in place? There are agencies you can turn to in situations like this. If it's money you're worrying about . . .'

'She doesn't need money,' he said. 'They need *me*, both of them . . . for as long as it takes.'

Maurice blew through his lips, a sudden expulsion of air that made them quiver. His expression was less than inscrutable for once. A nervous tic twitched at the corner of one eye as he worked his way through the implications of Kavanagh's insistence on standing his ground.

'As long as it takes?' He gave a short laugh which somehow conveyed frustration, irritation and confusion in equal measure – anything but amusement. 'That's a bit of a blank cheque, wouldn't you say? I need you to be a wee bit more realistic than that. We could be looking at years here. Old people nowadays, especially if they've looked after themselves – they could both struggle on for another ten years or so. You can't expect us to be able to cover for you indefinitely.'

'I don't,' Kavanagh replied. 'I'm not asking for cover.'

He forced himself to look Maurice in the eye.

'I'm saying I'm done here.'

A dozy and apparently suicidal bluebottle made one lazy fly-past too many and was slapped out of the air by Maurice, who followed up quickly and stamped on it as it hit the floor. Then he rose from his seat without saying a word and limped over towards the French windows. He stood in the doorway for a moment, staring ostensibly at the mower as it chugged back and forth across the lawn but in all probability focusing way beyond that. When he next spoke, it was with his back still turned to Kavanagh.

'I can see why you didn't want Vic here,' he said. 'At least you've made one good decision today.'

Kavanagh could feel his legs starting to cramp up. He thought about getting to his feet, maybe wandering over to join Maurice at the window, but that seemed presumptuous and intrusive somehow. He felt awkward, wished he could be anywhere but here, groping his way through these complex negotiations. For some reason the country lanes around his grandparents' cottage flashed into his mind and he remembered those carefree afternoons he'd spent there as a teenager, running, running, free as a bird and with all the worries in the world rushing past him in the opposite direction. That was where he'd be right at that moment if he could choose, but that was a prize still to be earned. He knew these were still the early skirmishes of a much tougher battle.

'You do know what he'd say if he was here, don't you?' Maurice continued.

Kavanagh did his best not to shudder. The day he was able to access the thought processes of a psychopath like Vic Abraham and make sense of them it would be definitive proof that he had been doing this job for too long. Maurice stepped out onto the balcony, clapped his hands and called, 'Ginny – here, girl.' Seconds later, after more vocal encouragement, a small Pomeranian scuttled across the patio and leapt into his arms, licking his face in the excitement of having been summoned.

Maurice buried his nose in the dog's fur, then came back inside.

'He'd say, *This is not the effing army*, or something to that effect,' he said, resuming his seat. 'He'll tell you no one walks away from the Syndicate.'

'There's always a first for everything.'

'I didn't say no one had tried.'

And there it was. Maurice could do this when he needed to. He could switch in the blink of an eye from the affable guy two doors down who always stops at the gate for a chat on his way to get the morning paper to a cold, intimidating loner with a glare that could pin you to your seat. He only ever revealed brief glimpses of this side of his nature but then again that's all it took as a rule. He let the dog jump down to the carpet where she immediately started growling and tugging at Kavanagh's laces. He wasn't much of a dog lover himself, had no time whatsoever for small, pampered pets, and had to rein in his natural instinct to nudge Ginny away with his shoe.

'I thought you were happy here,' Maurice said, shaking his head more in feigned confusion than genuine disbelief.

'I have been,' he said, choosing his words carefully.

'So what's changed?'

'I've told you – I need to spend time with my family.'

'No . . . I don't buy that,' said Maurice. 'I thought we were your family. You know how much your work here is valued. It can't have escaped your attention that a lot of opportunities have been put your way. More than would usually be the case.'

'I know. And I appreciate it.'

'And this is how you intend to reward us for the time and effort we've invested in you? Don't play dumb with me, son. You know what that was all about. I'm not going to be doing this forever. I'll be sixty at the end of the year. In a fairer world, Sean would have been working alongside me by now with a view to taking over in ten years or so and I could have sailed off into the sunset and enjoyed a peaceful, stress-free retirement. I haven't given up on the idea that Jimmy will be able to step into my shoes eventually but he's sixteen and we both know he's light years away from being ready for that level of responsibility right now . . . and, let's face it, he's going to need a lot of help to get there.'

Amen to that, thought Kavanagh. A *miracle* was the word he'd have chosen.

'As soon as he's left school I want him working here and learning the ropes alongside someone I can trust, someone who will set the right example. It can't be Vic – he's not exactly in the first flush of youth and he's not going to be around forever. You're not daft, son. You know – you *must* know – I've been hoping Jimmy might have you there alongside him until the time's right for him to take over. There's no way we can afford to let you go.'

Kavanagh took a sudden interest in his shoelaces, keen to keep his thoughts to himself. This was pure fantasy. Admittedly he was not a father and had come to terms with the fact that he was never likely to be but, if the opportunity were to arrive, he'd like to think he'd be able to rise above the fits of self-delusion that so often seemed to go hand-in-hand with parenting. Anywhere away from his son, Maurice was a sharp, perceptive operator in a world where taking the measure of a man was a crucial pre-requisite for survival. The loss of his eldest son in such desperate circumstances was always going to cloud his judgement to some extent, but the fact that he could allow himself for one moment to imagine that Jimmy might one day magically acquire the qualities needed for leadership simply beggared belief. Ageing was one thing, maturing quite another. Jimmy Hayes had an IQ fixed firmly at room temperature and an intellect rivalled only by garden furniture. If further evidence were needed that Kavanagh was doing the right thing in getting out, this insight into the way things were heading provided it in spades.

He leant forward, hands clasped between his knees. *Respectful but firm*, he reminded himself.

'I'm sorry,' he said, maintaining eye contact. 'I didn't come here to ask your permission. I'm leaving this evening. I've got a number of things to sort out before I go but I've told my grandparents they can expect me later tonight.'

Maurice muttered something to himself, tossing back the remnants of his drink before hauling himself to his feet and heading over to the bar for a refill.

'It would be nice to think, after all we've done for you, you could at least extend me the courtesy of being honest with me about what's happening here. I'm going to get a wee bit personal here, son, and if you don't like it I'm afraid that's tough because one of us isn't being entirely honest and it's not yours truly.'

He poured himself a measure that was at least twice the size of his previous one and came back to sit eye to eye with Kavanagh.

'There's no nice way to put this – you have commitment issues. Your grandparents – they took you in and gave you a good solid home by your own admission. How did you reward that act of kindness? You took the first opportunity that presented itself to get away. Joined the army, for God's sake. You know I'm the last person to sing the praises of our armed forces but at least they provided you with a base and a new home. So what did you do?'

Maurice shaped as if to take another sip, then stopped himself. He was in full flow now, white specks appearing at the corners of his mouth.

'You upped and left them too because you thought, on the strength of one short conversation with a complete stranger, that we offered the prospect of a better life here. And you were right, as it happens. You're earning good money, you've been fast-tracked. We've looked after you, given you a new home. It was a total shot in the dark, a leap of faith if you like, but you got lucky.'

He shifted further forward in the seat until he was perched on the edge of it, uncomfortably close from Kavanagh's perspective.

'And what happens?' he continued. 'You decide it's time to move on again . . . and you've got the gall to use – as a pretext for this restless disposition of yours – those same grandparents you left to fend for themselves all those years ago and have hardly bothered to visit since. Ungrateful? That's not even the half of it.'

He paused. Kavanagh counted off the seconds. Each one that passed would bring him closer to the moment when he could leave, walk away from this life for good. He just needed to ride the storm for the next few minutes. He could do this.

But Maurice hadn't finished.

'I have to say I find your capacity for disloyalty quite breathtaking. The least you can do is be honest about the real reason you're leaving. You owe me that much.'

'I've told you,' he said, his voice unwavering.

'No, you haven't. It doesn't make sense. The timing of it . . . I know what's at the root of all this. We both know it's those teenagers.'

Now it was Kavanagh's turn to pause. This wasn't part of the plan. He'd been hoping, perhaps naïvely, that there might be a way to avoid acrimony and finger-pointing, that Maurice might be prepared to let him go without dragging up things from the past that could only turn this discussion into something more adversarial. It was very much in his best interests to leave on the best possible terms. Unfortunately, it was starting to look now as if that wasn't going to happen.

'Which teenagers?'

'Don't play the innocent with me, son. Never kid a kidder. You know damned well which teenagers. The ones arrested yesterday for that arson attack in Hendon a few months back.'

So, thought Kavanagh. Maurice was determined to go down that road. He wasn't sure tackling him head on was necessarily the wisest move, but at least a small part of him was pleased not to be leaving all of this unaddressed. The unwarranted attack on his loyalty, after everything that had happened, was beginning to bite deep.

'You mean the arson attack Leon Murphy was supposed to have carried out?'

'Meant to? There's no *meant to* about it. He killed that family.'

'So where do these two boys come into it then?'

'They don't. The police have got it wrong as usual – either that or they're trying to flush the guilty party out somehow. If those boys played any part in it, it was never more than peripheral, I can assure you of that. Murphy was the person responsible. And he's the one who put the petrol bomb through the window.'

'Why?'

Maurice gave every appearance of being genuinely puzzled by the question.

'What do you mean, why?'

'Why would Murphy do that? You never once told me and I never bothered to ask because it wasn't my place. Because it was enough for me that the instruction came from you. But I'm asking you now, even if it is a bit late in the day. What was Murphy's problem with that family that meant he was prepared to go to such lengths?'

Maurice tried to shrug it off and just for a moment he looked less than convincing. Clearly the possibility that he might actually be asked this question hadn't occurred to him.

'I have no idea. I don't concern myself with these petty rivalries. Some drug deal gone wrong maybe – who cares? The *why* doesn't matter. Your job was to concern yourself with the *who*.'

'As long as it's the right who,' said Kavanagh, refusing the implicit invitation to move on. 'What made you so sure it was Murphy?'

'I know everything that goes on around here, son. Everything,' he said, leaning on the word. 'I know for instance that you were in The Grosvenor when you first heard about the arrests and that there was a certain amount of conjecture at the bar until Lennie put a stop to it. You think I wasn't expecting you to come here looking for reassurances? I knew before you yourself did.'

'That wasn't all you knew though, was it?'

Maurice shook his head.

'You've lost me, son.'

'You knew how I felt about that side of my job. How I've always felt. You remember Munir Sirhan? He was the first person I ever killed out of uniform. Max Judd? Eddie Larner? With each of them I managed to square it with my conscience because I knew what they were and that there was only one way to stop them. I told myself it was a question of damage limitation, serving the greater good. But Murphy was the first one I'd never met, didn't know from Adam. I remember asking Vic how come I'd never even heard of him and being told it wasn't my job to ask questions, just get on with it and stop whingeing. Then suddenly you're there, telling me all about this family he's killed and I thought at the time it was a bit insensitive of you, given what happened to my family when I was a kid, but it certainly helped to focus the mind a little. The little pep talk served its purpose.'

Maurice linked his hands behind his head. He was tight-lipped, almost ashen, clearly taken aback.

'You think I'd do that?' he asked. 'Use a personal tragedy to . . . what? Motivate you to do a job I could just order you to do anyway? You think I'd stoop to those depths?'

There was a knock at the door.

'Not now,' Maurice barked.

The door opened slowly and one of Maurice's accountants poked his head round it.

'What part of *not now* don't you understand?'

The unfortunate victim swiftly withdrew his head and closed the door.

Maurice ran a hand across his face, then waved it in apology for having lost his temper. He conjured up a smile from somewhere. Unnatural didn't do it justice. It reminded Kavanagh of the father of the bride at a shotgun wedding.

'Take tomorrow,' he said, for all the world as if the previous discussion had never occurred. 'Tomorrow and the weekend. Go visit your grandparents and put in place whatever they need. If you're back here first thing on Monday, we'll say no more about this. Chalk it up to a bad day at the office.'

Kavanagh shook his head.

'It's not going to happen.'

'Take your time and think very carefully. You know how this works. You're either inside the tent or outside. If you opt for the latter it will be assumed you're pissing in, if you'll pardon the expression. We don't allow any of our people to place themselves in a position where they may be vulnerable to approaches from the authorities or other interested parties. We can't run the risk of anyone being coerced into operating against our best interests. You know all this – you need the time to think seriously about the implications of what you're proposing to do.'

'I'm leaving,' said Kavanagh, getting to his feet.

'Then you'll be making a very grave mistake.'

'Like Leon Murphy did?'

That struck home. Kavanagh could see it, the momentary confusion that flashed across Maurice's face.

'More riddles?'

'Lennie or whoever was reporting back to you from The Grosvenor obviously didn't brief you well enough. The conversation went on for a while before I got involved, but I could hear what was being said all the same. That's how I found out that they all knew Leon Murphy. Because he used to work for the Syndicate.'

Maurice paused, then burst out laughing.

'That's the big secret? Of course he worked for the Syndicate. You name me one person involved in this business who hasn't worked for us in some capacity or other, even if only indirectly.'

'What happened, Maurice? Did Leon want to leave too? Is that it?'

Maurice's expression changed instantly, reverting to the mask he'd been wearing all morning.

'No, that's not it. I've told you what he did and why he needed to be dealt with. But if you seriously believe that was why I sent you after him, maybe that ought to give you pause for a moment, before you make the same mistake.'

To Maurice's obvious surprise, Kavanagh's face creased into an approximation of a smile.

'He'd better be good, whoever he is. And anyway, no one will be coming.'

'And what makes you so sure of that?'

'I'm better prepared than Murphy was.'

'Meaning?'

'I've had time to think about this. It's not a spur-of-the-moment thing. I've known I needed to get out of here for a good while now, long before I had reason to suspect I'd been shafted over Leon Murphy.'

He took a step towards Maurice's chair.

'I always was grateful to you for the privileged position you put me in but never more so than in the past few weeks.'

'Stop grandstanding, son. Spit it out if you've something to say.'

Kavanagh had hoped it would never lead to this but a deterrent was of no practical value unless he was prepared to use it.

'You don't seem to have realised that I'm not just sneaking off and hiding away somewhere. If I'm going to enjoy the rest of my life and put it to good use, the last thing I want is to be looking over my shoulder, wondering where you are and who's coming after me. I'm telling you right now, to your face – I'm going to be in Wareham. I can give you my address and phone number if you like. If I ever move on from there, I'll be sure to let you know exactly where I'm going. I don't imagine we'll be exchanging Christmas cards or arranging reunion lunches or anything like that but you will always know exactly where I am.'

He paused, preparing himself for the next part of a speech he'd been polishing for a while now. He knew it had to be pitch perfect.

'And you can forget about me. I'm not going to be any sort of threat to you or the Syndicate because the only way I can hurt you will be to drop myself in it at the same time. I'm implicated in everything that can be thrown at you. It's the perfect stand-off in a way. We don't need to have anything to do with each other because there's no mileage for either of us in creating a problem for the other. But you have to understand this.

'The reason I'm grateful for the head start I was given is because I've used it well. You'd be surprised the quantity of compromising material that comes my way on a daily basis. Conversations I can record. Documents I get to sign off on. Names, places, transactions. Shipments of people and weapons. I've used the time to put together a dossier that will cause you considerable embarrassment if I'm ever forced to use it. I don't know whether it will be enough on its own to put you away personally because I know how sharp the legal boys are and they may well be able to get a lot of it thrown out.'

He leant forward until his face was no more than inches away from the man he'd once looked upon as a father figure.

'But you're not going to come out of it unscathed, Maurice. It's going to hurt like hell and at some point you're going to ask yourself if it was worth destroying this empire you've built for the sake of bringing some upstart rogue employee to his knees.'

He pulled back, satisfied that he had made his point.

'And the beauty of it all,' he continued, 'is that there's abso-lutely no reason why the dossier should ever see the light of day. Leave me well alone and it will be destroyed the moment I no longer need it. But the first sign I get that you're coming after me – even if it's just someone snooping around, asking questions and checking out the lie of the land – I'll disappear and send instructions for the dossier to be released.'

Maurice gave another forced smile. Kavanagh knew how much he'd be hurting inside but there was nothing on this Earth that would make him show it.

'And presumably, if something happens to you before you can do that, there is someone authorised to see to it all on your behalf?'

'We understand each other,' said Kavanagh, straightening. 'It's really quite simple. Remember the Cold War? The mutual deterrent? There's no reason why it can't work just as effectively for us.'

'As arrangements go,' said Maurice, raising a finger in objection, 'it strikes me as loaded rather more in your favour than mine. What happens for instance if we respect the terms you've outlined and you get hit by a bus or die of a heart attack or something that lies entirely outside our control? What safeguards do you have in place for an eventuality such as that?'

'I don't,' said Kavanagh. 'But it won't be my problem, will it?'

This time Maurice's smile didn't come close to convincing. It bristled with menace.

'I'm just thinking about Vic and what he'd have done if he'd been in here,' he said, once he'd pulled himself together. 'He's so very protective of me. It's going to be difficult to persuade him that this arrangement is in all of our best interests.'

'Then I suggest you find a way of controlling him,' said Kavanagh. 'A loose cannon isn't much use to anyone ... and he's been more of an embarrassment than an asset for some time now.'

He turned and headed for the door, counting the steps that would take him into a new life.

'You're bluffing,' Maurice called out from behind him. 'About the dossier and tapes. I know you're bluffing.'

'So call me on it.'

'I was right about one thing,' Maurice said. 'Jimmy could have picked up such a lot from someone like you.'

Kavanagh paused in the doorway. A parting shot concerning Jimmy's capacity ever to pick up anything of value flashed through his mind, found its way to the tip of his tongue. And died there.

'Goodbye, Maurice,' he said.

And walked out.

11

May 2018
Dorset

The ghost village of Tyneham lies nestled in a secluded valley in the Purbeck Hills, no more than a ten-minute drive from Kavanagh's cottage on the outskirts of Wareham. Whatever may be happening in the world around it, Tyneham is always preparing for Christmas 1943. The village knows nothing of men walking on the moon, the Cold War or 9/11. No vehicles are allowed beyond the car park at the entrance to the village. No concession stands or tourist shops have sprung up to tempt unsuspecting visitors into parting with their money. It's frozen in time, which effectively stopped one day in November when the villagers received notification that Tyneham was to be requisitioned by the War Cabinet *in order to give our troops the fullest opportunity to perfect their training in the use of modern weapons of war.*

Its 225 inhabitants were given twenty-eight days' notice to leave and settle elsewhere for the duration of the war. One unfortunate couple received this news on the same day they were informed that their son was missing in action. As they left the village, his mother pinned a poignant note to the door of the church, asking that the buildings be treated with care.

We have given up our homes, she wrote, *where many of us have lived for generations, to help win the war to keep men free. We will return one day and thank you for treating the village kindly.* Her touching faith in a world governed by justice and decency proved to be misplaced. The moment the villagers had vacated their homes, the army moved in and began training for D-Day, subjecting the buildings to repeated shelling and manoeuvres designed to prepare the troops for a war zone. Then, after the war had ended, the army was reluctant to lose what was now regarded as a valuable training ground and the villagers were denied the opportunity to return and pick up the threads of a life that had been so cruelly ripped from their grasp.

Tyneham has always been something of a siren call to Kavanagh, who understands what it is to feel frozen in time. Here, he always experiences a sense of wonder, allied to an inner peace he's never managed to find elsewhere. Other regions around the world will presumably have their own idea of what constitutes God's Own Country. For him the village of Tyneham embodies every subtle nuance of the phrase, from the views out over the rolling hills to the sun dipping over Worbarrow Bay, as he listens to the whispering voices of the restless spirits roaming from ruin to ruin in search of a past that once belonged to them in a way the future never would. He makes a point of coming here at least twice a week to eat his packed lunch, indulging his fascination with the old black-and-white photos on display boards which seek to resuscitate what was once the beating heart of a community. Coming here, it's impossible not to appreciate just how much the villagers lost that fateful day.

Parking is free for visitors but there's a sign at the entrance to the village that suggests a voluntary contribution of two pounds. As he does with each visit, Kavanagh takes a ten-pound note from his pocket and posts it through the slot. Some days he heads straight for St Mary's Church to refresh his memory of the numerous individual histories preserved there. Today though he heads for a bench which is set back a few metres from the path. It's become his favourite place to take stock, something he feels an overwhelming need to do today, because so much has happened since last night, when he finally heard from Adrian Lowe.

More than two weeks had elapsed since he'd first enlisted his help and he'd known better than to pester him every five minutes for updates. But as the days dragged by and the end of April drifted into May with still no word from him, Kavanagh was just starting to wonder whether this might prove to be one of those rare occasions when Lowe might actually be unable to come up with the goods.

Then the call finally came late last night.

He'd found Jessica Murphy.

Kavanagh didn't sleep well, prodded every few seconds by the few details Lowe was happy to divulge over the phone. As soon as it was daylight, he took the earliest train to London and it's only now, with his pack of sandwiches and Lowe's detailed dossier next to him on the bench, that he's able to sit back and take stock of events. He can't allow them to run away with him but at the same time he knows that if he's going to go through with this, it has to be now, while his eyes are up to the challenge. He needs a few months, that's all. Then he'll submit to whatever testing and treatments and operations they can throw at him.

But the girl comes first. Jessica. The events of that fateful night at Murphy's house nearly thirty years ago have been haunting him more and more of late, scratching away at his conscience like an old woollen blanket. He spent all those years in London, believing that the men he'd taken out on Maurice's orders were the scum of the earth – that the act in each case was justifiable in the wider scheme of things. He still remembers them all as if it were yesterday.

Munir Sirhan – ruthless conman who, until Maurice tracked him down in Maspalomas, thought he'd got away with embezzling not just a significant sum of money from the Syndicate but also the life savings of a number of elderly couples across South London.

Max Judd – a dealer responsible for the death in a night club of two students, one of whom Maurice had represented to Kavanagh as the daughter of a close personal friend.

Eddie Larner – trafficker of women and young girls from Eastern Europe, some of them as young as eleven. He'd been arrogant enough to ignore a clear warning that he needed to leave London. Thought he was untouchable.

Leon Murphy was meant to belong in the same company and it was a lie. Not a miscalculation, but a deliberate attempt to deceive. Murphy's only crime was trying to leave the Syndicate without the necessary insurance in place, a mistake Kavanagh took great care not to repeat. Murphy paid the price for his carelessness but he's not the only one who's been punished. His daughter has lost her mother to a drug habit and her father to a hired killer who trusted the wrong people. He has a detailed dossier from Adrian Lowe that details her movements since then. It sounds as if, on the face of it at least, she's come through relatively unscathed, may even have carved out a better life for herself than would otherwise have been the case – had he not intervened that night and dragged a three-year-old girl through a door that was not of her own choosing.

But if Kavanagh has learnt one thing from his years with Maurice, it's that *on the face of it* isn't good enough. You have to look beneath the surface, poke around in the corners and flush out what is really going on. He has set himself one ground rule that will take priority over all else – that nothing he does from here on in will ever have a negative impact on Jessica Murphy ... or Anna Hill, as he'll have to get used to calling her now. The moment he senses that things are sliding beyond his control, he'll back off and leave her to continue with the life she already has. But if he can get close enough to assess for himself whether she's happy and comfortable in this life he's inflicted on her, he'll find a way to set her up for the future and then walk away. She'll never know a thing about it. And if it turns out that she needs help, he'll be there to protect her. It's the least he can do, nothing he wouldn't have done for his little sister if he'd had the chance.

And as the sun disappears behind a cloud and the spirits of the village begin to close in around him, he senses there is a new one among them, nodding his grudging approval.

Maybe in time Leon Murphy will even go so far as to forgive.

12

1964
Spencer Street, Bristol

He groped under the pillow for his torch and switched it on, directing the beam at his wristwatch.

Quarter past eleven.

Peering closely to make sure he hadn't misread it, he slammed the torch against his pillow. He'd come to bed an hour after Katy because, even though she'd be four tomorrow, he was five years older and allowed an extra half hour of TV. He'd checked his watch regularly since then, convinced each time that no more than ten minutes could have passed, and it was always at least twice that. Time was racing by and it seemed so unfair. He remembered the night before his own birthday – he'd spent half the night lying there, wishing the time away, and it had dragged on forever. Now he needed it to slow right down because he was meant to be at The Cross at midnight and there was no way he could sneak out until his parents had gone to bed.

He'd been lying in bed, trying not to listen as they jumped straight from one argument into the next. His mum had been in a bad mood all evening, obviously upset about something, but she'd waited till he and Katy were both in bed before having a go at his dad. The brakes on her bike hadn't been working properly for weeks – did he want her to have an accident or something? Then there was the shed – it was a week ago she'd told him about the broken hinge, which meant the door was hanging off at an angle. How many reminders did he need before he got off his backside and did something about it?

She'd started crying by the time she got to the twenty pounds which she said was missing from the holiday fund. She kept it locked in a money box under their bed and the two of them were the only ones who knew where the key was. She wanted to know what he'd spent it on and whether he'd got himself a fancy woman. Jonny had only the vaguest idea what one of those might be but didn't think checking with either of his parents in the morning would be a very good idea.

His dad had already had a couple of pale ales even before Jonny came upstairs, and he knew the shouting and tears were going to get worse with every additional bottle he opened. It seemed to be happening a lot lately. Normally Jonny would lie there, doing his best to ignore it, knowing that if he pulled the blanket over his head he'd fall asleep eventually. But he can't afford to do that tonight. He has to stay awake.

At least his mum has gone to bed now . . . at last. She came up a while ago and put her head round the door to check he and Katy were both OK. His sister was already asleep, birthday tomorrow or not. He pretended he was too, because he didn't want his mum to know he'd been listening. He lay there with his back to her and eyes shut tight, waiting till he heard her close the door and make her way across the landing to the bathroom. The moment he was sure it was safe, he flicked the torch on again.

Twenty past.

That was never five minutes!

If he didn't make it to The Cross by midnight, Griff and Tony would be gone ... and so would his chances of joining the Spartacus Gang. If Griff said midnight, he meant it. They were both two years older and he'd been trying for ages to persuade them to let him in. He could tell Griff wasn't all that keen on the idea, probably because he'd moved on to the Grammar School now and didn't want to be seen hanging around with primary school kids. Tony was more relaxed about it, because he'd known Jonny for longer. He was the one who persuaded Griff to let him tag along, do a few dares for them to show how useful he could be.

He'd gone through all the usual things like nicking sweets from the corner shop when Mrs Bowen wasn't looking and putting a brick through one of the greenhouses at the local allotment, but that was kids' stuff really and he didn't think Griff was that impressed. Then, out of the blue, Tony had told him they were planning a test for him which, if he managed to do it, would mean he could join – he'd become Spartacus 22, as long as he came up with the ten-bob membership fee. He knew Griff and Tony were Spartacus 1 and 2 but had never seen them with any other members of the gang. He could only guess numbers three to twenty-one were friends from the Grammar School because he knew no one from Westlands Juniors had been allowed in. And if he was honest, he wasn't sure exactly what this whole Spartacus business was about. He knew there was a film a few years ago but his parents hadn't allowed him to see it because he was too young. From the little he'd managed to pick up, it seemed to involve a lot of jumping up from a seated position and shouting, I am Spartacus! *but just as he was sure* there had to be more to it than that, he was equally convinced that asking for clarification would mean the end of his chances of joining.

He was a bit nervous about the challenge, to be honest. They wouldn't tell him what it involved.

'The enemy doesn't tell you when it's coming,' Griff had said. 'We need to know you'll be there to back us up, whatever happens.'

He'd already decided that if it was a fight, he'd go through with it. He was big for his age, another thing that probably helped earn him this chance. He'd been in two fights at school, neither of them his idea but his dad had always told him never to let anyone push him around and the two boys who'd called him out so far now knew he was someone you didn't mess with. So even if he had to fight a bigger boy from another gang, he'd do it. The worst that could happen was a black eye or a bloody nose. But to prove himself, he had to be at The Cross at midnight or he'd never get another chance.

HAD TO.

He reached for the torch again. This time, when he turned it on, it flickered and went out before he had time to check his watch. He shook it, banged it several times with his hand, tried taking the batteries out and putting them back in again. No use. He held his watch in front of his face. When he'd opened his birthday present a couple of months ago, he'd been hoping for one with a face that lit up when you pressed a button or one with hands and numbers that glowed in the dark like Tony's. This one had neither and even though he squinted at it, he couldn't say for sure what time it was.

He could see, from the glow beneath the bedroom door, that his mum had left the landing light on, so he swung a leg over the *protective rail and placed one foot carefully on the ladder. Normally, especially if his parents weren't around, he'd have jumped from the top step, but he couldn't do that without making a noise and the last thing he needed was to cause a disturbance. Instead he negotiated the four rungs as silently as possible and stepped down onto the cold floor. Then he tiptoed across to the bedroom door and tugged on the handle, praying the door wouldn't creak as it opened.*

The moment he stepped out onto the landing, he knew his luck was in. The snores echoing around the staircase were enough to wake the dead. He decided to investigate, knowing that even if his dad happened to wake it wouldn't matter. He'd just say he needed to pee or wanted a drink of water or something. But as soon as he was halfway down the stairs and able to peep through the railings and into the lounge, he could see his dad was out of it, sprawled across the sofa, one hand draped over the side and dangling as if groping for the beer bottle or ashtray on the floor next to him. There was a blanket over him and he looked as if he was there for the night.

Jonny gave a silent cheer. He had no way of knowing how long he'd be out with Griff and Tony, but whatever this challenge might be, he couldn't see it taking more than a couple of hours. His dad was going nowhere and, if he woke for some reason, checking on him and Katy would be the last thing on his mind. As long as he could get out of the house without causing a disturbance, he'd be in the clear.

Time, though. That was what he needed to worry about. A glance at his watch told him it was now gone half past. Hardly daring to breathe, he helped himself to his dad's torch which was kept in the drawer underneath the TV. Then he tiptoed back into his room and silently pulled the door to behind him before stepping swiftly out of his pyjamas and reaching for the pile of clothes his mother had put out ready for the morning. He had about twenty-five minutes to get to The Cross. Should be OK, he thought, as he pulled a sweater over his head and stooped to fasten the laces on his shoes.

And then Katy woke.

It was the rustle of the sheets that first alerted him and he wondered for a moment whether she was just rolling over in her sleep. Then he realised her eyes were open and she was staring at him.

'Shhh,' he whispered, putting a finger to his lips and sitting on the floor next to the bottom bunk. 'Shhhhhhh.'

He stroked her forehead and she closed her eyes immediately. He continued for a while, mentally counting off the seconds, imagining the minutes racing by. She hadn't woken properly. If he could just get her to go back off to sleep, there was still time. But when he decided he'd given it long enough and stopped stroking, she opened her eyes immediately.

'Bugger,' he muttered under his breath. 'Bloody, bloody bugger.'

Katy stared at him, at his clothes, at the pyjamas on the floor next to the bed.

She pointed at them.

'Go back to sleep,' he whispered, stroking her head again. Why hadn't he carried on for just a couple of minutes longer? But this time, instead of closing her eyes and relaxing, she propped herself up on one elbow and pointed with her free hand at the clothes he was wearing. Then at the pyjamas. Then back at his sweater.

'I know,' he whispered. 'I have to go out. You need to go back to sleep. It's not time to get up yet. It's still dark.'

He eased her back under the covers and tucked them in once more.

'Listen,' he said, as an idea occurred to him. 'It's your birthday in the morning. If you get a good night's sleep, the next time you wake up you can have all your birthday presents. That'll be good, won't it?'

She nodded.

'But if you don't go back to sleep, it won't be your birthday for a long time. Understand?'

She nodded again.

'Don't wake Mum or Dad, OK? If you do, they'll be really angry and might even cancel your birthday. Then you'll have nothing to open. Look . . . I've bought you a box of Maltesers – if you go back to sleep, I'll open it and you can have one now. Would you like that?'

He stepped across to his underwear drawer and took the box from it. Normally the cellophane wrapper wouldn't have been a problem but his fingers couldn't seem to work properly.

Tick tock.

Eventually he managed to open the box and took two Maltesers out, popping one in his mouth and bringing the other over to her.

'Here,' he said. 'Open up.'

She did as he asked and he dropped the Malteser into her mouth. When she'd swallowed it, she closed her eyes and rolled onto her side.

'Happy birthday,' he said. 'Remember . . . don't open your eyes again till morning or no presents.'

He waited for what was no more than a few moments but felt like hours. Then he turned and pulled back one of the curtains just far enough to open the window. The cold air took him by surprise but he swung a leg over the windowsill and stepped out onto the roof of the porch above the front door. He had no way of fastening the window so he just pushed it to. There was no wind to speak of and this wasn't the first time he'd sneaked out at night.

Once he'd made it onto the roof of the porch, he shinned down the drainpipe, careful to make as little noise as possible. Then he turned to make sure his movements hadn't disturbed his parents and there, standing at the window, stood Katy. In one hand she was holding Mister, the battered old teddy bear which had once been his. With the other she was dragging his paw up and down.

Waving.

13

May 2018
Zelda's Bookshop, Wareham

When Miriam Cunliffe gave up the lease on Niche in 2004, six months after her husband's heart attack, the more pessimistic among the locals interpreted the demise of this small, but tasteful craft shop as symptomatic of the way things were heading. It was all anyone read about in the papers at the time – so many businesses going to the wall, and not just the small ones either. Even the retail giants were having to cut their cloth a little more judiciously. The thought of another property remaining vacant for any length of time, junk mail and fliers piled up inside the door and gathering dust, felt like one more nail in the High Street's coffin. The gloomier among the local population were already envisaging tumbleweed drifting down the road.

So there was considerable relief when it was announced that a new bookshop would be opening on the same site in time for Christmas – and no little curiosity about its owner. The intrigue intensified rather than dissipated once customers had met him in the flesh. Even after a few visits, they knew his name but precious little else, a fact which many found difficult to explain. It wasn't as if he was rude or standoffish or anything like that.

Even evasive would be too harsh a word for the way he managed to duck out of conversations the moment they strayed into more sensitive areas. He just had this way, without giving offence, of marking out boundaries and making sure everyday chit-chat never found a way to penetrate them. The locals felt they could respect that.

They guessed there was more than a touch of shyness about it. That scar couldn't have done much for his confidence, that's for sure – dear me, it was alarming. If he were to smile every now and then, it might help to soften his features a little and drag everyone's gaze away from it but smiling seemed to come to him no more naturally than small talk. It apparently hadn't done him any favours with the ladies either as there was no Mrs Kavanagh, nor even a hint of any significant other for that matter.

The name of the shop did at least give rise to a certain amount of speculation that this might not always have been the case. You didn't come across many Zeldas nowadays and the usual suspects predictably came up with any number of theories to explain it away. Fanciful though these conjectures were, however, they did little to make him seem any more accessible.

If social skills were what you wanted, you went to Conor for that. Conor Mitchell was almost the polar opposite of his employer – warm, always smiling, never too busy to stop and chat with customers, irrespective of whether they were actually there to buy a book or browse or merely while away part of the morning. No one had a bad word to say about Conor, a local lad who had gone off to university and read History but had never given up on his roots. He'd done all the right things as far as everyone was concerned: returned to his home town, married a local girl and never been tempted to move from the area, despite the discouraging lack of job opportunities that might allow him to apply the skills he'd spent so long acquiring. He was happy to tread water for a while, trying his hand at a number of manual jobs without really feeling that was what he was seeking. Then he heard about the new bookshop and never looked back.

Kavanagh was quick to appreciate what an asset he had on his hands. In no time at all he decided that he himself was better off staying in the background. It was Conor who dealt with anything requiring the personal touch, Conor who hosted the occasional panel event and socialised with the authors taking part, Conor who formed a reading group, which met once a month in his front room eating cakes thoughtfully provided by his wife, Claire. Kavanagh was content for his part to hug the shadows, managing the finances and keeping everything ticking over smoothly.

It's been fourteen years now since the two of them started their double act and Conor suspects he ought really to have moved on some time ago if he's ever going to aspire to anything in life. The thing is, he's not sure ambition features much in his DNA. He enjoys his work and, as Claire is quick to point out, if he has to aspire to something, there are worse things he could prioritise than job satisfaction. Kavanagh has been good to him. He pays well – more than he was earning elsewhere at any rate. Over the years he's been given more and more responsibility, encouraged to make decisions without having to seek approval for each and every one of them. Their relationship may not be based on friendship in the traditional sense of the word, but there's a bond of sorts, underpinned by a healthy dose of mutual respect. He understands that not everyone is as fortunate in his choice of employer.

Today they're going through a quiet spell so Kavanagh has gone into the back room to work. Conor is in the main shop, unpacking books from the boxes that came in first thing this morning and finding space for them on the shelves. Hearing the front-door bell ring, he leaves what he's doing and walks over to the till. A man in a long black coat closes the door, then turns the sign round so that it will read *Closed* to anyone outside on the pavement.

Puzzled, Conor leans back against the desk and folds his arms, smiling as he takes stock of this presumptuous stranger. He wonders if he's a little eccentric – his entrance is certainly more than a little unorthodox. It's difficult to determine his age with any degree of certainty. The lived-in face with its multiple creases, allied to his slightly awkward posture, as if favouring an arthritic hip perhaps, might persuade the casual observer to put him somewhere in his mid- to late-seventies. Closer inspection however strips several years away from that initial estimate. Wrinkles notwithstanding, it would be difficult to come up with any other trace of frailty in his make-up.

The visitor turns to face Conor and flashes a smile revealing teeth that are almost certainly not his own. In this respect they are a perfect match for the smile itself which disappears the instant it's served its intended purpose.

'Lunch hour,' he says in a gravelly voice.

'We uh . . . we don't close for lunch, actually.'

'You do today.'

Conor smiles, pushing himself away from the till and moving past the stranger with the intention of turning the sign back to *Open*. As he does so, his arm is caught in a grip that stops him in his tracks, the strength of it taking him by surprise. He notices for the first time how huge the stranger's hands are.

The fake smile is back again.

'I wouldn't do that.'

Conor looks pointedly at the hand on his arm, waiting until the pressure is released.

'What are you doing?'

'I'm here to have a few words with your boss.'

South London at a guess, thinks Conor, trying not to flex his arm. Some of his friends at university used to speak with the same lazy drawl and he'd spent so much time in their company that it had crept into his own speech patterns for a while, much to the dismay of his family when he returned home.

'He's busy,' he says. 'Can I help?'

'You think I'd be interested in anything the organ grinder can tell me?'

Under different circumstances Conor might laugh at this muddled analogy but something tells him it wouldn't be a good idea right now. He's met one or two people in the past who had something about them, an edginess that came off them in waves. Elderly he may be, but this man has more than a whiff of it himself.

Conor hears a noise behind him and turns to see Kavanagh standing in the doorway to the back room.

'It's OK, Conor. I'll see to this gentleman.'

'The door sign . . .'

Conor waves an arm to make his meaning clear.

'Leave it as it is,' says Kavanagh, his voice controlled, reassuring. 'We'll take a break for now. Maybe give us an hour or so?'

Conor turns to look at the visitor who, having made his point, has apparently dismissed him from his thoughts altogether. He's moved across to one of the display tables and is flicking idly through the pages of a book he's picked up.

'Are you sure?' he asks. He's not happy about leaving the two of them together. He has no idea why this stranger is here but he's pretty sure buying a book doesn't feature high on the list.

'Come back at one,' says Kavanagh, showing him to the door and giving what is clearly intended to be a reassuring pat on the shoulder as he does so. 'We'll re-open then.'

Conor steps outside, pausing briefly as Kavanagh closes the door behind him, drawing the bolt across at the same time. Walking away feels disloyal and for a moment he's tempted to stay where he can keep an eye on things, but Kavanagh's composure suggests he has the situation under control.

He watches a minute or two longer as the two men turn to face each other, then reluctantly walks off down the High Street.

Vic puts down the book and perches his backside on the edge of the table. Kavanagh decides to keep a respectable distance between them, not because he's necessarily expecting any trouble, but because he's learnt in the past that close proximity and perspective make for poor bedfellows. There are times when a little bit of personal space can make a world of difference. This, he feels, is one of them.

'So this is the dream you were chasing,' says Vic, with something of a sneer as he looks around him. 'You seriously trying to tell me you gave it all up for *this*?'

Kavanagh ignores the provocation.

'It's my home,' he says.

'It's a fucking shithole is what it is. You know how long it took us to get here? They never heard of dual carriageways around here?'

'What's going on, Vic?'

'We lost internet coverage about ten miles back,' Vic continues, ignoring him. 'It's like we're back in the 40s or something. What do they do for a good night out around here? I bet they got a fucking maypole, right?'

Kavanagh says nothing. Vic's the last person in the world he'd want to see here but if he pushes too hard for an explanation, all that will do is give him a button he can press. Far better to wait and see where it will lead.

Vic shrugs his shoulders – if he's disappointed at the lack of response, there's nothing in his manner to suggest it.

'Bet this has made your morning,' he says. 'Surprise, surprise, eh?'

'It's the monkey,' says Kavanagh.

Vic frowns.

'What is?'

'It's the monkey you don't want to talk to. The organ grinder's precisely the person you *do* want to talk to. He's the one with the answers.'

Vic thinks about it, then laughs.

'Still think you're fucking Bamber Gascoigne then. You always *were* a pain in the arse.'

'You were about to tell me why you're here,' Kavanagh reminds him.

'Jesus Christ – lighten up, why don't you? We haven't seen each other for years. How about offering me a drink?'

Kavanagh isn't in the mood to be deflected.

'We had an understanding.'

'Understanding?' Vic assumes an expression which is the very definition of disingenuous. He puts his forefinger to his lips and gazes at the ceiling – no one hams it up quite like Vic

Abraham. There's usually a random, totally disproportionate act of thuggery to back it up. Kavanagh has seen it so often, he's ready for anything.

'Can't think what understanding that would be ... unless you mean the one you struck behind my back all those years ago. The one I didn't even get any say in.'

'There was a reason for that.'

'Sure there was – you knew if you tried to pull a stunt like that with me in the room, I'd have ripped you a new one.'

'Is that supposed to impress me?' asks Kavanagh, and Vic smiles quietly to himself, as if imagining an opportunity that somehow got away.

'Sure,' he says. 'Easy for you to grow a pair, now I'm an old man.'

'Maurice and I needed to reach an agreement,' Kavanagh says, determined to keep the conversation moving forward. 'I didn't want you there because you would have been a distraction.'

'Agreement? Sounded more like blackmail to me, sunshine. And I'd have been more than a fucking distraction, I promise you that much.'

'QED,' says Kavanagh, pausing before adding: 'Point proven.'

'I know what QED means, college boy.'

Vic's self-restraint, always a relative concept at the best of times, is showing signs of fraying at the edges. Kavanagh senses he needs to be less confrontational if he wants to find out what this visit is all about. It's one thing to remind Vic that his presence here is bang out of order, quite another to keep prodding him with a sharp stick.

He takes a deep breath. Several. Tells himself it doesn't matter that Vic will undoubtedly misinterpret this as further proof that he's backing off, still intimidated by him. That kind of posturing is futile, irrelevant. What *does* matter is this gentle way of life in rural Dorset to which he's grown accustomed, surrounded by kind-hearted, generous people, miles away from the lethal circles of hell he used to patrol on a daily basis. He doesn't want to lose what he's worked so hard to build here.

'Who's we?' he asks, sidestepping to take some of the heat out of the conversation.

'What?'

'You said *we* lost the internet on the way in. Who else are we talking about?'

Vic screws his face up in disgust.

'Jesus Christ, you know what? I'd forgotten how much that used to piss me off, the way you let a question stew in your mind then suddenly throw it into the conversation half an hour later. Do you do that just to wind people up?'

'Who else, Vic? Is Jimmy here?'

'No. I dug up Maurice's coffin and brought it with me. Of course it's Jimmy – what sort of a fucking question is that? You think I'm going to drive all this way for anyone else?'

'So where is he?'

'It's all right, Shirley. If the big bad man wanted to hurt you, he'd have done it already. You wouldn't even have seen it coming and he certainly wouldn't have sent me here to tip you off. I dropped him off in some place called Swanage. He's in a meeting all day.'

The tone of voice, allied to a slight curl of the lip, makes Swanage sound like a village in some Third World country.

'So why aren't you with him?'

'Like I told you – he's in a meeting all day. Thought I'd just drop in and see how you're getting on, kill a bit of time. Maybe take in a bit of Morris Dancing – they do that here, right?'

'Does Jimmy know you're here?'

The mere fact that Vic has set foot in Wareham, let alone the shop, is a major concern. This is a gauntlet if ever he's seen one and he's being challenged to do something about it. They may be just dipping a toe in the water but it's a reckless gamble nevertheless and the last thing he'd have expected after all this time. He can't afford to let them think they can keep nibbling at the boundaries like this.

'He wants to meet,' says Vic, getting to the point at last. 'There are a few things he wants to discuss with you over dinner tonight.'

'I'm not interested in talking to Jimmy.'

'Well, maybe you should be. I was going to say you know what he's like but of course you don't. Let's just say he can be very persistent when he wants to be.'

'He can be as persistent as he likes,' says Kavanagh. 'I made it clear to Maurice that I was to be left in peace and that if anyone came sniffing around it could have serious consequences . . . for all of us.'

'Yeah, well. I'm sure that's one of the things Jimmy will want to talk about,' says Vic, practically yawning he's so unimpressed. 'He's booked a table at some pub in Swanage. You want my advice, you might as well say yes now cos if you blow him off today, he's not going to just swallow it. He'll keep coming back until you change your mind.'

'Not going to happen,' says Kavanagh. 'You need to tell him he's already made a big mistake in sending you here. It's a risk Maurice would never have taken.'

'What am I, your messenger boy?' says Vic, draping his coat over his arm and heading for the door. 'You can tell him your-self tonight – seven o'clock, The Black Swan. You don't want to turn up and talk with him? That's your funeral. I should give a shit.'

Kavanagh feels himself wavering for the first time. Vic's use of the word *funeral* is no accident. This pact with Maurice was supposed to ensure that neither side came after the other but even nuclear deterrents are only as reliable as the ability of those with the finger on the button to see the wider picture. Maurice had always been able to. Jimmy? Kavanagh's not sure.

Within twelve months of taking over from his father, he seems intent on redefining an agreement that has acted as an effective buffer for nineteen years. It's brinkmanship at best and although Kavanagh wants no part of it, he has no choice but to stand his ground. If the life he's built here is going to come under threat, the timing could hardly be worse. He's going to have to put Jimmy straight on a few things. And he can only spell out a few of life's realities if he agrees to meet with him, however unappealing the prospect might be.

But one thing he's absolutely sure about – it's not going to be at The Black Swan.

'The Quay Inn is just down the road from here,' he tells Vic. 'I'll phone and book a table for two – just Jimmy and me. Tell him seven fifteen. If he wants to meet, that's the only way it's going to happen.'

There's an important principle at stake here. Kavanagh has been out of the game so long that he's struggling to remember the unwritten rules that govern it, but one thing he hasn't for-gotten is how important home territory can be. It's not so much that he's concerned about what he might be walking into if he accepts Jimmy's invitation and meets him in Swanage. What Vic said earlier makes sense – if they were planning to take him out, the last thing they'd do would be to give him advance warning. But the choice of venue for the meeting . . . that sends out subtle messages about who needs this more and is prepared to work for it. Jimmy needs to understand that Kavanagh is serious about maintaining the agreement as it stands and not inclined to budge one inch. If anyone is going to be the petitioner, it's Jimmy.

Vic knows this as well as anyone.

'He's not going to like it,' he says.

'The Quay Inn,' Kavanagh repeats. 'Seven fifteen. And make sure you leave plenty of time if the roads are such a problem.'

Vic shakes his head as he turns and unbolts the door.

'We'll be in touch,' he says, closing the door behind him.

Kavanagh watches as he crosses the road, then turns the sign on the door back round so that it's facing the right way.

Normality restored.

He feels better already – for now.

He doesn't recognise Jimmy immediately. He's been keeping an eye on the door, checking each time it opens, and it's only as he approaches the table that Kavanagh realises who it is. He hasn't seen him since around the time of the incident in The Grosvenor all those years ago. Inasmuch as he's given any thought to him since then, the subconscious image he's retained has been that of a wiry teenager with Maurice's skinny frame and a shedload of attitude. If put to it at some stage in the intervening years, he'd have come up with a beefed-up version, a gym rat, pumping weights and steroids in equal measure, filling out his frame in all the right places with all the wrong intentions. Without really giving it any real thought, he's been on the lookout for baggy jeans, trainers and hoodie with inverted baseball cap to set it all off.

So the sharply dressed professional who approaches the table – fifteen minutes late, almost certainly to make a point – comes as something of a surprise. His hair is fashionably cut, short at the sides, long on top and complemented by a short stubble beard that is too well-groomed to be the result of a few lazy mornings without shaving. His shirt is unbuttoned at the neck, revealing an eye-catching gold chain, chunky and clearly expensive. The powder blue suit looks tailor-made and the light brown shoes gleam as if he's been polishing them in the car on the way here.

His physique though suggests he's been chasing an image without the reserves of energy and discipline required to see it through. Jimmy has indeed filled out but there are few signs of a gym having played any part in it. He has the fleshy, pasty look of someone who spends too much time indoors and has fallen foul of a surfeit of business lunches and snacks taken on the hoof. His lack of self-discipline is several light years removed from that of Adrian Lowe, but it's certainly not just muscle that is putting the shirt buttons and seams under pressure.

The Quay Inn is as packed as ever and the waitress appears almost immediately, having presumably been on the lookout for him since Kavanagh placed his own order. She proves to be a handy distraction, getting them past the awkward preliminaries. Jimmy casts a dubious glance at Kavanagh's soft drink, then orders a bottle of Médoc for himself. It comes across almost as a reflex.

He takes a look around at the other diners, tables pressed tightly together to make maximum use of every available bit of space. Checks out the unlit fireplace, and the mounted photos on the wall.

'This your local then?' he asks, turning back to face Kavanagh.

'I suppose so.'

'How often do you drink here?'

'I don't. This is where I come if I want to eat out.'

'So who cooks for you at home?'

'I do.'

'There's no Mrs Kavanagh then, I take it?' It's phrased as a question but Kavanagh has the impression Jimmy knows the answer anyway. He's looking straight at the scar as he asks it.

'I think that particular ship sailed a while ago.'

'Yeah,' says Jimmy, his gaze still fixed on Kavanagh's face as if fascinated by it. 'I'm a shit cook myself – don't mind admitting it. Luckily Lihua's really talented that way – you won't have met her, of course. She's my fiancée. Chinese. You want to see a photo?'

Kavanagh doesn't, but takes the phone from him anyway. Jimmy and Lihua, wrapped up in thick coats, scarves and woolly hats, faces pressed together to combat the numbing effect of the cold air.

'She's very pretty,' he says.

'Fo' sho,' says Jimmy drawing the words out with no apparent awareness of how incongruous this sounds in a Dorset pub on the lips of a fleshy businessman in a suit. He makes it sound more like a Chinese dish than street. 'You'd like her. One of the reasons Vic and I are heading home tonight, actually. There's nothing like knowing a good-looking woman is waiting there for you at the end of a rough day.'

It's either tactless or deliberate. Kavanagh hasn't had any contact with Jimmy for some time but doesn't have any problem in deciding which.

'I always meant to ask you,' says Jimmy, leaning forward and tilting his head to get a better look at the scar. 'Does that still hurt? I mean, I'm guessing you've had plenty of time to get used to it over the years but do you still get a lot of people wincing when they see it? You know, staring . . . that sort of thing?'

He becomes aware of the woman at the next table who has clearly been taking an interest in their exchanges and is frowning her disapproval.

'You all right there?' Jimmy asks, turning to face her. 'Want me to pull up a chair for you?'

She looks away quickly. Her husband – if that's who he is – wonders briefly whether or not to say something but decides instead to concentrate on his meal. Moments later they ask if they can move to a table by the window.

'Did you come all this way to talk about my scar?' asks Kavanagh.

'Bit of banter, that's all,' says Jimmy, reaching across the table and giving him a playful slap on the shoulder. 'Just breaking the ice. We haven't seen each other in a while, have we?'

He looks around for a sign that his wine is on its way. Shoots his cuffs. Tugs at the collar in an attempt to get comfortable. He nods at Kavanagh's glass of Diet Coke.

'You still drinking that shit?' he says, screwing his nose up in disgust. 'Bad for you, you know. I saw this thing on YouTube where they left some old coins in a glass of Coke and it stripped them clean in no time. Hate to think what it must be doing to your insides.'

Kavanagh says nothing. The sooner these preliminaries are over, the better.

'So how did it go with Vic this morning?' asks Jimmy. 'He behave himself?'

'Vic was Vic.'

'Bolshie?'

'Not by his standards.'

Jimmy laughs. 'Yeah . . . I thought you guys were supposed to mellow with age but I swear he's getting worse. If I'm honest, I was in two minds about sending him on his own. I'd have come with him, made sure he behaved himself, only there was this bit of business I had to deal with.'

There's a barely hidden agenda in this. It's difficult to escape the impression that what he's drawing attention to is not so much Vic's short fuse, with which they're both more than familiar, as the fact that it's now Jimmy who has him on a leash. Kavanagh wonders if there might be an element of insecurity mixed in here. He remembers what Nanna Belle used to say about empty vessels.

'Where is he now?' Kavanagh asks.

'Gone off to find a chippie somewhere. I told him to pick me up in an hour or so. I figured we wouldn't need much longer than that.'

'I'm sure that made his day,' says Kavanagh, trying to imagine that particular conversation. 'He spent most of this morning complaining about being left out of the original discussion.'

'Yeah . . . I'd steer clear of him for a while if I were you. You're not exactly flavour of the month. Not that you ever were, mind you.'

One of the bar staff arrives with the wine. Jimmy makes a great show of tasting it and nodding his approval, a little piece of theatre that Kavanagh has never understood and which he's sure is now being performed more for his benefit than anything else . . . just in case he thinks he's still dealing with a sixteen-year-old tearaway.

'You'll excuse me for being blunt,' Jimmy says, swirling the filled glass around in front of his eyes, 'but I thought it was a bit shitty of you not to show up at the funeral.'

Kavanagh nudges the knife and fork into better alignment.

'I thought it was for the best.'

'For you, you mean?'

'For everyone.'

Jimmy shakes his head.

'You'll have to explain that one to me.'

Kavanagh takes a sip from his drink. Picks his words carefully.

'I've been away for a long time now. I wasn't sure how appropriate it was for me to be there and didn't want to cause any unpleasantness.'

'So you thought, *fuck it. It's only Maurice.*'

'I didn't mean anything by it. I just chose to pay my respects in a different way.'

Jimmy nods.

'Sure you did.'

He clearly doesn't believe it. Kavanagh wonders whether to tell him about his visit to the cemetery the following day and the wreath he left but decides against it. *Methinks he doth protest too much.* It doesn't matter that it's the truth – if Jimmy would rather not believe it, there's precious little he can do to alter that.

'We went to The Grosvenor after the ceremony,' Jimmy continues. 'Quite a few of the old faces were there and your name came up a few times. They were surprised about the no-show. Thought you were sticking two fingers up.'

'I'm sorry if it was interpreted that way.'

'I mean, he thought the world of you, my old man. Always holding you up to me as some sort of example I should be following. *Jon this. Jon that.* Drove me up the sodding wall, to be honest.'

'I had a lot of respect for him too.'

'Strange way of showing it though, wasn't it?' says Jimmy, chin resting on cupped hands, elbows taking the weight. 'I mean, he took you in, treated you like one of the family. I swear there were times when I honestly thought he saw more in you than he did in me and then you go and shaft him like that – threatening him, walking out. I was only a kid at the time, never understood how you could do that. Still don't, as it happens.'

Kavanagh is grateful for the arrival of the food. This raking over coals which should have been allowed to die out years ago isn't going to achieve anything positive. Once Jimmy's request for a variety of condiments has been satisfied, Kavanagh decides he's had enough of all the feinting and parrying. Neither of them is here for the pleasure of each other's company.

'I presume you're not in any doubt about what Maurice and I agreed?' he says.

'In doubt? No.'

'So you know the risk you're taking in coming here?'

Jimmy nods, then suddenly opens his mouth in surprise. He reaches for a glass of water, emptying it in one go.

'Shit, that's hot,' he gasps, fanning his mouth with one hand. He squeezes the tip of his tongue between thumb and forefinger, then pours another glass of water to replace the one he's emptied.

'You haven't answered my question,' says Kavanagh.

'Is that what it was? Sounded more like a threat to me.'

'So why are you here?'

'Stop pissing about, will you?' says Jimmy, dropping his knife and fork on the plate with a clatter. 'That agreement was between you and the old man. You never came to any understanding with me and, as far as I'm concerned, whatever the two of you managed to cobble together expired along with him over a year ago. If I want to come to Dorset for the day – fuck it, if I want to buy a holiday cottage and spend the whole summer here – I don't see why I should have to run it past you first.'

'Then Maurice didn't explain it well enough.'

'Ooohhh. Here we go.' Jimmy fakes a shiver. 'Is this where you feed me that pile of horseshit about some pack of evidence you're supposed to have squirrelled away? Do me a favour, will you? Credit me with a bit of intelligence.'

Kavanagh forces himself not to blink.

'You don't believe it?'

'What do you think?' Jimmy snorts. 'You can lump Santa and the tooth fairy in there while you're at it. I know bullshit when I smell it. As if I give a shit anyway.'

He scoops another segment of Steak and Studland pie onto his fork, blows theatrically on it and shovels it into his mouth. Kavanagh turns to his own meal, carving up the sirloin steak with laborious attention to detail. This is no time to rush anything or allow his pulse to find a momentum beyond his control.

'You think Maurice got where he was and managed to stay there all those years without knowing the difference between a full house and a bluff?' he asks, as if playing down the significance of the question.

There's a brief disturbance as four men arrive to take the table recently vacated next to theirs. Jimmy shifts his chair so that his back is to them. He makes a point of lowering his voice to avoid any more intrusive eavesdropping.

'You want to know what I *think*?' he says, smiling and jabbing the air with his fork to emphasise each point as he makes it. 'I think losing Sean changed the poor old sod forever. He did his best to keep his shit together but his own judgement took a fair bit of the shrapnel that killed my brother and he was never the same again. That was never more obvious than when it came to dealing with you, and you know what? I wouldn't mind betting even *he* didn't believe you had any evidence worth having, but it was a straight choice the way he saw it. Calling you out would have been tantamount to admitting he was wrong to place so much trust in you in the first place, and he couldn't do it. Not if it meant going after Golden Boy. That's what *I* think. But hey, what do I know? I'm still just the gobby teenager, right? Nobody's ever cared what I think.'

Kavanagh looks on as Jimmy aims a sharp stab at a potato that has fallen from his fork. He's come a long way from the troubled adolescent whose immediate response to any sort of challenge was to take a wild swing at it with both fists. He's capable now of delivering what are obviously pre-rehearsed arguments in what he thinks is a convincing manner. There's no shouting, no histrionics. He's learnt to moderate his tone of voice, lace his answers with the occasional smile, and he's all the more convincing for it. He's confident. In control. But Kavanagh isn't fooled. Every so often the body language lets him down, a hint of anger flashing at the corners of his eyes. Traces of the quick-tempered juvenile are still lurking in there somewhere and the insecurities won't be far below the surface.

Kavanagh shakes his head.

'Do me a favour, Jimmy. If you knew for a fact I was bluffing, you'd have taken me out the moment Maurice wasn't there to stop you. Vic said as much this morning. There wouldn't have been any threats – I wouldn't even have seen it coming. So the fact that we're having this conversation right now . . . that tells me you *think* there's nothing to it, you may even be pretty sure, but you can't know for certain. Maurice was shrewd enough not to call me on it, because it would have been counter-productive. He knew I wasn't a threat to him as long as I was left alone and the same applies to you if you're smart enough to recognise a good deal and keep your distance. There's a line there, Jimmy, and it's worked well for a long time. Tell me what either of us has to gain from you stepping over it. What's changed?'

Jimmy puts down his knife and fork again, more quietly this time. He leans back in his chair and chooses his words carefully.

'OK, I'll tell you what's changed,' he says eventually. 'This deal the two of you cooked up may have had some sort of twisted logic to it back then, but that was getting on for twenty years ago. You were . . . what, forty-something at the time? Now you'll be drawing your pension before long. You're not the safe bet you used to be. The risk factor has increased significantly and that makes me feel very exposed all of a sudden.'

'Exposed how, exactly?' Kavanagh asks. 'I made it clear to Maurice that I've set things up in such a way that nothing will ever be released unless something suspicious happens to me. Stay well away and there really isn't a problem.'

Jimmy is tackling his side order of wings now, using his fingers and tearing at the meat with his teeth.

'So you say ... but some deaths can be a bit ambiguous, right? Look, let's be honest for once – this always was a crap deal from our point of view. I mean, we could stick to our side of the bargain, never come near you and still get shafted. All it would take is for you to have an accident. Some drunken arsehole could hit you head-on or you could get careless crossing the road. Pick up some mystery virus maybe. It wouldn't have anything to do with us but we'd be the ones left sweating on whether these mysterious friends of yours are going to misinterpret what's happened, think we had something to do with it and shit all over us anyway. That sound like a fair deal to you?'

It does. In fact Kavanagh suspects it's the only thing that's kept him alive since he left London.

'I didn't start this,' he says. 'All I did was try to leave and make a new life for myself somewhere else. The threat came from the Syndicate, not me. All I've done is take out an insurance policy, nothing else.'

Jimmy picks at a piece of meat that's lodged in his teeth and drops the rest of the wing onto his plate which he pushes away from him.

'So how about if there's no threat?'

'I'm not with you.'

'You say the threat is what started all this. What if it's no longer there?'

Kavanagh is thrown by this. From the moment Vic showed up at the bookstore this morning, he's been expecting only one outcome from this meeting with Jimmy and that's for the pressure to be ramped up in some way. He was sure he'd come this evening armed with threats, ultimatums, determined to strengthen his hand. The possibility that he might actually come suing for some sort of peaceful resolution hasn't even occurred to him. He's not sure where this will lead. Where it *can* lead.

'Still not with you,' he says, eyes narrowed. 'You'll have to explain how that works.'

'OK . . . cards on the table.' Jimmy removes his jacket and fits it over the back of his chair. 'Just hear me out. If you don't like what I'm going to propose, fair enough. But just remember . . . I didn't start this whole fucking mess. That was down to you, Vic and the old man. I was just a kid when this all kicked off but I'm the one having to deal with it twenty years down the line so at least give me credit for that and take my proposal seriously, OK?'

'Go on.'

Jimmy rolls his shirt sleeves back a couple of folds and leans forward, lowering his voice.

'You say I've broken the agreement by coming here today, right? Trust me – and don't shoot the messenger – but the agreement was broken a long time ago. You didn't honestly think you could walk out carrying a time bomb that could blow up in all our faces and not have Vic and the old man keep tabs on you, did you? This is the Syndicate, for fuck's sake. They've known every little thing that's happened to you from the moment you left London – the bookshop with the funny name, the weedy-looking guy who works with you – Conor, is it? His wife and little boy, those early morning runs of yours . . . everything. They're the ones who set it up, not me. All I've done since I took over is keep it going while I got my feet under the table, and I've come to the conclusion that it's plain fucking stupid. It doesn't come cheap and I really couldn't give a shit about your visits to the optician or whatever the fancy word is. It's a drain on our resources and quite honestly I'd rather focus my attention on more important things than you.'

Kavanagh allows this all to soak in. He's annoyed with himself. He's been careless. He's assumed that with the passage of time the need to be alert would diminish. The level of detail Jimmy has casually lobbed his way is alarming. If there's a surveillance team at work here, he should have spotted something, but his guard has been down for so long now. On the one hand he can't believe they've been following his every move since he left. On the other, he knows he should have expected something at least, instead of allowing himself to take his eye off the ball like that. He's not happy about the casual reference to Conor and his family either. That will have been anything other than incidental. He also wonders exactly how much of his activity in the past couple of weeks they know about.

Jimmy has paused, as if expecting him to give voice to his outrage. He seems encouraged by the fact that there is no comeback as yet.

'The thing is,' he continues, 'it's easy for both of us in a situation like this to lose a bit of perspective. There's barely a month goes by without Vic chuntering away about you over something or other, telling me you're an accident waiting to happen, pressing me to do something about it. Me, I spent nine years working alongside the old man before I took over and I never once questioned what the hell we're doing pouring money down the drain in return for reports on a life that, to be frank, would make me want to slit my wrists if that was all I had to look forward to each day.

'Then there's you,' he says, pausing to shake his head to dismiss the waitress who has come over to take away their plates. 'You've spent all this time clutching your little bag of evidence to your chest like a security blanket, like that's going to do you any good. The old man would never have come after you. Neither would I, believe it or not. I'm not going to pretend I like you – I don't. I resented you like hell growing up and hated you with a vengeance during my teenage years, but put a contract out on you? Do me a favour. Everything I do is reduced to percentages on a balance sheet. What exactly would I expect to gain from that?'

'Maybe it's not you I'm worried about.'

'Yeah … OK. I get that,' says Jimmy, settling into his new persona as the voice of reason. 'The only person who's turned this into something personal, who'd leap at the chance without batting an eyelid, is Vic … but think about it, will you? Do you honestly think that insurance policy of yours would stop him? For one thing, he thinks it's bullshit anyway and even if it wasn't he'd still want to rip your head off for making the threat in the first place. Ask yourself why, in all these years, he's never done it.'

'Because Maurice said no,' says Kavanagh.

'Exactly. And it's me who's holding him back now. Vic is many things but above all else he's loyal. Syndicate through and through. That's why he took it so badly when you thought you could just walk away. He'll rant and rave but he'll do whatever I tell him to do. You don't need this insurance policy of yours. You never did. We're not the problem. You can't know this because you're isolated out here, a million miles from what we're doing every day, but if it wasn't for the shadow of this potential threat hanging over us, there wouldn't be any reason why we'd even think of you. No disrespect but you're just not that significant. You run a small bookshop in the back of beyond. You say that package is the only thing that's kept you alive? I'd say it's the only thing that puts you at risk. It makes you relevant. Take that out of the equation and you're not even a blip on our radar.'

He's good, thinks Kavanagh. He remembers Vic saying something this morning to the effect that he didn't know Jimmy now and he was right. He's been expecting a full-frontal assault with all the subtlety of a sledgehammer. Instead he's almost been undone by an attack that has sneaked up on him from the rear, whispering all the buzz words he wants to hear. So he *is* Maurice's son after all. He may not share his policy of eschewing gratuitous vulgarity and he certainly doesn't have his father's measured temperament but there's a sharp mind at work all the same and he knows how to put together a convincing argument. Kavanagh would like nothing more than for this to be genuine. But Jimmy's not the only one who doesn't believe in the tooth fairy.

'That's all well and good,' he says, 'but I'm struggling to see where this is heading. Are you seriously expecting me to just hand over everything I've got?'

'Why would that be such a terrible thing?'

'Because the only protection that would leave me with is your assurances that I'll be left alone. No offence but that's one helluva leap of faith.'

Jimmy smiles.

'None taken. I get it. I'd probably have the same concerns in your position. But I'd like to think I'd also see the bigger picture. Someone's got to make the first move if we're going to get out of this. If you can think of anything else I could be doing, tell me what it is.'

'What happens if I prefer the status quo?'

Jimmy shook his head and flopped back into his seat.

'There is no status quo. That's off the table. I told you, I've had enough of trying to go about my everyday business with a knife at my throat while you sit around reading books and going for runs and making plans to wander off into the sunset without a care in the world. We've had years of that and the balance has to change. We've been so discreet until now, you didn't even know you were under surveillance, did you? But I'm here to tell you that if we don't manage to come to some sort of understanding tonight, you won't be the only one who knows we're around, if you take my meaning. You've got a nice little set-up here. I'd have thought it was worth doing what you can to keep it that way.'

He reaches for the bottle for a third time.

'I'm just asking for a bit of give and take, that's all. You see to your side of the bargain and you get to keep your spotless reputation as far as the locals are concerned and enjoy a happy and peaceful retirement. If that's not enough for you, ask yourself whether it's fair to make that decision for Conor and his family as well.'

And there it is. That's more like it. That's the full-frontal he knew he could expect if he held out for long enough. To his dismay, he realises he's being outflanked here. He's been telling himself all along that he holds all the cards, that Jimmy can moan and bitch as much as he likes but there's nothing he can actually do about it unless he's prepared to take a major leap into the unknown. But it's not just about him now. This new life has brought with it a shared responsibility for others – innocent people about whom he cares a great deal and who do not deserve to come within a thousand miles of the seamy world that Jimmy Hayes and Vic Abraham represent. He can't allow them to be drawn into this never-ending saga and used as pawns.

And Jimmy's smart enough to know it.

Only a few moments ago he was daring to hope that there might be a peaceful way out of this, that Jimmy would be receptive to some sort of compromise. Now it's clear that he's digging his heels in. He's not going to accept any deal that doesn't include handing over the evidence.

And that can't happen.

Not yet.

'You expect me to trust you,' he says, playing for time, 'and the next minute you're throwing around thinly veiled threats.'

'Threats never hurt anyone,' says Jimmy. 'They're just words. I don't like it any more than you do but I have to have a bargaining tool of some sort, same as you. You can't expect me to come to the table empty-handed. That line of yours is still there – it's just moved a bit nearer the middle, that's all. If you can live with it, that's all those threats will be . . . just words.'

Kavanagh thinks. Thinks again.

Comes to a decision.

'You're not going to back down on this, are you?' he says with what he hopes will sound like a touch of resignation.

'I never back down. Not when I know I'm in the right.'

'And you're always in the right, I suppose.'

Jimmy allows himself a smile at this.

'More often than not.'

Kavanagh sighs.

'So let me make sure I've got this right. If I agree to hand over the documents – *if* I agree to it – you, Vic, the whole Syndicate will stay well clear of here. Is that right?'

'That's right.'

'And you'll make sure everyone at your end knows and respects this. Including Vic. Him *especially*.'

'You have my word.'

'For what it's worth.'

Jimmy rolls his eyes.

'For what it's worth.'

Kavanagh picks up the salt cellar and draws a small face with it – outline, eyes, nose, mouth. His expression is a picture of concentration . . . or at least he hopes it is. Then, after what he feels is a suitable interval, he sweeps the salt from the surface of the table and looks up. He wants to read every possible nuance in Jimmy's reaction.

'All right,' he says.

'Yes?'

'Like you said – one of us has got to make the move. It's not like you've left me with much choice.'

'So we've got a deal?'

'On one condition.'

'Which is?'

Kavanagh is not a superstitious man. If he were, everything under the table would be crossed right now.

'I need the summer.'

Jimmy frowns.

'Meaning what exactly?'

'I'll go along with it. I'll get together everything you want and I'll trust you to stay true to your word. But it's going to be September before I can get it to you.'

'September's a long way off. Why's it going to take you nearly four months?'

'It's personal.'

'So give me a clue.'

Kavanagh sighs.

'I've got plans for the summer. I'll be travelling, getting some sun. I'm having an eye op towards the end of September and I've been told I need to rest leading up to it.'

Jimmy's eyes make it clear he's far from convinced.

'I don't get it. What's to stop you getting everything together and then having your holiday? Change the booking.'

'Why? What's the problem? You said yourself we've been living with this for nearly twenty years. What difference is three months going to make?'

'Are you going to start dicking me around, just as things were going so nicely?'

'Three months, Jimmy.'

'How do I know you're not going to be pulling some stroke the moment my back's turned? You could be using the time to make other copies of everything you're meant to be handing over to us.'

'Copies of something you tell me doesn't exist?'

'Don't fuck around with me. You know what I mean.'

Kavanagh laughs as he pours himself a glass of water.

'I know exactly what you mean. You don't like the idea because you think you've got me over a barrel right now and you're worried that if I have time to think about it I may just change my mind. There are so many things wrong with that, I hardly know where to begin.'

'Like what, for instance?'

'For one thing, if I wanted to make multiple copies, I'd have done it already. For another, you're expecting me to trust you *literally* with my life and yet you're not prepared to extend the same courtesy to me. And lastly, there's no way I can afford to cross you on this because you've already hinted at the lengths you're prepared to go to if I do. You know how much this place and these people here mean to me. You think I'm going to run off and leave them to fend for themselves?'

One of the men at the table next to them gives a shout and shows his phone screen to the others. An early goal in one of the play-off matches. He clenches his fist in celebration and narrowly avoids knocking his glass over, grabbing it at the last minute. The others laugh, clapping sarcastically.

Kavanagh smiles, then turns back to Jimmy.

'You've made your offer,' he says. 'I've accepted it and asked for one small concession. Swallow it, Jimmy. It's non-negotiable. One summer.'

Jimmy seems to take an eternity to come to a decision. Eventually he gets to his feet and peels his jacket from the back of the chair. As he puts it on he reaches into an inside pocket and removes a fifty-pound note from what appears to be a hefty wad of them.

'September the first,' he says, slipping it under his plate. 'Ring this number. Don't disappoint me.'

He slaps a card on the table. Kavanagh has a brief flashback to Maurice doing the same thing so many years ago. So much water has flowed under the bridge since then. A reservoir. Jimmy pushes his chair back under the table. There's no handshake on offer from either of them. They both know the situation doesn't warrant it . . . even if each of them is carrying away from tonight a different interpretation of where they stand. The game is on.

'One summer,' Jimmy says as he turns and heads for the door.

The word *last* never actually leaves his lips.

But they both hear it.

14

1964
Bristol

When he finally reached The Cross, Griff and Tony were nowhere to be seen. Bent double, his breath coming in short bursts and beads of sweat forming on his brow, he checked his watch. Two minutes to midnight.

He straightened up as his breathing began to settle back to normal and looked around, wondering where they were. He wasn't late – Tony had definitely said midnight. He'd run as fast as he could, keeping to the alleyways and back streets as much as possible because he didn't want to take a chance on being seen. There wouldn't be many people about at that time of night but all it would take was for one of his dad's mates from the pub to spot him or one of the teachers from school maybe, and it would get back to his parents. That would mean no trip to Eastville to watch Rovers play Luton on Saturday. He knew it would have been quicker if he'd run right through the middle of the park but you couldn't see a thing in there at this time of night and besides . . . everyone knew Old Bogle slept in the bushes. He was only a disgusting old tramp with a wooden leg and as long as you saw him coming you could get away easily but he'd heard hushed whispers at school of what happened if you got careless and let him get too close. He didn't believe most of them but it wasn't worth the risk for the sake of a couple of minutes. Instead he'd stuck to the path which skirted the edge of the park and then sprinted the last couple of streets, arriving just in time. Or so he thought. His watch wasn't slow, was it? He'd checked it earlier that evening, wound it to make sure it was accurate.

Where were they?

It was at least a quarter of an hour before he decided they weren't going to come. Once he'd resigned himself to this, he felt angry and frustrated. He'd been looking forward to the chance to prove himself, taken risks to get there on time, and now it looked as if it was all for nothing. He wondered if all this was just a joke, whether they'd ever had any intention of letting him become Spartacus 22. They were probably tucked up in their beds, laughing at the thought of him standing there at The Cross, waiting for them like a dummy. He was close to tears as he turned to head home.

He'd gone no more than a few yards when he got the shock of his life as something slammed into the wall just behind him, missing him by inches, then rebounded, bouncing off the pavement and into the street. He instinctively yelled out in alarm until he saw the tennis ball rolling into the gutter and two figures emerging from the shadows. Tony was almost doubled over with laughter. Griff looked less than impressed as he stepped forward and retrieved the tennis ball, stuffing it into his trouser pocket.

'We've been watching you for ages,' he said, 'and you didn't even know we were there. If you want to be a Spartacus you'll have to do better than that.'

Jonny was still recovering from the shock, his heart pounding beneath his sweater. For some strange reason he felt as if he ought to say sorry but he wasn't sure what for. He was the one who was here on time and didn't think he'd done anything wrong. If it was just Tony he might have said something but he didn't know Griff well enough to feel confident with him. And apart from anything else, it was Griff not Tony who would make the final decision about whether or not he could join. Criticising him didn't seem like a good idea.

'Should have seen your face,' Tony laughed, offering a friendly punch on the arm. Jonny laughed too, to suggest they hadn't really scared him, even though the squeal had probably given him away. He tried to return the punch but Tony knew it was coming and was too quick, skipping out of range.

'Come on,' he said. 'It's this way.'

Griff was already twenty yards down the road and they jogged to catch up.

'Where are we going?' Jonny asked.

'You'll see when we get there,' said Griff, tugging at the neckline of his black sweater. 'And keep the noise down.'

There was something about him that made Jonny feel uncomfortable. Unwelcome. He was always so serious and Jonny wished he could do or say something that would make him smile for once, give some sign that he was willing to accept him as a friend. Tony had told him some of the things Griff got up to at school and they sounded amazing – bunking lessons, swearing at teachers. Nothing scared him. He'd only been there three months before he was caned by Mr Bridges, the deputy head, for putting a dead rat in a teacher's briefcase. Two nights later he'd sneaked into the playground with a tin of white paint and splashed FUCK OFF BRIDGES in huge capitals across the walls of the reception block. Tony said he was a real laugh. Jonny hoped he'd be allowed to see that side of him soon.

He realised they were more or less retracing the route he'd taken less than half an hour earlier. If he'd known that was what they had in mind, he could have arranged to meet them somewhere nearer home and saved himself a lot of panic. He said nothing though, having been tipped off earlier by Tony that Griff didn't like newcomers with too much to say for themselves. He was getting excited now – nervous maybe, but in a good way. They still hadn't said anything about what his challenge would be but he decided he was ready for it, whatever they had in mind. How hard could it be if others had managed it?

When they reached the park, Griff squeezed through a gap in the perimeter railings and beckoned to the others to follow him. Jonny realised they were heading for the central path that ran up a slight slope through the middle of the park. The one he'd avoided earlier. The bushes . . .

'Griff's not scared of Old Bogle,' Tony whispered as they headed up the slope.

'Neither am I,' said Jonny, forcing himself not to look around, and he realised as he said it that although this wasn't true exactly, it wasn't a complete lie either. As long as he had Tony and Griff there with him, he felt a lot safer.

They left the park once they reached the far side, using an alley that fed into Cormorant Road. His friend, Frankie, lived in a house on the corner and they'd spent an entire afternoon cycling up and down the street, with some of his dad's playing cards pegged to the spokes to make their bikes roar like an engine. Jonny paused to look up at the bedroom windows, wondering if Frankie might look out and see him.

And who he was with.

Out in the streets after midnight.

Then he realised the other two hadn't stopped and raced after them as they ducked into another alley which gave access to the rear gardens. Griff came to a halt outside the one with the number 33 painted on it.

'This is it,' he whispered, holding a finger to his mouth to remind the other two to do the same. His choice of words suggested Jonny should have some idea now as to what he was supposed to do next.

'What is it?' he asked.

'Crudshit's house,' said Griff.

'What?'

'Mr Crutchett,' Tony explained. 'He's our Science teacher. He's a Sadie.'

'Sadist,' muttered Griff.

'He gave Griff a detention after school. He had to miss football practice because of it and write two hundred lines instead. Tell him what you had to write.'

'If manners maketh man, mine promises to be a prolonged adolescence,' *said Griff, pulling a face.*

'I don't even know what it means,' *said Tony.*

'Shhh,' *hissed Griff, turning to face them both.* 'I'm going in. You two wait here. And not a sound, OK?'

They both nodded, looking on as Griff turned the gate's brass handle and eased it open before disappearing into the garden. On his own! Jonny wanted to see what he was doing but it was so dark he would've had to shine the torch and he knew better than to do that. He waited impatiently for some indication that he would be called into action sometime soon.

'What's he doing?' he whispered, putting his lips to Tony's ear to make sure he couldn't be overheard.

'Scouting.'

'What's my challenge?'

'He'll be back in a minute. He'll tell you then.'

'Oh.'

The unexpected hoot of an owl nearby made him jump. He could feel his hands starting to tremble, not so much anyone would notice but he stuffed them in his trouser pockets just in case. Until a few minutes ago, all he'd felt was excitement. If they'd just hurry up and tell him what he had to do, he'd be fine.

Almost as if responding to his silent plea, the gate swung open and Griff was back.

'It's on,' he whispered, putting one hand on Jonny's shoulder. 'Are you ready for your challenge?'

'Yes.'

'Are you sure? This isn't a kid's game.'

Jonny nodded.

'OK. Raise your right hand and repeat after me. I, Jonny – what's your surname?'

'Kavanagh.'

'Right. I, Jonny Kavanagh . . .'

Jonny followed him through something that sounded like 'the oath of the legions', repeating every short phrase as it was dictated to him. It was just as well they were forced to whisper as he wasn't sure how strong and confident his voice would sound. But when they were finished, Griff gave his shoulder an encouraging pat and said: 'Well done, soldier.'

And at that moment all the nerves flew off into the inky night sky and Jonny felt he could run through a brick wall if he had to.

Well done.

Soldier.

He was inside the house. In the kitchen, with one foot in the sink and the other on the draining board. The back door was locked but a small window above the central pane of glass had been left open, just enough for him to put his arm through and reach the handle of one of the larger ones either side of it. Griff and Tony had given him a bunk up and then held his legs while he was perched on the ledge. It was so narrow, he wasn't sure how easily he'd have managed it otherwise.

Once he'd scrambled through the gap, he turned and gave the thumbs-up to the other two. Tony held up both hands – twice. Fingers and thumbs splayed. They'd agreed to meet up in twenty minutes back at the alley which led to the park. Jonny wasn't sure why they couldn't just wait outside the back gate in case he needed to check something with them, but decided it was probably part of the test. He nodded to show he understood, then watched them walk away, their bodies immediately swallowed up by the dark.

Now that he was on his own, the hammering in his chest was back, stronger than ever. This felt different. Very different. He hoped Griff was right about the dog. Tony had raised the possibility that there might be one but Griff had been very quick to squash the idea.

'They'd never let someone like him have a dog,' he said. 'You have to have a licence from the police and they don't give them to sadists. It's against the law.'

It had sounded reassuring enough when Griff said it but in there, with strange shapes looming up out of the darkness as his eyes slowly adjusted to his surroundings, these assurances felt a bit flimsy. He decided it might be an idea to wait for a couple of minutes before getting down from the sink unit. The first hint of a growl or even just the sound of paws padding across the lino and he'd be out of there like a shot.

Once he'd managed to convince himself that everything was OK, the first thing he did was go to the back door. According to Griff, a lot of people leave the key in it when they lock up at night. He said it was always worth unlocking the door and leaving it open in case he needed to get out of the house in a hurry. Jonny had been impressed with the way he seemed to think of every little detail. He wondered whether one day he himself might be leader of a gang.

But when he checked the door, there was no key in the lock – not only that, but he couldn't find one hanging up anywhere near it either. He risked switching the torch on for no more than a couple of seconds because they'd told him several times he should use it only in an emergency, in case someone happened to see it. No sign of a key though, so he reached over the sink instead and pushed the window open as wide as it would go. Then he moved through into the next room as silently as possible.

In here it was even darker. He wondered how this was possible, then realised that at each end of the room the curtains were closed. He told himself this was a good thing as he'd be able to use the torch and was about to switch it on when he suddenly thought better of it, stopping dead in his tracks. He remembered standing on the landing, less than an hour earlier, looking down at the sleeping figure of his dad, sprawled across the sofa. What if someone was sleeping in here too?

He stayed where he was for a few moments to allow his eyes to adjust until he was sure he could find his way around the room without causing a disturbance. Then he tiptoed his way into the heart of the lounge, confident that he was entirely on his own in there. He turned on the torch for long enough to check his watch and was alarmed to discover that six minutes had already slipped by. Fourteen minutes left. If he was going to do this, he'd have to get a shift on.

So.

The challenge.

Griff had said it could be anything, as long as it would look good in the trophy cabinet. That wasn't a lot of help really as Jonny had never even known there was such a thing, let alone what was in it. Griff had explained that every Spartacus had to bring something back from his challenge. Money wasn't allowed. Thieves stole money. Common criminals. If money went missing, everyone would know instantly that it had been stolen and the police would be called in. Far better to choose something that wouldn't be missed for a few days so that when they finally noticed it wasn't where it should be, they'd think it was just mislaid somewhere. Bound to turn up eventually.

Jonny could have done with a few examples of what they had in mind but was worried it might sound as if he couldn't think for himself. Far better just to get on with it. If he didn't find something soon, he was going to fail the challenge anyway. He needed to start searching.

Reassured by the thickness of the curtains, he switched the torch on so that he could have a better idea of the layout of the room. Almost the first thing he saw, over in the far corner, was a large cupboard with a series of drawers, a bit like the one in his grandparents' cottage in Wareham, which was crammed with all sorts of things. He decided that was as good a place to start as any.

He shone the torch into the first drawer and found himself rummaging through a jungle of elastic bands, paper clips, biros, drawing pins, Sellotape – every piece of stationery equipment you could think of, none of it remotely suitable.

The second drawer was no better. This was clearly a sewing and knitting drawer with a number of patterns, needles and a silver thimble like the one Nanna Belle used when she was darning. He couldn't imagine himself handing over a thimble as his trophy. Griff didn't strike him as someone who would be that easily impressed.

The next drawer was larger and at first he thought that was going to be no more useful because it seemed to be stuffed with board games and old photo albums. But at the back of it he found a small box and even before he'd opened it he knew what he would find inside.

It was a service medal, with King George's head on a silver coin, attached to a ribbon in the colours of the Union Jack. He recognised it instantly because Grampy Joe was given the same one for fighting in the Second World War. He actually had two other medals as well. One was called the Atlantic Star and the other was for winning a clay pigeon shooting competition. Every time they went to visit him he got them out the moment they arrived and gave them a good polish. Then he'd tell them the same tales every time, which made his parents roll their eyes. They always had a good laugh about it in the car on the way home.

He took this medal out of its case and looked at it closely, wondering whether it would be right for the trophy cabinet. He couldn't decide for sure so he put it back in the box and stuffed it into his pocket for now. It might have to do if he didn't come across anything better.

He'd just opened the next drawer when his father's torch began to flicker. He shook his head in disbelief – not again, surely! He fiddled with the batteries, tried banging it against the flat of his hand and the light gave one last flickering sigh before plunging the room into darkness.

Now what? He took a step back from the dresser, and almost immediately stumbled over something that caused him to lose his balance. At the same time an awful screeching sound ripped through him, scaring him half to death, as something shot past him and into the kitchen. In his panic, he grabbed at the dresser to steady himself but knocked something with his arm as he did so – just a glancing blow but enough to send whatever it was crashing to the floor where it shattered on impact.

He forced himself to stay where he was for a moment, hardly daring to breathe. Then he heard footsteps in one of the upstairs rooms and a door opening. Next thing he knew, a thin ribbon of light appeared in the gap under the door and he heard a voice upstairs, grumbling: 'It'll be that bloody cat, you mark my words. Did you leave the kitchen door open again?'

A woman's voice answered but he couldn't make out what she was saying and the moment he heard footsteps coming across the landing, directly above his head, he knew he had no choice but to make a run for it. He raced into the kitchen, hitting an armchair on the way, any concerns about being heard the furthest thing from his mind right then. All that mattered was getting out of there while he still could. He leapt up onto the draining board and flung himself out of the window, almost in one movement. It was only something like a four-foot drop to the patio but he mistimed it, caught one foot on the window frame on the way out and was thrown off balance. He hit the ground awkwardly, waves of pain instantly shooting through his ankle but the adrenaline rush was enough to get him across the garden and out into the alley, away from the angry shouts and the dazzling lights now coming from the kitchen.

He was thinking clearly enough to know it wouldn't be a good idea to run back the way they'd come in, just in case the owners went to the front door and grabbed him as he ran past. Instead he relied on his knowledge of the local area, taking two more back alleys that led him away from Cormorant Road, trying to ignore the pain in his ankle. It was all so unfair – everything had gone wrong, just because of the stupid cat. Every time he thought back to the awful noise it made and the shouts that drove him out of the house, it spurred him on to keep moving, no matter how much his body might be urging him to stop and allow his ankle to recover.

It was a couple of minutes before he slowed to a walk – more like a hobble now – hoping he'd managed to put enough distance between himself and any possible pursuers. What he needed was to get back to the park and find Griff and Tony. He wondered how they'd view what had happened. Would they be excited by the drama of it all and the fact he'd so nearly been caught, or angry because he'd messed up and was returning empty-handed? Treading on a cat and knocking over a vase probably wasn't what they expected from a Spartacus. Maybe he ought to come up with an exaggerated version of events that would present him in a more heroic light. A dog perhaps, rather than a cat. A big dog, one he'd had to fend off with his feet as he scrambled through the window. He'd have the injury as well to back it up. That would make for a better story.

And then he remembered.

He had got a trophy of sorts . . . even if it wasn't a really big one.

Dipping his hand into his pocket, he pulled out the small box containing the medal. It would be better than nothing, wouldn't it? If Griff and Tony wanted something for a trophy cabinet, what could be better than a medal? He remembered how proud Grampy Joe was of his own collection, how he polished them every day; the way he seemed to come to life and looked as if he might even cry whenever he talked about his wartime experiences. He told himself Griff and Tony would have to be impressed by that – he'd chosen well.

He was about fifty yards from the park when he heard the first siren. He barely had time to duck into the driveway of the nearest house as a black police car with rotating blue light flashed past. He waited until the coast was clear, then hurried as best he could to reach the sanctuary afforded by the dark alley where Griff and Tony would be waiting for him.

Only they weren't.

Again.

This was a bit much, he decided. For someone who was supposed to place a lot of importance on punctuality in others, Griff seemed very slack about it himself. This was the second time in the space of an hour or so that they'd kept him waiting. He needed to tell them what had happened, warn them about the police car in case they hadn't seen it. More than anything else, he wanted the security of having someone else there to tell him what to do instead of leaving him to decide everything for himself.

WHERE WERE THEY?

He stepped just inside the park and sat on a bench where he'd be able to keep an eye on the entrance to the alley and spot them the moment they appeared. He also had a good look around in case they were hiding somewhere in the park, planning to sneak up on him as they'd done earlier. He wasn't going to fall for that a second time. And if they were playing games with him, he'd say something this time. He would.

While he waited, he took his shoe off and rubbed his injured ankle. He wished he knew what to do to make it stop throbbing. His dad would know – footballers injured their ankles all the time. He was pretty sure the frantic dash through the garden and the back streets hadn't done it much good, but it wasn't like he had much choice. If there was any consolation in Griff and Tony being late yet again, at least he could sit here and let it rest for a bit. Maybe that would help.

Now that he was no longer on the move, he realised he was starting to feel the cold. A stiff breeze was disturbing the trees and bushes just inside the entrance, causing the leaves to make a rustling sound that made him think there might be someone moving about in there. He tried not to think of the path that led through the middle of the park, past the bushes where Old Bogle slept. He was safe here, he told himself. There was too much open ground for the old tramp to cover – if he kept his wits about him, he'd see him coming long before he could get anywhere near, and even with an injured ankle he'd be able to outrun an old man with one leg. Even so, he put his shoe back on and made sure he stayed on the alert.

Still no sign of Griff and Tony. He picked up a stone and threw it as hard as he could at the gate. They were the ones who'd said twenty minutes, not him. He looked at his watch, brought the dial up as close to his face as he could in an attempt to make out the position of the hands but it was useless. It must be more than twenty minutes though, surely. He told himself he'd give them just a bit longer and if they hadn't arrived by then he'd leave without them and they could keep their stupid gang. Any sense of excitement had long since drained from his system and fatigue was creeping up on him with every passing second. All he wanted was to get home, sneak back in through the bedroom window and hope his ankle would stop throbbing long enough for him to get some sleep.

Then he heard more sirens in the distance and started to panic. He didn't think they were anything to do with him but he knew they were bad news anyway. He still had to get home and the last thing he needed was for some passing police car to stop to ask why he was out so late. Was that why Griff and Tony weren't here? Had they heard the sirens and run maybe? Had they panicked and dashed off home, leaving him here to take his own chances?

The idealist in him, the team player, did its best to say no and mean it. Running away wasn't what any Spartacus would do, let alone its two leaders. And they always protected their own. What was that bit in The Oath of the Legions about loyalty? Let down a fellow soldier and you let down yourself? You couldn't believe something like that and then run off at the first sign of danger, leaving a new member at risk.

Could you?

But another voice was starting to whisper suspicions that Griff might not be everything Tony claimed he was. What had he done so far that was so brilliant? Spotted an open window? Given him a bunk up? Big deal. He'd said the house was safe . . . and OK, it was a cat not a dog, but what was the point of him acting so brave and scouting the place first if he wasn't going to get it right? Just how carefully had he checked? And now he came to think about it, he only had Griff's word for it that this teacher was so awful *and deserved to have his house broken into. He'd moaned about the detention and missing the football practice but he hadn't said what he'd done wrong in the first place. He'd made it sound as if the teacher had picked on him for no reason but was that what really happened?*

And this teacher had a medal from the war. He couldn't be all that bad, surely. They gave medals to heroes, not bullies. Images of Grampy Joe started crowding out all other thoughts for a while. If someone broke into their cottage in Wareham and stole his medals, he'd be heartbroken. The uncomfortable realisation began to dawn on him that this teacher might not be any different. For some reason the whole Spartacus thing was starting to seem pointless all of a sudden. He knew he'd probably feel differently about it in the morning after a decent sleep but the way he felt at that moment, he didn't want the medal to end up in some stupid trophy cabinet where no one but Griff would ever see it. He'd rather sneak out another night and post it back through the teacher's letterbox, where it belonged. At least he'd earned it.

He told himself he'd count to one hundred. If they hadn't turned up by then, he'd leave and they could keep their stupid gang. Weariness was sweeping over him in waves and he'd have given anything to be in his bed right then.

And that was when he first noticed the strange orange glow above the rooftops.

15

May 2018
Clapham

Anna has never been one to ponder life's great questions as to the true nature of things. The way she looks at it, when your mother walks out on you barely a month after you turn seven and your father effectively withdraws from family life, abdicating responsibility for you and your younger sister, you barely have time to draw breath, let alone indulge in philosophical speculation. When she was at school, her friend Cassie had a ring binder and on the front it said something like: *When you are up to your neck in alligators, it's easy to forget that the goal was to drain the swamp.* She never had any trouble working out what it meant. At fifteen she was doing *nothing but* fighting off alligators and eight years later they're still coming at her in droves. And the swamp, as far as she's concerned, can look after itself.

Every so often though, there is a chink of light, a parting of the clouds that makes it possible, however fleetingly, to believe that beyond the chaos and random nature of life, there just might be some underlying sense of order, a pattern that brings everything together in a coherent and convincing way if only you can find the time and space to see it. And today has been one of those days.

As she lies back in the bath, with the steam working on her pores and the bubbles foaming under her chin, she closes her eyes and reflects that there just might be a God after all. She signed the contracts for Praia D'El Rey a week ago and is due to fly out in just over a fortnight. Her flight is booked, she's spoken to the manager of Cristi's about her accommodation and what she'll need to bring with her. At work they were a little on the shitty side but even they aren't closing any doors for good and they suggested, albeit grudgingly, that there may even be a way back in for her if she needs it in the autumn. For the past few days she has been walking on air, smiling her way through the tours even as the rain hammered on her umbrella and found its way inside the upturned collar of her raincoat. She can do that, knowing it won't be for much longer. Everything is set fair. No clouds on the horizon.

Except one.

Every morning since Ches broke the news to her that evening in The Ascot Lounge, she's promised herself that she'll ring Emmie and let her know. And every evening, she's found herself bottling it. Her sister's term finishes towards the end of next month and she's got a holiday job lined up at a local dance school in Northampton where she's worked for the past two summers, helping with the younger children. She'll be working there until she goes back for her final year at the Dance Academy – apart, that is, from a two-week break when she's booked time off to come to London and live it up with her big sister.

In one of her blue-sky spells, Anna is able to persuade herself that this doesn't have to be a problem. Emmie can just come to Praia D'El Rey instead of London. She can soak up the sun, relax on the beach, swim in the sea. Anna can help her out with money for the flights if necessary and even though she'll be working most nights they'll have the days together. It will be fun. Who wouldn't jump at the chance?

Well, Emmie for one. The realist in Anna knows this is not going to work. Emmie isn't much of a sun-worshipper. If she travels abroad she avoids beaches in favour of big cities with as extensive a choice of nightlife as possible – and the wilder the better. Praia D'El Rey is 106 kilometres from Lisbon – she's looked it up – and although there are other places nearer such as Obidos and Peniche, they're going to seem a bit *Eastbourne on a wet weekend*, not at all what Emmie will have in mind. Added to that, she'll have no way of getting there other than by taxi, which will cost her a fortune, and she'll be on her own almost every evening which, as Emmie would surely be quick to point out, is a curious definition of spending two weeks together.

And the final nail in the coffin would be plain old-fashioned jealousy. Emmie loves her, she knows that, but she's always been the ultimate competitor. She decided even before she reached puberty that she was going to be a dancer and even though her priorities in recent years have swung away from traditional to jazz, street and contemporary, she's never compromised on that ambition . . . and has the talent to back it up. They often tease each other about which of them will be first to smash it and it's always good-natured on the surface, but however much they both want the best for each other, Anna suspects her sister's confidence and self-esteem will take something of a battering if her big sister is the first to make the breakthrough. She's been dreading the moment when she has to tell her.

And then, out of the blue, the whole thing is solved, which is as close enough to divine providence as makes no difference.

Emmie had phoned, excited beyond belief, to say she'd been given a provisional three-month contract with a professional dance company specialising in cruise ship entertainment. They're booked to fly out to Vancouver a month from now, have five days in the city for rehearsing and bit of sight-seeing, then sail up the Alaskan Inside Passage to Seward. She'll have to miss the last week of term but the Dance Academy have been great about it because they know what an opportunity it is.

Emmie had burbled on for about ten minutes, listing places she'd get to see in Alaska, other cruises which are scheduled to follow, and a number of practical arrangements. If she was at all concerned for Anna's feelings, there were precious few indications of it during that brief call, and Anna wondered why she'd been quite so worried about breaking her own news. That was Emmie, though – once the tap was turned on, it ran full-bore until there was nothing left in the tank. It was taken as read that everyone else would be thrilled for her. Any suggestion of remorse or empathy would come later.

When Emmie finally took a breath long enough to apologise for having to take a rain check on their fortnight in London, that would have been the perfect opportunity to pass on her own good news, but still she'd held back. This was Emmie's day . . . and she deserved her moment in the sun because she was talented and had the right work ethic. Anna didn't want to dilute that in any way so she decided her own news could wait. She'd give it a couple of days and then ring her, make out it had only just happened. Allow Emmie to believe she'd made the breakthrough first. In the wider scheme of things, it really wasn't that important. What matters is that the worry which has been tick, tick, ticking away inside her brain for the past few weeks has disappeared like the bubbles foaming around her throat. Pop. Gone.

Things are coming together at last.

And someone, somewhere is definitely smiling down on her.

16

1964
Bristol

Three roads out from Spencer Street, he knew exactly what the glow was because it provided a backdrop for clouds of smoke as flames reached high into the night sky. A few more painful steps and he knew for sure it was his road, and his imagination automatically went into shutdown, refusing to allow him to go there. There must be at least sixty houses in Spencer Street, seventy probably.

The closer he got to home, the greater the number of houses that had lights on. Some people had even come to the end of their drive to see what all the noise was about. Others had drawn back the curtains and were leaning out of upstairs bedrooms. He crossed to the other side of the road where he'd be less visible under the overhanging branches.

By the time he made it to Spencer Street, it was almost like a street party and his chances of getting home without being seen had all but disappeared. For all he knew, his parents were probably outside as well, watching from the front gate. There was so much noise, not even his dad would have been able to sleep through it.

A policeman was standing at the entrance to Spencer Street, talking to a few of the neighbours and preventing anyone from going past. Jonny hovered close enough to listen as he explained that there were emergency vehicles further up the road at the crown of the bend, and the officers needed to be sure everyone was behind the barrier to allow them to get on with their work unhindered. Jonny knew this would be a problem. From this end of the road he could see as far as the first couple of police cars and an ambulance but beyond there the street bent round to the left and doubled back on itself before disappearing down the hill to the main road. From where he was standing he couldn't see the other half of the street so there was no way of telling which of the houses was actually on fire.

Someone nearby was talking about the Hepworths, an elderly couple who lived over the road from his family, and his heart gave a sudden lurch. They were always kind to him, said he reminded them of their grandson who lived in New York. Gave him biscuits and the occasional sixpence for doing a few odd jobs in their garden. His mum liked Mrs Hepworth – they went to bingo together. She'd be really upset for her friend.

'Went up like a bloody firework factory,' a man was telling a group of curious onlookers who'd just been turned back by the policeman. 'Never seen anything like it. Those poor sods . . .'

He decided he couldn't stay where he was until the show was over. If his parents had been woken and gone outside to see what was happening, maybe there was a chance after all that he'd be able to sneak into the house through the back without being noticed. But first he'd have to find a way to get there. To enter Spencer Street from the other end, he'd have to walk right round the block and his ankle was really hurting now. There wasn't any *point anyway – there was probably a policeman at that end too. His best chance was to sneak into one of the back gardens while no one was looking and try to work his way from one property to the next until he was close enough to see whether the coast was clear. It was risky but he had to try something. He couldn't stay out here all night.*

But before he could move, he heard someone call his name, the voice rising at the end as if unsure. He turned and saw Mr Yallop who worked with his dad at the post office. He was staring at him in disbelief. Almost immediately a woman he knew by sight but whose name he could never remember stooped in front of him, kept repeating, 'Oh my God' and 'You poor mite' as she removed a blanket from her own shoulders and wrapped it around him. She pulled him into a hug and suddenly everyone was speaking at once and the policeman was there and questions were flying at him from all angles, questions he couldn't understand, didn't want to understand and someone else ran up the road to report that he was safe – it was a miracle.

Shutting out the questions, he tried to focus on snatches of conversations that had broken out around him, hushed whispers hinting at dark things, and he couldn't help but notice how everyone was staring at him with this weird expression on their faces as if they'd seen a ghost. Somewhere on a deeper level an awful suspicion was begging to be let in and before he knew what was happening he was crying, whining softly at first, then calling for his parents, then yelling with all his might as the panic set in with a vengeance. He struggled to get away but Mr Yallop was holding on tight to his arm. They were wrong, he was desperate to make them understand, as if shutting them up might somehow hold reality at bay. His dad was fast asleep on the sofa. His mum had gone to bed ages ago. Katy . . . it was Katy's birthday. He'd bought her Maltesers. She loved Maltesers. And it was Mr and Mrs Hepworth's house anyway – he'd heard someone say so.

An ambulance man was there now and they were backing the vehicle down the road with the policeman waving his arms to guide the driver and at one point – when they thought he'd given up on the idea of getting away from them – he managed to wrench his arm out of Mr Yallop's grasp and he was off and running free for no more than a yard or two before he collapsed on the ground, clutching his ankle and screaming in pain.

He was still screaming as they lifted him into the ambulance and they moved his foot oh so gently, removing his shoe to try to make him more comfortable.

As if his ankle was the reason he was screaming.

17

26th June 2018
Praia D'El Rey

Music has never assumed a position of any great prominence in Kavanagh's life. It's not that he is averse to it exactly. He's as partial as the next person to a strong melody but he's never been one for whistling and is cursed with a singing voice that is between registers, causing him to miss more notes than he would hit. As for the wider music culture, it's not something he's ever bought into. He's never played an instrument, never owned a music player of any description, and downloading songs is as alien a concept to him as quantum mechanics.

His formative years, when music might have gained some sort of foothold, were too fragmented, punctuated by one upheaval after another. Back then he had more pressing things on his mind than choosing between the Beatles and the Stones. It might have been different if Nanna Belle had been as obsessive about music as she was about books, but there was only room for one passion of that intensity in the cottage at Wareham and music never really gained a foothold. Over the years it's become almost incidental, little more than a distraction, pulling him out of whatever novel he's trying to read.

So when it comes to deciding on the merits or otherwise of a performer, he doesn't feel he's in much of a position to offer an informed opinion. Even so, in the unlikely event that someone should ask him, he'd have to say she's good.

She's *very* good.

This is his second night here but his first at Cristi's. A gentle half-hour stroll from the heart of Praia D'El Rey, it's far enough for those who believe a night out only merits the name if you actually leave the resort, but not so far that you have to choose between forking out for a taxi or falling foul of Portugal's stringent drink-drive laws.

Its huge windows on both levels look out over landscaped and immaculately maintained grounds that have been reclaimed from the surrounding woods and scrubland. Downstairs is a restaurant, upstairs the Cabaret Lounge with its much larger bar, comfortable seating, subdued lighting and, at the far end, a stage just large enough for a piano and performer.

He was originally intending to come here last night but the flight brought on one of his episodes – a milder form, certainly, but his vision was hazy for a while and his balance was slightly off all evening, leaving him with another of these migraines that have been an intermittent problem since the bomb blast but much more persistent of late. As a result he spent his first night in Portugal lying in his room hoping to sleep it off.

He felt much better when he woke this morning and spent a couple of hours walking around the resort, familiarising himself with the layout, then cooling off in the sea which was sharp enough to take his breath away. Back in his room he worked his way through the welcome pack, picking out a handful of leaflets for Cristi's. These consisted of the usual lunch and dinner menus, cocktail and wine lists and the promise of first-class entertainment in the Cabaret Lounge courtesy of its resident musicians. Guest attraction for the summer: a promising newcomer from the London cabaret scene.

Anna Hill.

This afternoon he decided against a run. Instead he found himself returning again and again to the photo inside the pack. Attractive face, the slight kink in the bridge of her nose somehow drawing her features into a coherent whole, like the flaw in a diamond. Jet black hair, presumably dyed, and a quiet smile accentuated by the soft lighting. He wondered then if the photo had been airbrushed at all but from where he's sitting now, no more than ten yards away from her, his guess would be no. No need.

He'd opted for an early dinner in the restaurant downstairs and for the past hour or so he's been ensconced in one of the comfortable chairs in the Cabaret Lounge, a well-thumbed copy of *The English Patient* on his lap and a glass of Sagres on the low table in front of him.

He'd have been happy losing himself in the novel for a while, were it not for the distraction caused by one of the local musicians, who was thrashing away at an acoustic guitar and singing of his love for some woman named Maria. If his facial contortions were anything to go by, it was a toss-up as to who was suffering more, the singer or the audience. The moment Anna came on stage though, the book was put to one side. He missed her entrance, didn't know she was there until the main lights went down and a single spotlight picked her out, fingers hovering over the keys.

For some reason he couldn't quite understand, he actually felt nervous for her when she started playing. Every so often he found himself looking away from her and checking the expressions on the faces of everyone else in the room to see how her performance was being received. While the poor, tormented guitarist was baring his soul a few minutes earlier, there were pockets of conversation breaking out everywhere and if his agonies had proved terminal, few would have noticed, let alone cared. But the moment Anna started playing the conversations died away. The only form of communication was the occasional nod exchanged between partners as if to acknowledge that this was different and he knew then that he could relax and enjoy it. He wasn't sure why it mattered either way. It just did.

To his admittedly untutored ear, she has something about her. There's a haunting quality to her voice – an ache, almost – which reaches out to the audience, and she has a disarming way of almost drifting off in the quiet, reflective passages, as if she's totally unaware she's in a lounge full of people.

Those moments have awakened something inside him. He knows loneliness when he hears it.

When she reaches the half hour interval, the response from the audience is more than appreciative and Kavanagh is surprised to discover how much that means to him. He reminds himself that he's here to check on her, try to discover what sort of life she's managed to fashion for herself in the real world beyond the dry pages of the dossier Adrian Lowe prepared for him. He knows it's unrealistic to hope that her life has been entirely unaffected by events she probably can't even remember. It's even more inconceivable that he will ever be able to fill in the gaps for her and find some form of absolution for his actions. What he can do though is try to get to know her over the next couple of months, decide for himself whether there is anything at all he can do to restore some sort of parity to his moral balance sheet. But to do this, he needs to be dispassionate – there's no room for sentimentality.

It's this mental dressing-down that persuades him he'd be unwise to approach her just yet. Apart from anything else, one of the bar staff has brought a cocktail over to her the moment she stepped down from the stage and a member of the audience – a lad who must be about the same age as Anna – has been quick to move in and take her to one side. Kavanagh decides there's no hurry. There will be other evenings and besides ... maybe it wouldn't be a bad idea to wait a week or so, give her a chance to get used to him as a regular in the Cabaret Lounge, see him around the resort every now and then before he thinks of striking up a conversation.

He knows from experience that his social skills are going to present a problem. They've been a constant drain on his confidence. It's too easy to blame it all on the scar, just because that automatically unsettles anyone meeting him for the first time. He knows it goes deeper than that. He's never mastered the art of small talk. Light and trivial is beyond him. He envies those blessed with the ability to flit from one humorous observation to the next. He'd love to be able to fire off instinctive, witty remarks and relax in the company of others. Then again, he'd also like to cure cancer and eliminate world poverty at a stroke. He needs to focus on what he *can* do. Wait for the right opportunity to present itself. Find a way to earn her trust, rather than scare the living daylights out of her. *Patience*, he tells himself. With any luck, they'll have the whole summer ahead of them. That's more than enough time to find out what he needs to know and decide what to do next.

Anna Hill. He realised earlier this afternoon, when he was committing every little detail of Lowe's dossier to memory, that he's going to have to be very careful if he ever manages to gain her trust. He knows so much about her background now – it would be so easy to let something slip that he should have no way of knowing. There are some things even she isn't aware of. If the dossier is accurate – and when was Lowe anything but thorough – she believes John and Colette Maitland-Hill are her natural parents, has been told nothing about being adopted soon after her fourth birthday. If that's the case, it's probably a blessing. He can't think of anything she'll gain from being introduced to events that belong firmly in the past.

It happens so quickly he almost misses it. Anna has just thanked everyone and announced that this will be her final song of the evening. When she says she hopes everyone has had a good time, there's a spontaneous burst of applause and he looks around to share in the audience's appreciation. Two tables away the fair-haired man in his mid-twenties, who spent the whole interval talking to Anna, has just returned to his table. Sitting on his own, he now has two drinks in front of him. One is a pint glass which he's almost emptied. The other is a cocktail not dissimilar to the one Anna was drinking during the interval – some complicated affair with an umbrella, a straw and random pieces of fruit spilling out of the top.

If he'd been less furtive in the way he went about it, Kavanagh probably wouldn't have noticed, but he's turning his attention back to the stage when some instinct tells him to take another look. He can't be one hundred per cent certain in the dim lighting but the cocktail is now being stirred. And of course, taken in isolation, the gesture looks completely innocent, distracted, something to do with your hands while your mind is elsewhere. If he looks around, Kavanagh will probably see two or three other people doing the same thing at this very moment. But his mind retains a vague impression, no more than a fuzzy picture, of something being slipped into the glass moments earlier. It was done swiftly, almost surreptitiously, with a quick look right and left as if making sure no one was watching. He was right the first time – furtive is the word.

The stalker – as Kavanagh feels inclined to view him now – looks up at that moment and catches Kavanagh staring at him. He slowly drops the cocktail stick into the glass and pushes it away. There's no embarrassment there, no guilty averting of the eyes. Instead he holds Kavanagh's stare and smiles. And there's something brazen about that smile. It almost feels like a wink.

Once the final notes of the song have drifted away, Anna takes the applause and leaves the stage. Stalker intercepts her before she's reached the bar, all effusive praise and tactile overtures. He waves an arm in the direction of the table where he's been sitting, alerting her to the cocktail he's bought for her and inviting her to join him.

Kavanagh, who is too far away to make out what's being said, watches with more than a touch of schadenfreude as it becomes clear that this is not going to be Stalker's night after all. Anna's not some rookie. She may be young but she's obviously been in the business long enough to know how to deal with unwelcome attention from punters without giving offence. She's running through her repertoire of polite brush-offs – the smile never leaves her face for one moment but her body language makes it abundantly clear that socialising with members of the audience is not on the agenda. Instead she leans across the bar and asks one of the staff to pass her a large hessian bag which he assumes she left there earlier. Then she excuses herself with another smile and disappears into the Ladies restroom, leaving Stalker to contemplate the pile of rubble to which his plans for the evening have been reduced.

Kavanagh loses track of him for a moment in the crowd at the bar. Then he spots him making his way back through the tables, carrying another bottle of lager. He's clearly not happy about the way he's been sidestepped. If ever a parade was rained on, it was here tonight. He takes a couple of hits from the bottle, presumably in an attempt to drown his sorrows, and it's only then that he notices, with a classic double-take, the cocktail he'd bought earlier for Anna. The glass is there on the table in front of him. Empty. He picks it up, staring at it as if an explanation might be printed on the inside of the glass, then whips round to check the other tables. Someone, somewhere is having a laugh at his expense and he looks as if he's in the mood to find out who.

His eyes finally settle on Kavanagh, the only person looking his way. He picks up the glass and holds it out at arm's length, scrutinising it as if it might reveal some clue as to what has happened. Kavanagh says nothing. Instead he turns back to his book, wondering whether the pot plant next to him will start to feel drowsy anytime soon. He's pleased with the way he's handled it, views it as a positive sign. Years ago he'd have wanted Stalker to know, pointed at the pot plant. Returned the smug grin Stalker had flashed in his direction earlier. Maybe thrown in a wink to wind him up a bit. But he's no longer that person and understands that beating the crap out of someone doesn't have to be the only response.

'Un-fucking-believable,' Stalker mutters, only for his attention to be drawn immediately to the restroom area where Anna has emerged, dressed now in T-shirt, shorts and trainers. She makes a point of going back to the bar, embracing each of the staff and returning the smiles and nods of appreciation from some of the customers. Then she disappears into the stairwell, taking the hopes of the highly disgruntled Stalker with her.

Or maybe not.

He stays where he is for thirty seconds or so. Then, as if coming to a decision, he drains the bottle in one go before pushing off from the table and making his own way towards the staircase. Without thinking, Kavanagh leaves the same sort of interval, then picks up his book and follows him.

It's possible of course that Anna drove here earlier – if that's the case, he's not going to be following either of them for long. His interest in Stalker ends the moment Anna is away and safe. But the change of clothing into something lighter and more comfortable suggests very strongly that she'll be on foot. He's sure she's walking but there's no point in speculating when he can check for himself. Better safe than sorry.

When he steps outside into a night which is still mild, he can't see either of them. A car drives past the entrance and out of the car park but it's an open-top with a middle-aged man at the wheel and the woman in the passenger seat is definitely not Anna. Apart from that, there's no obvious sign of any activity outside the building. He makes one last check, then sets out on foot to follow them back to Praia D'El Rey . . . because he's sure that wherever she is, Stalker won't be far behind.

He leaves the car park and crosses the road so that he'll be facing any oncoming lights. There's no pavement and the overhanging trees mean that even a cloudless sky leaves the road surface no more than dappled with moonlight. At first he can't make out any shapes up ahead but then a car flies past and its lights pick out a figure a hundred metres or so further on. Even with the recent deterioration in his eyesight, he's pretty sure who it is. There's no sign of Anna but the lights disappear as the road bends round to the left and he decides she must have already passed that point. His instincts tell him she'll definitely be somewhere up ahead. Stalker's abrupt departure seems like too much of a coincidence otherwise and the furtive way – that word again – that he hustles through the occasional patch of light does little to persuade him he's misreading the situation. He copies Stalker, hurrying through any moonlit stretches, hugging the very edge of the road in case his quarry should happen to glance over his shoulder. There seems to be little chance of that happening though – he appears to have only one person in his sights at the moment.

Kavanagh keeps his distance as the three of them make their supposedly separate ways towards the edge of the resort. He breaks into a jog when Stalker disappears around the bend as well, careful not to make any more noise than can be helped. When he reaches it himself twenty seconds or so later, he takes one look and immediately presses himself up against one of the bushes. Anna is about fifty metres away, standing in the middle of the road, bag in one hand with the other resting on her hip. Facing the oncoming Stalker. Challenging him almost. She doesn't say a word, merely stands her ground, waiting for him to walk past. It feels like a foolishly defiant thing to do at such a late hour on an unlit and supposedly deserted road. Presumably she feels she's now close enough to the resort to shout for help if she has to but it still feels like an unnecessary show of bravado.

Stalker walks right up to her . . . and stops.

'Nice of you to wait for me,' he says, his words carrying clearly to Kavanagh across the still night air.

Anna looks unimpressed.

'I'm waiting for you to go on ahead,' she says. 'Nothing personal – I just don't like being followed down dark roads by someone I don't know.'

'Oh . . . and there was me, thinking we're friends.'

If he's hoping it's not too late, even now, to win her over with what passes in his mind for smooth talk, he can't be picking up on any of her responses because Kavanagh can read her body language just fine.

'When you're ready,' she says, in the absence of any suggestion he's about to do as she's asked.

'What . . . you think I'm following you?'

'What would you call it?'

'Not guilty,' he says, spreading his arms. 'I'm going back to my apartment. Only one road in and out – how else am I supposed to get there?'

'So it's a coincidence then?'

'Yep.'

'So walk ahead of me,' says Anna, waving him through. 'That way we don't have a problem.'

Now it's Stalker who's not impressed.

'Fuck me, you really are up yourself, aren't you?' he says, laughing without conveying the slightest trace of humour. 'What's happened to all the smiles and come-ons all of a sudden? You were free enough with them during the interval . . . or do you just trot them out when you fancy a drink and need to be told what a great singer you are?'

If Anna is concerned by the abrupt change of tone, she does a good job of hiding it.

'I'm sorry you wasted your money,' she says calmly, 'but nobody asked you to. And if you think buying me a drink means I have to put up with a load of shit from you, you can think again. Now can you walk on ahead, please? I've had enough of looking over my shoulder every five paces.'

'You think I'm going to jump you or something? Is that it? Like you're so special?'

Kavanagh doesn't like the way this is going. He's impressed by her composure under fire and her refusal to be intimidated, but he edges closer to the pair of them just in case, using the bushes at the side of the road as cover. He's met enough of these cocksure, self-preening bullies in his time to suspect Stalker's not going to respond well to being dismissed in such an offhand way. His sense of entitlement doesn't allow for summary rejection.

'No. I asked you a question,' Stalker snaps, catching hold of her arm as she turns away from him. 'What makes you so special, eh? I mean, it's not like they haven't got better karaoke singers back home at The Fletcher's Arms. Who did you have to fuck to get this gig in the first place?'

She looks pointedly at her arm. Instead of letting go, he pulls her closer.

'That's it, isn't it? Where's this talent of yours? In here maybe?'

He laughs as he tugs at the front of her blouse and peers inside, then jerks his head back suddenly as he sees the slap coming, far too late. The crack as the flat of her hand makes contact probably shocks him as much as the blood that immediately starts to trickle from one nostril. He dabs at it with his fingers, looks up slowly and the two of them stand there for a second or two, staring at each other. Then, as she reaches into her bag, he launches himself at her, but before he can do anything he's stopped in his tracks by an arm around the throat which lifts him up onto the very tips of his toes, almost choking him. He flings one arm back to try to make contact with his attacker's face, misses, and is immediately punished for his mistake as his arm is grabbed and driven up between his shoulder blades . . . just high enough to dissuade him from trying something similar with his free hand.

'Give me a reason to break your arm,' says Kavanagh in a voice that is all the more threatening for the calm and measured way in which it delivers the message. 'Nod your head to show me you understand.'

'Fuck you.'

'I said nod your head.' The last word is emphasised by a further tug on his wrist.

Stalker evidently has one last rush of blood in response to a desperate appeal from his ego to do something to save face. He draws one foot forward, then slams his heel back, hoping to make contact with his attacker's shins but he's telegraphed the move and hits only thin air. His reward for this indiscretion is for his arm to be squeezed even higher up his back until it feels as if it's going to be wrenched out of its socket. At the same time the pressure on his throat tightens still further.

'OK, OK,' he gurgles, nodding frantically and letting his body go limp.

Kavanagh lets go and takes a step back just in case Stalker is a very slow learner but the moment he's released, it's clear all the fight has been driven out of him. He moves out of range, grabs his injured arm and tries to manipulate it. Then he looks up and realises for the first time who the Good Samaritan is.

'Jesus,' he laughs, shaking his head. 'It's the fucking bookworm.'

'You might like to watch your language.'

Stalker looks across at Anna who is inspecting her arm for bruises.

'Why? Because there's a *lady* present?'

'Because I used to work for someone who'd have kneecapped you for swearing in his presence and I'm starting to understand his take on things.'

'So this is – what?' he says, peering round Kavanagh to address Anna directly. 'You've got a bodyguard, for fuck's sake?'

'That's strike two.'

'Well boo-fucking-hoo, grandad,' he says, nodding at the book that Kavanagh is picking up from the road. 'What are you going to do – read me to death? Ah, Jesus.'

He groans as he tries to lift his injured arm into a position it's clearly not prepared to contemplate just yet. 'I think you've dislocated my shoulder.'

'How are your legs?'

'My what?'

'You've been asked very politely to go on ahead. You've got five seconds to start running.'

Stalker stares at him as if he's speaking a foreign language.

'Four . . .'

'You are joking, right?'

'Three . . .'

'How am I supposed to run when you've crippled me?'

'Two . . .'

It's at this point that bravado and ego lose out to a tidal wave of support for the concept of self-preservation. He turns away from them both, shuffling in a curious crab-like style with one shoulder bent over and cradled by its opposite hand. It's ungainly and strips him of any dignity that has not already been drained from him by his previous humiliations. Kavanagh watches him go and only when he's a safe distance away does he turn back to Anna.

'Thank you,' she says. 'I really appreciate it.'

'You OK?'

'I'm fine. Better than he is anyway. That was very good of you. Some people might have thought twice about getting involved, you know?'

She holds out her right hand.

'I'm Anna.'

'I know,' he says, shaking it. 'I was at the show just now.'

Her face lights up.

'Really? You were there? I'm sorry I didn't see you. It's not that easy with the spotlight. You just see shapes really. I hope it was OK.'

Kavanagh nods his head. Tells her he enjoyed it and he can see she's pleased.

'Well, thank you,' she says with a disarming tilt of the head. 'I'm sorry . . . I didn't catch your name.'

'Kavanagh.'

'Kavanagh,' she says, as if rolling it around on her tongue and trying it out for size. 'That's not your first name, is it?'

He hesitates, trying to remember the last time he was asked that question. It feels like an eternity since anyone outside a professional context was sufficiently interested. He's lived a life that borders on the reclusive – a hermit in plain sight. Now he can't even decide which version of his name to use. Jon? Jonny? Jonathan? They all sound alien somehow.

He opts for Jon and she says it suits him. He's not sure why that should be the case but reminds himself this is small talk. It doesn't have to make sense.

He finds her composure puzzling. No, more than that. It's disconcerting. He's just pulled her out of a potentially dangerous situation that may not have been of her own making but to which she made a significant contribution. Stalker may have built the fire and struck the matches but fanning the flames the way she did was reckless. He'd feel a lot more comfortable if she showed signs of having at least been shaken by the ordeal.

'You don't think walking down dark roads on your own at night is asking for trouble?' he says.

Anna blinks and comes out with something that's half laugh, half gasp.

'Excuse me?'

'It's not safe for a woman,' he says, aware even as he says it that he may be expressing himself clumsily. 'Not on your own.'

'This is the twenty-first century. I should be able to walk down a dark road at night if I want to.'

'And you did. So how did that turn out for you?'

Anna takes a step back and looks quizzically at him.

'Look, I'm really grateful for your help but I can assure you I come across this sort of harassment every day of the week back home. The day I can't handle some tanked-up loser who fancies his chances, I'll choose another line of work.'

'That's what you were doing, was it? Handling him?' Kavanagh doesn't mean it unkindly and he's picked up on the irritation in her voice, but her safety's an issue here and she needs to think seriously about what happened a few moments ago . . . and the possible consequences if he hadn't been there.

Anna doesn't reply immediately. Instead she opens her hessian bag and reaches inside to find a small handbag. Opening the latter, she takes two items from it and holds them up in turn.

'Pepper spray,' she says. 'Whistle.'

There are so many things he can say in response to this. These self-defence accessories are only as effective as the notice she's given. It's taken her four or five seconds to get them out of the bag. What is someone like Stalker meant to be doing in that time –standing around with his hands in his pockets until she's ready? Supposing she does have enough time – how difficult does she think it will be for him to take them from her before she can use them? This unshakable belief in their invulnerability that young people wave like a guarantee of safe passage is as alarming as it is unrealistic. Life has a way of proving such people wrong. He doesn't have to dig too deeply into his own experience for proof of that.

He *could* say all this but doesn't. He can tell from her reaction that he's already gone too far. Anna doesn't want a lecture from a total stranger and if he's not careful he's going to undo any good work he's done in coming to her rescue. He's annoyed with himself for being so clumsy but having spent his life putting up barriers, he can't expect to come out from behind them and fit in seamlessly. Anna is twenty-three, he reminds himself – young enough to be his granddaughter. He's going to have to learn quickly how to strike the right note because he's been handed a gift-wrapped opportunity to get closer to her. The last thing he needs is to balls it up by offering unwanted lectures.

'Are you going to report him?' he asks, trying to dig himself out of a hole by reminding her of the *real* villain of the piece, the person who *should* be the focus of her anger. 'If you want me to come with you . . .'

'No,' she says, shaking her head. 'I don't think that would be a good idea. I've hardly been here any time at all. The last thing I want to do is kick up a fuss that might embarrass the management in some way. I've worked hard for this opportunity. I'm not going to let some clown like him jeopardise it.'

He shrugs his shoulders.

'He spiked your drink.'

That gets her attention.

'He what?'

'Your cocktail. The one he bought for you and was trying to get you to drink. He put something in it.'

'What was it?'

'I don't know. I poured it into a pot plant.'

She stares at him for a moment, mouth agape. Then she bursts out laughing.

'You poured it into a pot plant?'

Kavanagh isn't sure whether she's laughing at him or with him. He looks at the ground.

'Just letting you know what you were dealing with. He's a bit more than a clown. He's likely to try it again with someone else.'

Anna thinks about this, then shakes her head.

'We're not going to be able to prove anything. It's your word against his. The police aren't going to be interested and it'll just stir up a lot of bad publicity for Cristi's for nothing. They're not going to thank me for that.'

Kavanagh nods. Says nothing.

They've reached the outskirts of Praia D'El Rey now. He wonders where her apartment is.

'You OK from here?' he asks. 'I don't mind walking you back to your place if you'd prefer it.'

'You think he might come back and try again?'

'No,' he admits. 'Better safe than sorry though.'

'It's not far now. I'll be OK from here.'

'Sure?'

'Sure,' she says, starting to walk off, and he wonders whether the suggestion was yet another gaffe on his part. Then she turns and calls out to him.

'But thanks for the offer.'

And maybe, he thinks, he hasn't blown it after all.

18

28th June 2018
Praia D'El Rey

Anna is woken by the sound of her mobile ringing on the pillow next to her and realises instantly that she's been dragged out of a dream. The detail may be elusive but the lingering sense of anxiety tells her she's better off out of it – this is happening too often. She fumbles for the phone and checks the screen before answering. It's a Facetime call from Emmie. In Vancouver.

Still groggy, she blinks at the time.

03.57.

She rubs the sleep from her eyes and her sister's face swims into view, frozen for a second or two but springing to life as her voice rings out as clear as a bell from the other side of the Atlantic.

'Hiya Bubs,' she says. 'You OK? I can't see you. The screen's all dark.'

Bubs – Emmie's nickname for her ever since primary school. She took it from some character in a children's TV programme, a bossy child who's constantly telling her younger sister what to do. Over the years she's come to regard it as a sign of affection.

She gropes behind her and presses the light switch on the wall at the third attempt.

'Better?'

'Oh my God,' Emmie shrieks, her voice competing with a level of hubbub in the background. 'You're in bed. What time is it? What time is it, guys?'

She's looking over her shoulder. Anna hears a male voice in the background, telling her it's coming up to eight p.m.

'Time difference,' she yawns. 'I'm eight hours ahead of you, remember?'

'Shit. Did I wake you?'

Anna starts to sit up in bed, then remembers it's a Facetime call. Emmie's in a bar – if there's a chance someone's going to peer over her shoulder at the screen, they're not going to see her looking like this.

'It's four a.m. Yeah, you woke me. Is everything OK?'

'Sorry. Yeah, everything's fine. It's just . . . the cruise starts tomorrow and I thought I'd ring you while I've got the chance. I didn't want to leave it till then cos it's an early start. We're meant to be boarding around eight – that's eight our time, not yours – and it's going to be manic for the first few days so I don't know when I'll get to call. Jesus, I can't believe I woke you. Didn't even think. I'll let you get back to sleep.'

Ten minutes later, she's still talking. Buzzing. When Emmie's on an emotional high, as Anna knows from experience, there's no way of getting a word in edgeways let alone stopping her. Vancouver, for today at least, is apparently the greatest city in the world. She's been there for five days now and by the sound of things rehearsals couldn't be going better. She feels fully accepted by everyone at the dance company, now she's shown what she can do. Anna lies back on the pillow and listens as she burbles on about cycling the sea wall at Stanley Park and visiting the aquarium on her afternoon off. This is clearly the best thing that's ever happened to her.

She wishes she could see the world through Emmie's eyes right now and share in her excitement. Not so long ago, she was living her own version of the big dream and looking forward to swapping stories when they were next in touch.

She reminds herself that it's only six weeks or so since she was in London, slogging from one shitty bar to the next, grateful for half a dozen people who might actually be listening to her rather than trying to impress their date for the evening. Crap day job. Crap agent. Tenuous foothold on the property ladder. No relationship since Theo finally ran out of patience two years ago and no sign of any queue, orderly or otherwise, forming at her door in a bid to replace him. No wonder the whole Praia D'El Rey project turned her head when Ches laid it all out in front of her.

She holds the phone firmly in front of her, peering at the small screen and wishing she'd taken the call on her laptop instead, that the technology existed that would allow her to reach inside the screen and hug her baby sister, wrap her arms around her and never let go.

'How about you?' she hears Emmie ask, bringing her back to the Facetime call. 'Did it go well?'

She's asking about her set at the Cabaret Lounge two nights ago but the fact that it's the walk home that automatically springs to mind can't be a coincidence. She does her best to shut it out . . . just for as long as Emmie's on the phone.

'Yes . . . it went well.'

'That's good. Have you got to know anyone yet?'

'Not the way you mean, no.'

'Liar,' Emmie says. 'Show me the rest of the bed.' The laugh that punctuates these words is so happy, so carefree.

'Look, I'll let you get back to whatever you were doing. You look like death warmed up. Get some sleep, OK?' Not a hint of irony.

Anna's screen freezes for a few seconds. She taps it, calls out to Emmie, shakes the phone a couple of times before the picture swims back into view.

'You still there, Bubs?'

'I'm still here. Lost you for a second.'

'OK, I was just saying ... look after yourself, right? And before you start nagging, I promise I'll ring when I can.'

'You will be careful, won't you?' she blurts out.

'Yes, Mum,' says Emmie, tongue in cheek.

'Seriously. I mean it. Look after yourself.'

'It's a cruise, Bubs. I'm not backpacking across Australia.'

The male voice is back again and Emmie turns away briefly to explain. Against all the other background noise, Anna is unable to hear what he's saying.

'Who's that?' she asks.

'That's Luca, one of the dancers. He says to tell you not to worry. He'll look after me.'

She waggles her eyebrows suggestively.

'Got to go,' she adds. 'Love you.'

'Love you too,' says Anna, although the screen has already gone blank.

19

29th June 2018
Praia D'El Rey

'Hello again.'

Kavanagh is studying the pictures on cartons of fruit juice to work out exactly which flavour is which. He looks up to see Anna standing at the end of the aisle with an empty basket in her hand. Her smile looks a little tentative for some reason, her demeanour bordering on sheepish, although he can't imagine why that should be the case. If he hasn't seen her since coming to her rescue, the fault lies more with him than her. Cristi's has been relegated to a landmark he passes on his early morning run. He hasn't been back in the evening, either for a meal or to hear her perform, because he's not sure she would welcome the contact.

He's given a lot of thought to that evening and become more and more frustrated with himself for misjudging things so badly – for being so protective that he practically trampled all over her. He can see now how important it is for her to present herself as adult, liberated, able to make her own decisions. Advice is one thing but no one enjoys being lectured and made to feel stupid. She's even less likely to take it from someone she presumes to be a dyed-in-the-wool chauvinist whose view of the world is probably forty years past its sell-by date. He's frustrated by the fact that this is not at all how he sees himself but in this instance it's not *his* perception that matters.

He's made a point of staying away because he hopes that with a little time and space to think things through, she'll realise that however clumsy he may have been in expressing himself, his intentions were so much better than that. If, on the other hand, he's in the Cabaret Lounge every night with a front-row seat, he'll become a constant reminder of what happened. If he's not careful, she may even come to feel she's simply exchanged one stalker for another.

So for the past couple of days he's gone back into hermit mode, snuggling into a well-worn blanket which suits him just fine, not least because it's not so markedly different from the one he's used to back home. He misses the bookshop and swapping opinions on books with Conor, but replacing them with a patio, a comfortable sun lounger, unlimited sunshine and a stunning beach is not a bad consolation. He's not a sun-worshipper by any means but gradual exposure in small doses at the right time of day is already starting to have a positive effect on his colouring. Add to that a couple of swims a day and a gentle stroll along the beach as the sun goes down and he's probably never felt so relaxed in his life. He's even watched the golfers from his balcony and wondered about maybe taking a few lessons. He could get used to this. It's so seductive, it would be easy to forget why he's here.

Anna walks over to him and stands there, holding the basket in front of her in both hands as if selling primroses. The word *demure* springs to mind. Coy.

'I haven't seen you recently,' she says. 'At the Cabaret Lounge, I mean.'

She pauses, presumably to give him a chance to offer an explanation.

'No,' he says, colouring slightly. It's only a small, on-site supermarket and they're the only people in there apart from the elderly woman at the checkout, who speaks excellent English and can probably hear every word from where she's sitting.

'I wondered if maybe you were unwell but then I thought, that's stupid. Just because you haven't been to Cristi's for a few days doesn't necessarily mean there's anything wrong – there could be lots of reasons. So then I started thinking maybe it was something to do with what happened the other night.'

'I'm fine,' he says.

'I haven't upset you – you know, for not reporting that creep like you suggested?'

He takes a moment to try out his answer in his head before delivering it. He knows she's actively brokering some sort of peace deal here and doesn't want to say anything that is going to upset her again.

'Why would I be upset?' he asks. 'It's not my decision to make.'

'You were, though. I could tell.'

She puts her basket on the floor and takes a deep breath.

'I don't know why I'm holding this stupid thing,' she says. 'I'm not here to buy anything. The truth is, I followed you in and grabbed it so you'd think it was a coincidence, our bumping into each other like this. I just wanted to apologise, that's all. I'm sorry – I really am.'

He tries to process this. It's not at all what he was expecting.

'You don't have anything to apologise for.'

'Yes, I do. I have this terrible habit of getting on my high horse every now and then. My sister Emmie, she tells me if I get any further up myself, I'll be able to nibble my intestines. It's just ... I hate being talked down to and I thought that's what was happening, but when I thought about it afterwards I couldn't actually find fault with anything you said.'

'Just the way I said it.'

She laughs.

'Well ... maybe. I suppose so. But you were just trying to help. When I got back to the apartment I couldn't help thinking it was a pretty shabby way to reward you for stepping in like that, so I made up my mind that first chance I got, I was going to apologise. That's why I've been keeping an eye out for you at the Cabaret Lounge. I was so sure I'd offended you.'

He shakes his head. If it's a lie, it's no more than a white one. She doesn't need to know how much he's been beating himself up since then.

'I'm eating at Cristi's tonight,' he says, one lie apparently begetting another. 'I'll probably be in the Lounge afterwards.'

'Oh, I'm afraid I won't be there,' she sighs, and she looks genuinely disappointed. 'I get one night off during the week. It was supposed to be Wednesday but I was asked to do a swap tonight and I've arranged to meet up with some friends. I'll be singing tomorrow though ... if you've nothing better to do, that is.'

He nods and she places a hand on his arm as if to seal the deal before stooping to rescue the basket.

'What's your favourite song?' she asks, her eyes brightening suddenly.

He gives a mental gulp. He's not sure he has one. He's heard songs he likes, of course he has, but there's no way he's going to be able to come up with a title at such short notice. Then, out of nowhere, a distant memory crawls to the surface. A drinks reception Maurice had organised as one of his PR exercises – captains of industry, politicians, TV celebrities in attendance. Classical music in one room and a jazz quartet in the other with a female vocalist who included in her repertoire a song that actually registered for once, made it through all the barriers that normally kept his emotions under lock and key. He'd made a point of asking what it was.

'*Summertime*,' he says now.

Her face lights up.

'Perfect.'

'It's from a musical.'

'I know,' she says, smiling. '*Porgy and Bess*. It was one of my dad's favourites too. I love it. Billie or Ella? I can do either.'

Now she has him. Not a clue.

'You choose.'

'Ella,' she says decisively. 'Tomorrow night.' And she walks off towards the exit, adding the empty basket to the others stacked by the door. At the last minute, she turns as if something has just occurred to her.

'Just a thought,' she says. 'I don't suppose you've got anything planned for today, have you?'

Two hours later they're in the back of a taxi, heading for Obidos Lagoon. Kavanagh has offered to pay the fare, then tried to insist on at least going halves, but Anna's having none of it. She was going to the lagoon today anyway and having company will make the walk all the more enjoyable. Besides, it's her treat, a chance to make amends for her less than gracious behaviour of a few nights ago. It doesn't exactly sit easily with Kavanagh but he's prepared to let it go, rather than slip onto the wrong side of that precarious line between good manners and causing offence.

Luis, the taxi driver, must think they're very strange. He's used to tourists who insist on the shortest route possible and have more than one eye on the meter. When Anna asks if there's an alternative to the direct route which she took last week – one that will allow them to see a little bit more of the scenery beyond the resort – he can hardly believe his good fortune. Not slow to recognise an opportunity, he offers them his services for the day at a price he insists will be a lot cheaper than if she has to make a number of separate bookings. His expression, when she agrees, is a picture and he makes a point of kissing the cross dangling on a chain from the rear-view mirror before turning on the ignition.

The first three miles or so are familiar enough, replicating the outer leg of Kavanagh's early morning run. From there onwards it's all new territory – through the small parish of Serra D'El-Rei and then out along a succession of tree-lined roads, most of them gun-barrel straight and pointing the way ahead to Obidos. Luis, who clearly sees the role of tour guide as part of his newly acquired responsibilities, keeps up a constant stream of chatter, managing to find something to say about almost every building and farm they pass. Kavanagh remembers this is not a million miles away from what Anna herself does on a day-to-day basis and tries to picture her, shepherding tourists from one London landmark to the next. He nearly says something before remembering that he has no way of knowing this just yet. Not until she raises it in conversation. So many balls to keep in the air at the same time.

When they reach Amoreira, Luis picks up a minor road, which leads up through a small cluster of houses, the majority of them almost identical with their whitewashed walls and orange slate roofs. Out in the open countryside, they drive past a succession of farms, the landscape constantly changing: cultivated one moment, scrubland the next, then fir trees providing a temporary reprieve from the sun, strobe-lighting the way forward. If the scenery varies, the heat doesn't – it's unrelenting. Luis seems more or less unaffected by it but in response to Anna's request for the air conditioning to be turned up, he makes a few adjustments and the sudden influx of cool air helps to make the last few miles less arduous.

Eventually they arrive at a car park near the water's edge. Anna tells Luis he's welcome to go off and find a café while he waits – she doesn't imagine they'll be back for an hour and a half at least. He assures them both he'll be there whatever time they return, and she and Kavanagh walk down to join the trail which covers three sides of the lagoon. It's firm underfoot and well signposted for the most part. They're in no hurry and it doesn't take him long to appreciate why she's made such a swift return trip. It's an idyllic setting. Children are paddling in the crystal-clear waters of the shallows, their squeals of delight the only sounds competing with the birdsong and the chirping of cicadas in the woods alongside them. Further out, local fisherman are at work in battered-looking skiffs and every so often a flock of birds comes sweeping in, skimming the water before skidding to a halt and composing themselves all in one graceful movement. There are other walkers and the occasional cyclist but the further they stroll, the easier it becomes to imagine they have the place to themselves.

'There were flamingos here last week,' Anna says. 'Actual flamingos. About seven or eight of them, skipping through the shallows. I'd only ever seen them on TV and they were just these stupid birds, standing around on one leg. I had no idea they were so graceful close up – they're like ballet dancers, the way they walk.'

Kavanagh smiles. She seems relaxed and that's good to see.

'So tell me about yourself,' she says suddenly. 'I'd hate you to think I make a habit of inviting strange men to share a taxi with me or join me on long walks.'

'Good to hear.'

'Come on then. Who is Jon Kavanagh? Where are you from? What do you do? You don't mind me being nosey, do you?'

He shakes his head. Tells her he lives in Dorset, which it turns out she's never visited although she thinks she might have heard of Lulworth Cove. As for what he does for a living, he decides to keep it simple, telling her he's more or less retired now. When asked what he did before, he says he was in security and leaves it at that. He finds it interesting that his limited contact with her should automatically cause his mind to default to a period of his life which is long gone . . . as if the past twenty years have counted for nothing.

'You make it sound very mysterious,' she says, cocking her head to one side. 'Like you were a spy or something. Was it dangerous?'

'No, not really. It had its moments but most of the time it was really mundane and boring.'

'So that's not how you . . .?' She shapes as if to point at the scar, then drops her hand suddenly and gasps. 'Oh God, I can't believe I just did that. I'm so sorry – the mouth on me. I'm always doing things like that. I only have to think something and I find myself coming straight out with it. Theo – my ex – he used to say I must have some sort of filter missing.'

He says it's fine – he's used to it. People are bound to be curious. He'd much rather they asked than just stared. He tells her it's an injury he picked up when he was in the army.

'A lifetime ago.'

He doesn't offer any more than that, gently steers the conversation to her instead. He needs her to start revealing a few details about her own life so that he can add them to the list of things he's actually entitled to know. He's relieved when she starts talking about her family background, the problems she faced when her mother walked out and her father's distance-learning approach to parenting, which more or less amounted to a total abdication of responsibility. It feels like a foot in the door. He wonders if she's as calm as she appears to be, whether there's an underlying anger that wouldn't need much prompting to come to the surface.

Listening to her discussing it now, he's reminded of something in Lowe's dossier that struck him as slightly anomalous when he first read it. According to the notes, her sister Emmie was born in August 1998. It was only eleven months after this that Anna herself was brought into the family, having just turned four. That in itself strikes him as curious timing, but he accepts he's anything but an authority when it comes to relationships. Perhaps those eleven months were enough to convince Colette that she didn't want to go through it all again. Maybe Anna was a short-cut, a ready-made older sister who could act as a play-mate for Emmie and help to look after her. As Lowe suggested when Kavanagh queried it with him, analysing the relationships of other people is an exercise in futility. It's possible to speculate all day long and never come close to understanding them. *Who knows and who cares?*

In any case, that's not the strangest part of it, as far as Kavanagh is concerned. It's the speed with which the whole thing fell apart that he can't quite get his head around; the fact that only three years later, having gone to such lengths to have a family of her own, the mother should choose to walk out on them all in pursuit of a dream that was never going anywhere. Walk out for good, with never a backward glance. What was that all about? It's like a child with a short attention span. Novelty's worn off – time to move on.

And even if the father was stunned by this turn of events and found it difficult to cope on his own, his cavalier attitude to parenting once he was left to bring up the two girls on his own is little short of inexplicable. Whatever reasons may have prompted the couple to adopt in the first place, it's hard to imagine how they were considered suitable candidates and certainly doesn't cast the adoption process and its checking procedures in a very favourable light. He'd be interested to hear Anna's take on this but that can't happen without entering very dangerous waters. She already appears to have a fairly jaundiced view of her upbringing. He can only imagine what she'd make of it if she knew they weren't even her birth parents.

'So what brought you to Praia D'El Rey then?' she asks. 'I mean, I'd never heard of it. If someone said *Portugal* to me, I'd have thought Lisbon or the Algarve. What made you choose here?'

'I read an article in one of the travel supplements,' he explains. 'The golf doesn't really interest me but I saw all these photos of the beach and those waves and I thought it looked like the perfect place to spend the summer.'

Answers are so much easier if you can prepare them well in advance, he thinks.

'The summer? You're here for a while then?'

'Two months. With an option for a third. How about you? How did this opportunity come about?'

'No idea,' she says, flicking a small pebble with her shoe and watching as it rolls down to the water's edge. 'It came right out of the blue. Like I said, I couldn't even have told you where Praia D'El Rey was but the moment Ches said Portugal, that was good enough for me.'

'Ches?'

'My agent.'

Kavanagh stops. Looks at her.

'Your agent?'

Surely not, he thinks to himself. *Then again . . . London?*

'Yes,' she says, frowning slightly, clearly surprised by his reaction.

'Ches Headley?'

There's a pause before she replies.

'No,' she says, almost warily as if testing the answer out on herself. 'Why do you ask?'

'No reason. Someone I came across years ago, that's all. When I was working in London.'

Strange, strange man. Dress sense that was not so much idiosyncratic as just plain idiotic. Saw himself as a style guru, a fashion icon, always had a thing for cowboy outfits. Hadn't long started out in the business and was trying to engineer a foot in the door for his acts at one or two clubs in which the Syndicate had a vested interest. Kavanagh had been sent round to explain in person some of the protocols that Headley was failing to observe. Problem solved.

Ches, he thinks. Unusual name but then again London's a big place. He's about to ask her agent's surname but she's moved on already, skipping down the path and using her phone to take photos of the eucalyptus trees that border the lake.

'You know, this would be the most amazing place to run first thing in the morning,' she says, her eyes sparkling. 'I wish I was a runner like you. I'd get Luis to bring me out here two or three times a week. Crack of dawn, before everyone else gets here.'

And the moment has passed.

Luis, as good as his word, is waiting by the car when they arrive back, even though they're fifteen minutes earlier than agreed. Anna says they'd like to go to Obidos, spend some time strolling around the town, then have lunch somewhere cool and shady. Bearing in mind how hot they were in the car earlier, she opts for the most direct route and asks how quickly he can get them there. He says he can probably do it in thirty minutes – does it in twenty. When he drops them off this time, he offers to go with them and act as a guide. Anna shakes her head, says they'll be back at two thirty, and the disappointment comes off him in waves as she and Kavanagh set off to join the crowd of tourists making their way towards the main gate of the walled town.

Obidos, they soon realise, needs more than an hour or two to do it justice. Unfortunately it also lends itself better to cooler conditions than this thirty-degree heat which hasn't even started to flex its muscles as yet. The pleasant stroll they've been envisaging is trammelled at every turn by the apparently inexhaustible flood of human traffic, negotiating narrow streets that were never built to cater for crowds of this size.

The volume of tourists and the stifling heat are only part of the problem. For one thing, there's hardly a ten-metre stretch of path that is on the level. Everywhere they walk, they seem to be going down steps, or hauling themselves up sharp inclines that test their stamina and tug at tired calf muscles. Then there's the cobbled streets that are hard on the soles of the feet and make it difficult to descend with any degree of confidence. Kavanagh's shirt is stuck to his back long before they make it up to the castle walls but at least he can be distracted by spectacular views from here over the surrounding countryside and far out to sea.

On the way down they do all the touristy things – peer into tiny shops where there is only just room for the owner, let alone anyone else; drink Ginja from a chocolate cup, offered as free samples by street vendors. It's not long though before the thought of lunch – and in particular long, cool drinks from a frosted glass – proves irresistible. They duck into the first café that looks even half decent, grab an upstairs table in the shade and order sandwiches and a bottle of Sagres each.

Anna sits opposite him, dabbing at her face with a wet wipe. She offers one to him and he's grateful for it. He wishes he could change out of his shirt which feels clammy against his back but at least up here on the balcony and out of the direct sunlight he can feel the benefit of what little breeze there is.

She tells him, if it's OK with him, she'll head back once they've eaten. She's going out this evening for a few drinks in Peniche with some of the other musicians and wants to shower and grab a couple of hours' sleep before they leave. She asks about his plans for the evening and just for the briefest of moments he wonders whether she's going to suggest he might like to come along too. Then his sense of perspective kicks in – a night out for someone her age is going to be markedly different from anything he might choose to do.

He tells her he'll probably have a night in. Maybe finish the Ondaatje.

'Is that a book?' she asks.

'Michael Ondaatje. He's the author.'

He realises she's looking at him and assumes it's the scar that's caught her attention again.

'I was just thinking,' she says, breaking into a smile. 'About the other night. You don't mind me bringing it up again, do you? It's just . . . I can't get the picture out of my head.'

'What picture?'

'You and your book. I just remember you stooping to pick it up off the ground after you'd sorted that guy out and brushing the dust off the cover. It made me laugh later, when I remembered it. I mean, it just seemed so . . . what's the word?'

'Incongruous?'

'I don't know. If that means weird, then yeah. I mean, you looked like you were stroking it, like it was a pet or something. You must really love your books.'

He tells her they've always been important to him, explains how they provided companionship and a sense of possibilities for a lonely teenager with only his grandparents for company. Being Anna, she asks if something happened to his parents and apologises immediately for prying. He doesn't go into details, just tells her they died when he was young. He's never told anyone since Maurice and look where that got him. He knows from first-hand experience that the more you tell others, the more exposed you leave yourself. You make it easy for them to manipulate you, give them strings to pull.

This time she doesn't push it.

'I ought to read more,' she says, taking a bite from her sandwich. 'I keep telling myself I will. I bought a Kindle a few years ago and I keep adding new books to it but I don't suppose I've read more than a dozen or so. I brought it with me and haven't even taken it out of the suitcase yet. I suppose you hate Kindles.'

'I don't hate anything that encourages people to read. I definitely prefer books, though.'

'Well, you would, wouldn't you?' she says. 'Profit margins and all that.'

She stops and there's a moment, just a moment, when her eyes widen, almost as if in panic. Then she breaks into an extended coughing fit which she manages to bring under control only when he picks up her glass and hands it to her. She takes a couple of gulps from it and flaps her hand in front of her face, which eventually manages to conjure up a smile from somewhere. He thinks it looks a little strained.

'You OK?' he asks.

She nods, takes out another wet wipe and dabs at her brow. She holds the pack out to him once more but this time he shakes his head. He checks again that she's all right and she says she's fine. Serves her right for eating and talking at the same time.

'One of the few things Colette got right,' she says, the attempt at humour presumably intended to reassure him.

He wishes that was how he felt . . . but he doesn't.

Not quite.

When they're back in the taxi, heading for Praia D'El Rey, she says very little for the first five minutes. She's gazing out of the window, so obviously preoccupied that even Luis picks up on it and offers little in the way of conversation. Kavanagh is happy to give her the space if she needs it. She's not the only one with a few things on her mind.

When she does finally break the silence, her words are prefaced by a deep sigh that is loud enough for Luis to glance in the rear-view mirror.

'I owe you an apology,' she says. 'Another one.'

She's still looking out of the window, staring at the scenery . . . or maybe something way beyond it.

'Back at the lagoon, when we were talking about how I got this contract? I lied about my agent. That was stupid of me. It *is* Ches Headley. I'm sorry.'

Kavanagh waits until she turns to face him before replying.

'What made you say it was someone else?'

'Oh . . . I don't know,' she says. 'Embarrassment, maybe? I know it's no excuse but this place . . . it's the best thing that's ever happened to me. By a mile. I can't begin to explain what it's done for my confidence. Back home in London . . . well, I'm nothing really. Just another jobbing singer, hopping from one shitty bar to the next for chump change. I feel like some pathetic cliché, singing my heart out, hoping maybe tonight is the night, this time someone influential is going to be there and like what I do. And every night I'm lucky if half a dozen people are even bothering to listen.'

She runs the wipe up and down both arms and drops it into her bag when she's done with it.

'Then this chance lands in my lap out of nowhere. I come out here and everything changes overnight. I've got audiences who like what I do, who really listen. They even buy my home-made CDs, for God's sake. I've got top billing for the first time in my life and I'm a serious performer all of a sudden. But the moment you said you know Ches, I thought that's it – all over now. If you've met him, you'll know that anyone on his books can't be all that much. He's just a flesh peddler – need a body to wail away in the background for an hour or two? Ches is your man. So I lied . . . and I'm really sorry. I've been beating myself up about it ever since.'

She uses the heel of her hand to dab at the corner of one eye. She looks tired, as if the sun has at last taken its toll on her.

'He's not a friend of yours, is he?' she asks, forcing a laugh that sounds as if it could easily slip over into something else.

Kavanagh remembers his only encounter with Headley. *Don't go overboard,* Vic had told him beforehand. *Just make sure he gets the message.* He hardly had to lean on him at all. All mouth and trousers, as Nanna Belle used to say.

'No,' he says. 'You need to change agents, though. Find someone with a bit of ambition.'

'I know. I was planning to do just that and suddenly he came up with this contract. I thought maybe I'd misjudged him and things might be looking up.'

Kavanagh looks her in the eye to make sure he has her attention.

'Get a proper agent,' he tells her firmly.

She looks for a moment as if she's about to say something. Then she takes a deep breath, lifts his hand from the back seat and squeezes it in both of hers.

'Tomorrow night,' she says. '*Summertime.*'

The watery smile is probably intended to convince him she's OK but it falls well short of that. He hopes she has a good time with the other musicians tonight and that they'll be able to take her out of herself for one evening, because that's clearly what she needs. It will do her good to be in the company of others who understand how talented she is.

He's pleased she's come clean about the white lie she told. He doesn't see it as anything more serious than that but it *has* been bothering him. He sensed there was something off about it right from the outset, the way her expression ran the gamut from puzzled, through startled, to evasive before she skipped off down to the water's edge. It's good to know he still has an eye and an ear for that sort of thing and that his instincts aren't about to let him down any time soon. And it makes perfect sense too for her to be embarrassed. If he himself was in any way dependent on someone as flaky as Ches Headley, he wouldn't be shouting it from the rooftops either.

It's been a good day, he tells himself. Nine out of ten. They've spent several hours in each other's company without any real hint of awkwardness. They've swapped phone numbers to make it easier to get in touch with each other in future. Given his dismal track record when it comes to building relationships of any description, he doesn't think today could have gone any better. There were times when he actually relaxed and he's picked up a few things to add to what he already knows about her. Just by letting her talk and listening with a sympathetic ear, he's discovered that she lacks confidence in herself, something Lowe's fact-based dossier could never have told him. He senses that even she doesn't really believe in her own potential. If she's convinced herself that these three months in Praia D'El Rey are as far as she can go, then it will be. And as long as she has the likes of Ches Headley as an agent, there's nothing more certain.

He may not know the music industry but his years in London brought him into contact with others who do. And yes, twenty years is a long time but he's confident there are enough people who will remember him and be keen to point him in the right direction – even if it's only to move him on.

He's here in Praia D'El Rey because he wants to know if there is any way he can help her and he may just have found one.

Kavanagh's days have always been structured. Even on holiday, he's not someone who is happy allowing things to drift. He likes to fill his days, moving from one planned set piece to the next in an orderly fashion. It doesn't mean he's incapable of relax-ing. He's more than happy to spend an entire afternoon doing nothing but read and go for the occasional swim, but he likes to know in advance that this is how those hours will be spent. His early morning run, for instance, has been a priority for as long as he can remember – it may vary in length and intensity but if he finds himself unable to factor one in for some reason, the whole day feels out of balance somehow, and it's always there at the back of his mind, an itch that won't go away.

Since he came to Praia D'El Rey his evening walk has started to exert a similar hold over him, but tonight his routine has been seriously compromised by *The English Patient,* the last one hundred pages of which have taken him much longer to read than expected. By the time he's finished and is ready to set out, it's gone half nine. The sun will have slipped beneath the waves before he reaches the beach if it hasn't done so already. He even considers the possibility of giving it a miss for one evening but his legs have been curled up beneath him for ages and are making their impatience known.

The moment he steps outside the air-conditioned villa the warmth of the night leaps out of the shadows. The forecast earlier suggested there might be a storm on the way and for most of the day that's seemed inconceivable. It's not so difficult to imagine now though, judging by the clouds that have come rushing in under cover of darkness. It's not going to put him off walking or even persuade him to take a kagoule with him. A sharp downpour will be something to welcome if it washes away the muggy, oppressive atmosphere hanging over the resort.

He turns into the road that leads down to the expansive sandy car park at the foot of the hill, offering a sympathetic nod in passing to a couple who've just reached the sharpest part of the climb and are definitely struggling. The man gives an exaggerated grimace before breaking into a grin. The woman smiles too and says something in what he assumes to be Portuguese and he appreciates the gesture. He's starting to feel at home here.

When he reaches the foot of the hill, he crosses the road, heading for the parking area and the dunes that lie beyond it. He's not sure what makes him glance at the road that carries on away to his left. And then look again. It's the second look that does it because it's at that precise moment that the girl steps out of the shadows and walks directly under a street lamp. She's there for a second, maybe two, then she's out of its range again and about to disappear altogether around a further bend in the road.

He has nothing really to go on. He's seen her for a split second, no more, and knows it flies in the face of logic because Anna's in Peniche with some of the other musicians. Even so, he thinks it's her. He hesitates, tells himself it can't be, and walks a few paces further into the car park but his imagination, having concocted this unlikely scenario, isn't ready to give up on it just yet and he finds himself backtracking and rejoining the road before setting off in pursuit.

Somewhere inside, a voice is trying to reason with him, get him at least to slow down. If it's not her, being pursued by a strange man with a scarred face is going to scare some poor girl half to death. And if it *is* her, how is it going to look? Their paths have crossed purely by chance but this is the second time within a week that he'll have been following her and if that doesn't start to ring a few alarm bells it damn well should. She's already made it clear she can look after herself and doesn't need someone to shadow her every move. At best she'll see it as overprotective. At worst he'll come across as obsessed, if not predatory.

He crosses the road to where the trees and bushes offer more cover and picks her out again just in time because, to his surprise, she steps off the pavement and chooses instead a footpath that runs along the back of a cluster of villas, fringing the golf course. It's completely unlit and a ridiculous thing to do when reasonably well-lit alternatives are available. What on earth is she doing?

He's convinced now that it's Anna. He has no idea why she isn't enjoying a night out with her friends as she said she would be, or what it is that's brought her out here, but there's no time to worry about any of that now. The whys can wait. He can't shake the suspicion that something very odd is going on here and if it concerns her – particularly if it's going to put her at risk in any way – he needs to know what it is.

He follows her onto the path and the first spots of rain start to fall, isolated drops at first, then a sudden flurry as the heavens open and it starts to come down much more steadily. It's almost impossible to see anything in these murky conditions and he's worried she might slip into one of the back gardens without him even noticing. But away to his right, on the other side of the fairway, he sees a light which flashes twice and moments later there is the girl again, changing course and heading across the golf course towards it. He realises the signal came from an old abandoned house which he's walked past a few times during his evening stroll. He has wondered before now why it's been allowed to fall into such a state of disrepair because its location on the cliff top with a stunning view over the bay would surely make it a prime piece of real estate. Anna has clearly arranged to meet someone there . . . and rain or no rain, Kavanagh isn't about to leave until he knows who.

There's no way he can follow her across the fairway without being seen so he stays where he is for now, hoping that whatever has brought her here is not going to take long. He's completely exposed to the elements but the path is the only vantage point that will allow him to see them both when they leave so he's left with little alternative but to tough it out. He has next to nothing in the way of protection from the rain. He remembers how his T-shirt stuck to him while they were climbing to the castle walls earlier today. This one is now glued to him, front and back, and he wishes he'd been less cavalier earlier and brought a kagoule with him. He wraps his arms around himself and squats down behind the largest fence he can find in the hope that it will ward off the worst of the downpour. And waits.

It feels like half an hour, although it's probably no more than seven or eight minutes. Then two figures appear on the fairway directly in front of him. For a moment he thinks they're both coming back his way, but once they've crossed the fairway they split up. Anna is heading in his direction while the other figure continues straight on and disappears temporarily from sight, leaving Kavanagh with a decision to make. If he stays where he is, Anna will walk straight into him. If he goes back down the path ahead of her, he can find places to hide and let her go past without being spotted. But if he does that, by the time he gets back here he'll almost certainly have lost the person who was with her.

He picks the third option and steps over a chain-link fence and into one of the rear gardens. There are lights on upstairs but the curtains are drawn and there's a tall fence separating the property from the one next door. He presses himself up against it and waits for the girl to pass. And it *is* her. He can see her quite clearly now, no more than ten feet away. If she turns for some reason, she can't help but see him and there's no explanation he can think of that will sound plausible. He holds his breath as she scuttles past, no better dressed for the rain than he is. Counts to ten which is as long as he feels he can leave it before setting off in pursuit of the other shadowy figure.

He steps back over the fence and runs to the opposite end of the path and sees how it is that his quarry managed to disappear from view because there's another path here, one that links the golf course to the main road through the centre of the resort. There's no sign of him by the time Kavanagh gets there so he sprints the length of this path as well, then stops dead once he reaches the junction, taking care not to be seen as he decides which way to go.

The figure is off to the right, a good way further up the road, which is fortunately well lit. Whoever it is, he's come much better prepared for the weather and is wearing a plastic raincoat and a baseball cap, which is protecting not only the top of his head but also his identity . . . from this range, at least. Kavanagh, anxious not to be seen, makes no attempt to get any closer. There's no need. He has him now. He won't be losing him again.

He assumes he's heading for the clubhouse, which is not far away, but shortly before it comes into view the figure turns right into a small side road and Kavanagh picks up the pace to avoid letting him out of his sight for any longer than he has to. When he reaches the corner, the figure is much closer than expected because he's stopped at the rear of a white Seat Ibiza and is standing with his back to him, removing the raincoat and tossing it into the boot of the car. Next to go is the baseball cap and even before he turns sideways on and ducks into the vehicle, Kavanagh knows who it is.

And his heart sinks.

He's trying desperately to compute what he's just seen and can't come up with anything that doesn't bring a whole raft of serious implications in its wake.

It's bad enough that Anna, having been assaulted three nights ago, should choose a secluded location for a clandestine assignation at dead of night.

But what exactly is he supposed to make of the fact that the person she's meeting is none other than the same individual who attacked her only three nights ago?

All of a sudden a day that was a cast-iron nine out of ten has plummeted through zero and is still on its way down.

20

1st July 2018
Richmond

When Adrian Lowe is jolted out of a deep sleep at whatever ungodly hour this must be, it takes him a few moments to work out exactly what it is that's disturbed him. Then something butts against his chin and starts kneading the sheet before walking across his chest and flopping down onto the pillow next to him.

'Missy,' he groans. 'For God's sake. How did you get in here?'

She's not allowed in the bedroom. Lowe has always been mildly allergic to cats, which might make his choice of pet less than ideal in some people's eyes but then again, as he has pointed out on more than one occasion, it's not as if he chose Missy. She chose him. Came sashaying into the kitchen one day, bold as brass, and threw herself at him – there's no other word for it. Threading her way in and out of his feet, purring like the shameless hussy she is.

He knows nothing of where she was before invading his life, but she's been here now for over three years and they've come to an understanding of sorts, which in essence amounts to her doing exactly as she chooses. If she wants to stay out all night, bring in mice and birds and leave feathers and entrails all over the kitchen floor, he'll clean up after her. If she forgets herself occasionally at night and pisses in her basket, fair enough – she's not in the first flush of youth and he himself is probably only a few years away from being similarly indiscreet. The arrangement isn't entirely unconditional, though. She may think she has the run of the house but he draws the line at cats in the bedroom.

And yet here she is.

Having got into the room and made herself comfortable, she's not about to move any time soon. He's going to have to carry her downstairs and put her in her basket. This time he'll make damned sure the door is shut properly. He resists the temptation to check the time because he needs the sleep and knows, if it's any later than five o'clock, he'll end up lying there for ages debating whether it's worth it for the sake of an hour or two. Instead he'll just see to Missy, visit the bathroom, flop back into bed and if he can do it without opening his eyes any wider than he has to, so much the better.

He throws back the sheet and makes his first attempt to roll onto his side and swing his legs out of bed. Doesn't come close. Forget muscle memory – there's not even muscle. He tells himself for the fiftieth time that he needs a new mattress, one that doesn't sag in the middle like a hammock. He's about to try again when a voice says, 'I wouldn't move if I were you' – and although he's never been tasered, he knows this is as close as he ever wants to come to it. He instinctively grabs the sheet and covers himself before reaching for the light switch and turning it on.

But he knows who it is anyway.

He's recognised the voice.

And the sheet isn't going to offer any protection at all.

'Jesus Christ,' Lowe gasps, struggling to sit upright. 'Oh fuck! What the hell are you doing, Jon? You nearly gave me a heart attack.'

Kavanagh is sitting astride a chair, six feet away, arms draped over the backrest. He watches dispassionately as Lowe clamps a hand over his heart, a gesture that strikes him as more than a little theatrical, but there's nothing fake about the breathing, which is laboured and has an ominous wheezing note to it.

'Hands on top of the sheet,' he says. 'Where I can see them.'

'OK, OK.' Lowe holds them up to make it clear he's happy to comply, then lowers them slowly into his lap.

'Just so we understand each other . . . if they move from there I'll break every finger on whichever hand leaves the sheet. You ever had a broken finger?'

Lowe nods. Swallows. 'Once. The index one. It never healed properly. Still got a kink in it.' He holds it up to show him, realises his mistake and slams it back down onto the sheet.

'One's painful. You don't want four, trust me.'

Kavanagh's voice is quiet, measured. Most people make the mistake of thinking that shouting is the best way to intimidate because it can act like an assault on the senses, but they're wrong. Shouting means you've lost it and a person out of control is easier to outmanoeuvre than someone who stays composed, clear about what he's doing. It's the contrast between tone of voice and content that works best on the imagination.

Most people woken this way in the middle of the night would be badly shaken but Lowe is no novice. He looks as if he's recovering from the initial shock already. Kavanagh knows his brain will be scrambling for the right angle. He can talk for England and has probably persuaded himself he can reason his way out of this if he can buy himself enough time. It's a common enough mistake.

'What's this all about, Jon?' Lowe says. 'Aren't you meant to be in Portugal?'

Repeated use of the Christian name. All friends here. Nice try.

'What part of *client confidentiality* don't you understand?' he asks.

'What do you mean? I'm not with you.'

'I told you this was to stay between the two of us. One hundred per cent confidential. Couldn't have been any clearer.'

'Jon, I—'

'You got shirty about it, if I remember rightly. Acted like it was some sort of slur against your professional integrity. Started lecturing me about how discretion is your middle name. Ring any bells?'

'Look, any chance of doing this downstairs?' Lowe asks, a whine creeping into his voice. 'Lying here like this, it's a bit degrading, to be honest . . . not to mention what it'll do to my back.'

'I know what you did,' says Kavanagh, using both feet to scoot the chair a yard closer, causing Lowe to flinch. 'I'm not going to ask who it was you told. We both know it was Jimmy. What I *do* want to know is why?'

Lowe looks for a moment as if he's weighing the merits of denying the obvious but thinks better of it. He has no idea how much Kavanagh has found out or how, but it's obviously enough. Plan B then. Kavanagh watches him closely, following every twist and turn of his thought processes.

'What else was I supposed to do?' Lowe asks, putting his head in his hands until he realises what he's doing and frantically grabs the sheet again. 'Two of his Neanderthals were in my office no more than ten minutes after you left. He knew you'd been here so I had to tell him something. It's not like I went out of my way to tip him off.'

Which almost certainly means that's precisely what he did, otherwise why throw that in?

'So how did they know I was there?'

'I don't know, do I? Like they're going to tell me. My guess is they had a tail on you or something. First thing I knew about it, these two goons were in my office, acting like they owned the place. Said Jimmy wanted a word and you know what that means. Jimmy Hayes calls, you grab your coat and hat. You do *not* piss about. They took me straight to that basement room at The Grosvenor.'

Lowe shudders, recalling it now. He is piling it on with a shovel here, playing the sympathy card. Poor helpless victim, caught up in something way beyond his capabilities. Kavanagh isn't taken in. He's still weighing up the suggestion that he was tailed. Is that really what happened? He realises he's out of practice but it's not like he's forgotten everything he knew. He remembers taking the usual precautions at Waterloo, even though he thought it was overthinking things a bit after all this time. Was that where he went wrong? Has a touch of complacency set in?

His instincts tell him Lowe is lying, that he's the one who tipped Jimmy off in the first place, but it's not worth pursuing now. It's to be expected even. What else is he going to do in his present situation? A drowning man in a raging torrent is going to clutch at every overhanging branch on his way downstream.

'The dossier's a fake,' Kavanagh says, narrowing his focus.

Lowe doesn't bother to deny it. Just gives the slightest of shamefaced nods.

'You told them I was trying to find Jessica Murphy. Why?'

'I didn't want to,' he says, as if that fact alone should offer some form of expiation. 'What else was I going to say – you called in for a social visit? After nearly twenty years? Came all that way just to bring me some jelly babies? He's not stupid, Jon . . . and I'm not a brave man, in case you hadn't noticed.'

Kavanagh thinks about it. Shakes his head.

'No way,' he says. 'I'm not buying it. This is a print shop. I run a business. I could have been here for any number of reasons. You expect me to believe someone who's made a living out of wriggling and squirming the way you do couldn't come up with something better than that?'

'Jon, I swear to you—'

'Try again.'

Lowe shrugs his shoulders, his eyes beseeching Kavanagh to believe him.

'I don't know what to say. It's the truth. You want me to make up another reason?'

Kavanagh has been here so many times before. He always follows the same principle. If you're unsure, assume it's a lie . . . especially if the other person insists it's the truth. You'll be right more often than not. He pauses just long enough to encourage the tiny spark of hope that Lowe imagines he's ignited.

'Give me your right hand,' he says.

Lowe looks at him in alarm.

'Wh–what?'

'Keep your left where it is and it'll be just fine until you decide to lie to me again. Give me the right.'

Kavanagh extends his own right hand, reaching across the bed.

'Jon ... please,' says Lowe and he's starting to sweat now which is not something to encourage with someone his size in an enclosed space.

Kavanagh clicks his fingers at the cat, stretched out on the pillow and blithely ignoring everything that's happening around her.

'Here, kitty, kitty.'

Lowe gets the message and makes a tentative move to offer his right hand before snatching it back at the last minute.

'OK, OK,' he says, making sure to place both hands on top of the sheet where Kavanagh can see them. 'I'm sorry, OK. Really I am. Jesus Christ!'

Objective achieved, Kavanagh pulls his arm back and sinks both elbows onto the backrest again.

'You phoned him, right?'

He nods his head, resignation written all over his face.

'Why?'

'Because Jimmy has me over a barrel, that's why.'

'How?

'The bloody gee-gees, how else?' he snaps with a sudden burst of anger. 'The bloody horses. You know me, never could resist a punt. And don't give me that look – a guy's got to have something to do in his leisure time. You like running, I suppose. Working out in the gym? I like poring over form guides and visiting stables. It's harmless enough and I've come out ahead more weeks than not ... until a couple of years ago anyway.'

He sighs, making a mental trip back to a point where his life might have taken a much smoother course.

'It started getting away from me, all right? One wild bet too many, then doubling the stakes to try to cover the losses with one big win. Always worked before. I tell you, you wouldn't believe the run of bad luck I had.'

'You kept chasing the losses?' It's such a cliché, Kavanagh can hardly believe someone with Lowe's street smarts could possibly get sucked into such an obvious vortex. The definition of addiction – everything is under control until it's anything but.

'It's happened once or twice before – not quite so serious but bad enough – and I've been able to cover it from the business and build up a nice little cushion again. Ups and downs, you know? Shit happens. But the timing couldn't have been worse. I'd just bought Madame Chen's place next door – you remember she had this little fabric shop? – and that bastard Stelios had already made me pay way over the odds for that shitty little barber's place on the other side. I was forking out left, right and centre to finance the expansion and get the place refurbished so all my money was tied up.'

'And good old Jimmy was there to lend you enough to suck you in and make sure you never quite managed to pay off much more than the interest.' Kavanagh makes no effort to keep the reproach out of his voice.

Lowe hangs his head.

'Rub it in, why don't you? You think I don't wake up every morning and kick myself for being such a bloody idiot?'

'So how much are you into him for?'

'Ha,' says Lowe, rolling his eyes, 'now *there's* a question. Too much. If you want an exact figure, your guess is as good as mine.

I try to keep track of it but it's hopeless. I always thought I was pretty good with the financial side of the business but he's got these whizz kids working for him who are bloody unbelievable. They run rings round me. Let's just say he holds most of the paperwork on Excelsior Print Services and leave it at that. If he really wants to, he can probably pull the plug on me anytime he likes.'

Kavanagh thinks about it. He's genuinely surprised. Lowe isn't the first person to fall prey to the Syndicate and be swallowed up, but he'd have been well down the list of likely candidates. The dangers of complacency, he thinks to himself. Sometimes you can be too damn smart for your own good.

'He won't do that,' he says eventually.

'Do what? Pull the plug on me?'

'Not the way they operate. Why would he? Right now, you're exactly where he wants you. He's bleeding you dry and he's got you pretty much on call whenever he needs your services, right? He'll keep you dangling until the spreadsheet tells him you're more of a liability than an asset. You know how it works, for God's sake.'

It's a bleak assessment and one which Lowe has almost certainly managed to work out for himself. Kavanagh sees no reason to spare his feelings. This sad excuse for a human being has cost him time and money, quite apart from the emotional investment he has in his search for the girl. He'll have known about the first two and should surely have been able to pick up enough from their initial consultation to suspect the third. He'll be reimbursing him for all three, that's for sure.

Lowe is still fussing about his back, arching it every so often to demonstrate just how uncomfortable he is.

'So tell me,' says Kavanagh. 'What's the going rate for selling me out? Did you really think you'd get away with a stunt like that?'

It's not clear whether it's prompted by fear or the cold – a convincing case could be made for either – but Lowe is visibly shaking now. He uses the edge of the sheet to dab at the corner of his eye, careful to keep his hands out in the open.

'Rock and a hard place,' he says, his voice having developed a croak. 'You want the honest truth? When you wandered into my office after all those years, I was actually stupid enough to think it was the best thing that's happened to me in ages. Jimmy's had the word out for a while now. Anyone hears from you, or even just *about* you, they're to let him know. He's got a hard-on for you like you wouldn't believe! I thought it might be something I could turn to my advantage – you know, improve my situation with him. Maybe get some of the paperwork back. Then you told me why you were there and started swearing me to secrecy. Christ, you laid it on with a trowel, all that stuff about how it had to stay between just the two of us and I thought, *Shit, how do I get out of this mess?* I don't pass on something like that and it gets back to Jimmy somehow, I might as well dig my own grave, jump in and start pulling the dirt on top of me. And if I *do* tell him, and *you* find out about it . . . I mean, what was I supposed to do?'

Kavanagh can see the dilemma. But it's not his problem. And Lowe needs to know he came up with the wrong solution.

'So what made you choose him over me? I couldn't have been any clearer.'

The tears are now making his eyes sparkle, although paradoxically he appears, apart from the occasional sniff, to be more in control of his voice than at any stage since he woke.

'All things being equal? I'd have gone with you – you must know that. Jimmy's a hard guy to like, right? I don't know anyone who's managed to get really close to him. He's always going on about this Chinese girl he lives with, like they're this devoted couple, but you hear things, yeah? She'd be out of there like a shot if she had any say in it. He's a bloody psychopath, whereas you ... I never got to talk to you often but I always thought we got along OK.'

'You said all things being equal,' says Kavanagh. 'So what tipped the scales?'

Lowe swallows. Picks his words carefully.

'Like I said, I knew if I didn't tell him you'd been here, he'd find out somehow. And the moment that happened, I'd be a dead man.'

'You seriously think he'd kill you for that?'

Lowe forces a rueful smile.

'You think he wouldn't? You've been away too long. A lot can change in twenty years. It's not like it was in Maurice's day, that's for sure. In Jimmy's mind, if you're not with him, you're against him and can expect to suffer the consequences. Paranoid doesn't begin to cover it.'

Kavanagh sits upright. Stretches his own back. Makes sure the whole of his scar is clearly visible from where Lowe is sitting.

'And how safe do you feel right now with the choice you made?'

'Right this moment?' Lowe takes a deep breath in an attempt to control his breathing. 'Not so good. But give me a choice between having you or Jimmy sitting where you are right now, I'd go for you every time. Jimmy would kill me and not even blink. It's in his DNA. But you—'

He swallows.

'You might if you're provoked . . . but I've never really felt your heart was in it. I mean, you walked away, right? Bought a bookshop, for Christ's sake. Can you see Jimmy doing something like that? Seems to me, you left this life because you knew it wasn't you. Never was. I mean, don't get me wrong. I'm sweating buckets here because I know your reputation, but reputations get exaggerated, right? You keep yourself to yourself and people speculate to fill in the gaps. But personally I've never seen that side of you. And despite what I've done . . . I just don't see it. I hope—'

'Hope what?'

'I hope to God I'm right for once.'

Lowe is a gambler. The worst sort. He doesn't set limits and respect them. Chases his losses and plunges deeper and deeper into a mire of his own making. He may well be taking the most important gamble of his life right now with little more than instinct to go on. It's either a brave or reckless move on his part. Probably both.

It may also have turned his fortunes.

Kavanagh has been surprised by how easily he's slipped back into the role that used to be his. The enforcer. The hard man. The loner whose mere presence at dead of night was the stuff of nightmares. He hasn't been that person for twenty years and that knowledge has infused him with an inner calm and a sense of his own worth that he never wants to lose but also a deep sense of regret for the person he once was.

Or was he? He knows he's acting now but this is the first time anyone has ever suggested that it was no more than an act all along. The Kavanagh who killed four men, at least one of them with no justification at all; who used intimidation rather than moral authority to settle disputes; who put the fear of God into so many people, just as he's doing right now – was that Kavanagh merely being true to his DNA as he's always believed? Or was he just slipping into the persona he needed to adopt if he was to survive in a world whose values ran contrary to his true nature?

He knows which he'd rather believe, but it's going to have to wait for now. There's a lot more he needs from Lowe.

'Have you got a dressing gown?' he asks.

Lowe blinks in surprise.

'On the back of the door.'

Kavanagh gets up and removes it from the hook. He throws it to Lowe.

'Get up,' he says. 'We're going downstairs.'

'So what can you tell me about Anna Hill?' asks Kavanagh.

Lowe, in dressing gown and slippers, is draped across the settee, looking considerably less stressed than earlier. He'll be wondering whether they've passed the critical point and daring to hope he might come out of this relatively unscathed, although Kavanagh doubts he'll be breathing normally until long after he's left. Twenty years ago he wouldn't have been breathing at all.

Lowe has even offered to make tea or coffee to reinforce the impression that everything is fine here – just two old friends, shooting the breeze and playing catch-up. Kavanagh has been quick to nip that one in the bud, doesn't want him to get too comfortable. Lowe may have dragged himself out of the swamp but he's still got the woods to negotiate.

'Not a lot,' Lowe admits ruefully. 'Nothing to add to what's already in the dossier I gave you.'

Kavanagh raises an eyebrow – just the one.

'You mean the dossier that says she was Jessica Murphy for four years before being adopted?'

'I've already apologised several times,' says Lowe, huffing indignantly. 'I don't know what else you want me to say. I can be as brave as the next man in the abstract but if Jimmy's standing in front of you, telling you to do something, then that's what you do. It was nothing personal, Jon.'

Nothing personal. Kavanagh bites down on the momentary burst of anger.

'So take me through it step by step. When did he ask you to create a fake version?'

Lowe links his hands behind his head and looks at the ceiling, keen to demonstrate that he's doing his best to be accurate here.

'Must have been ... maybe three days after you were here? Another of his heavies turns up – just the one this time – and I get carted off again, only this time it's to Jimmy's place rather than The Grosvenor. I can't have been in there more than five minutes. He says to forget about Jessica Murphy for now. Instead I'm to do a similar job on this girl called Anna Hill. He gives me a date of birth and a sprinkling of other details to make sure I get the right person. Pretty much like you did, only I have to say – he was able to give me a lot more information up front. Made it a helluva lot easier, I can tell you.'

No surprise there, thinks Kavanagh. Jimmy will have got most of the basic details from Ches Headley.

'Says he wants me to find out as much as I can about her, flesh it out a bit,' Lowe continues. 'The full monty. Says I've got forty-eight hours, so I run all the checks, work my arse off, stay up half the night to put the profile together and get it back to him a day early. And I'm hoping that's it – maybe I've put a few ticks in the credit column, you know? Only the moment he's read through it, he hands me a list of things he wants me to change.'

'Like the first four years.'

'Like the first four years. All of a sudden, instead of being born on whatever date it was, she's born a couple of months later. And instead of having some couple in Kettering as parents, she's come into the world as Jessica Murphy, and surprise, surprise – those first few years just happen to match up exactly to what you already knew about the real one. Father dead. Mother a junkie in New Zealand. Only, in Jimmy's version, the girl gets adopted by this family just after her fourth birthday. He says when I've made these changes, I'm to run the whole thing past him before I send it back to you.'

He sits there with his mouth open, inviting Kavanagh to share in his bemusement.

'And I'm like . . . are you serious? You think Jon Kavanagh's going to buy this for one moment? There are any number of ways he can find out this is a crock of shit and where does that leave me? Not that I said anything, of course. There are certain things Jimmy Hayes doesn't want to hear and *you are fucking kidding me* is right up there. But I've been bricking it ever since I sent you the dossier. I just knew you'd see through it.'

'Yes,' says Kavanagh, mentally giving himself a good kicking. 'Well, unfortunately I didn't.'

'Didn't what?'

'See through it. I bought it all, the whole shebang. Didn't think to question it for one second.'

'Are you serious?'

He knows he's being hard on himself. He *did* pick up on the anomaly of the adoption and its timing in particular, coming so soon after Emily's birth. But instead of questioning the authenticity of the document, he was far too eager to attribute it to the collective failings of the parents and the adoption agencies. There's no escaping the fact that finding Jessica Murphy has become too important to him. She's got under his skin and distracted him in a way he would never have allowed to happen back in the day.

'I made the mistake of reading what I wanted to read. I screwed up.'

Lowe is staring at him in disbelief.

'Christ, Jon . . .'

They sit in silence for a second or two. Kavanagh is deep in thought, doesn't need Lowe to spell it out. He's painfully aware that he's slipping. Vulnerable. He's been manipulated and doesn't like it. Even so, he's a step ahead of Jimmy in one respect at least. He's fully aware he's been played. Jimmy has no way of knowing that and it's an edge that might yet come in handy . . . if he can find a way of using it.

'But that doesn't make sense,' says Lowe. 'If you believed what was in the dossier, how did you find out it was fake?'

Because the plan was a long way short of foolproof, he thinks. *Because it asked far too much of an inexperienced girl who wasn't up to it, who got careless . . . more than once.*

Slip one: letting him know her agent's name was Ches. She obviously realised as soon as the name left her lips that it was a bit too close to home. Having made that mistake, she should have cut her losses and stuck with it. Could have been a coincidence.

He's deeply suspicious about such things as a rule, but there wouldn't be a word for them if they didn't happen. Instead her first instinct was to say it wasn't Ches Headley. So now we have *two* music agents named Ches working the same clubs and bars in London? Hmm. And the supposed guilt trip that prompted the tearful confession in the taxi? Touching . . . but amateurish. If you're going to lie, stick to your guns and brazen it out.

Slip two: the business with the Kindle and her comment about profit margins. All very innocent on the surface, the kind of throwaway comment people make all the time. But he was pretty sure he hadn't told her anything about the bookshop at that stage. As far as she knew, he was recently retired from what he'd euphemistically described as *security work in London*. So why would she think Kindles would hit him in the pocket? Again, taken in isolation, it's not much, especially as he can't be one hundred per cent certain about what he told her. Maybe he *did* mention the bookshop at some point. But he doesn't think so and her instinctive reaction, the way her eyes had widened, and then the coughing fit which she used to disguise a quick change of subject . . . even if only on a subconscious level, it was artificial enough to unsettle him.

As for the clandestine meeting with Stalker – who should probably be referred to as Middleman now – her surreptitious behaviour alone should have been enough to give him the wake-up slap he needed. He wanted so badly to believe he was worrying about nothing, that it was merely long-dormant instincts struggling to reassert themselves, but he was starting to run out of excuses for her. And if there were any lingering doubts, they were removed the following morning when he let himself into her apartment while she was rehearsing at *Cristi's*.

Singing "Summertime", no doubt. Because under her pillow he found a photo of a dancer – clearly a recent one. She and Anna were so similar – same eyes, same athletic figure, everything screaming same genes – although Kavanagh was prepared to bet this girl was Anna's junior by three years. On the reverse side was a handwritten message: *a reminder, in case you need it.*

'What do you know about the sister?' he asks, ignoring Lowe's question.

'Same answer as before. Everything I know is in the dossier. Name's Emily. Twenty, if I remember rightly. She's done two years at some dance academy in the Midlands – forget where exactly but it'll be in there. Otherwise not a lot.'

'You think this academy will have broken up for the summer yet?'

'No idea. No one asked me to go into that sort of detail about *her*. Just Anna.'

'So you don't know where she'd be right this moment?'

'Not a scooby. Why?'

'No reason. Just thinking aloud.'

The questions keep coming. He just wishes answers would keep pace with them.

'Why Portugal?' he asks.

Lowe frowns.

'Not with you.'

'In the dossier you put that she'd signed a contract to work in Praia D'El Rey for the summer. That's how I knew where to find her. Where did you dig that up?'

'I didn't,' says Lowe. 'It was one of the extras Jimmy told me to include.'

'*Jimmy* asked you to put it in?'

'Yes.'

Kavanagh backtracks furiously, his mind racing now. Something's not right. He can sense it but it keeps squirming out of his grasp. He zeroes in on something Lowe mentioned just a few moments ago. Takes out his phone and turns to the calendar app.

'And that was four days or so after I came to see you, right?' he asks, scrolling back through the days. 'You said the meeting at his place was three days after I came to your office and you had the dossier ready by the following day. And that's when he gave you these changes he wanted you to make.'

'That's right. I mean, it might have been a day or two more. I can't be totally sure.'

'But no longer than a week, right?'

Lowe is becoming more wary with his answers by the second, trying to follow Kavanagh's line of reasoning.

'No . . . I wouldn't have thought so,' he says hesitantly.

'And how long did it take you to make those amendments? A day or two?'

Lowe bursts out laughing.

'You kidding? An hour or so tops. I was making a few changes to a Word document not writing a bestseller. I emailed the updated version back to him the same day.'

Kavanagh does the maths.

'So why the delay in sending it to me? I came to London to ask you to find her on . . . 22nd April,' he says, consulting the app. 'So that makes it somewhere around April 26th he had the final draft, right? And you rang me to say it was ready on 12th May. That's over a fortnight later.'

'I know,' says Lowe, looking relieved to be on safer ground, now that he knows what it is that's been troubling Kavanagh. 'But Jimmy told me not to ring you till he gave me the go-ahead.'

'Did he say why?'

Lowe just laughs – *get real. As if.*

'But he only gave you forty-eight hours to get it done initially, so why do that and then hang on to it for more than two weeks? What was he doing in the meantime?'

Kavanagh keeps working it.

'Unless . . . unless Jimmy's the reason Anna Hill has the job in Portugal?' he suggests, trying it out for size. 'I've been assuming she already had the contract for the summer when he picked her out, but if the whole Praia D'El Rey thing was Jimmy's doing in the first place, he'd need a week or two to set it up, wouldn't he?'

'What makes you so sure it was his idea?'

'Have you met Ches Headley? Think useless and go down a couple of notches. Anna told me herself she couldn't believe he managed to conjure up such an opportunity for her. I'll bet he's never come close to landing a deal like that in all his years in the business. No . . . it was Jimmy. He wants Anna in Praia D'El Rey for some reason. Presumably me too, since the whole point is for me to follow her. And he wanted to make sure it was all set up before he allowed you to send the dossier to me, which is why I had to wait so long.'

Lowe seems intrigued by this. His interest doesn't come across as artificial or contrived in any way. He's nodding along to every point Kavanagh makes, as if fully invested in this search for some sort of rational explanation behind Jimmy's behaviour.

'Which brings us back to my original question,' says Kavanagh. 'Why Portugal? I mean, he's got the girl out there for three months along with at least one middleman. There could be others I haven't flushed out yet. Probably some contact at this Cristi's place. This must be costing him a fortune and he's not even out there. He's sitting here in London, totally dependent on others for information. If he wants to keep a close eye on me, why not just leave her here in London where it would cost a fraction of what he must be spending?'

So many unanswered questions, breeding like rabbits. As soon as he turns to deal with one, another pops its head out of the ground. And another. They both think it through for a few seconds. It occurs to Kavanagh that Lowe will be loving this. *Teamwork.* His chances are improving by the second.

He realises all of a sudden just how tired he is. Maybe it's the constant reminders of how sloppy he's been that is wearing him down. On the other hand, he's been awake nearly twenty-four hours and he's not as young as he used to be. Lowe, on the other hand, looks more energised now than at any stage since he was dragged from his bed. The phrase that springs to mind is *he would, wouldn't he?* Even so, bouncing ideas off him is proving more than useful. Kavanagh can't do this on his own and, if nothing else, Lowe knows enough about the murky world of the Syndicate to make worthwhile contributions and keep him pointed in the right direction.

If . . . if he can be trusted to learn from his mistakes.

Maybe now's the time for coffee, he thinks, and sends him to the kitchen.

It's 05.30 when he finally leaves by the back door. It's no more than a precaution – he doesn't think there's any way he can have been followed here. He waited yesterday evening until he was in

Baggage Reclaim at Heathrow before he sent the text to Anna, explaining that he'd been called back to the UK on urgent business. She was probably performing at Cristi's at the time, wondering why he wasn't in the audience for "Summertime". By the time she'd read it and had the chance to notify Middleman, Kavanagh was already somewhere in Central London – on the loose, whereabouts and intentions unknown.

He wanted to make sure Lowe was dragged from a deep sleep and at his most vulnerable when confronting him, so he spent yesterday evening keeping as low a profile as possible. Watched a movie in a nearly deserted cinema. Ate a takeaway on a bench in a small square behind Regent Street. Took an Uber to Richmond just before midnight and walked past Lowe's house several times, waiting for the lights to go out. Then waited some more on a bench at the edge of Richmond Green until it was reasonable to assume Lowe was asleep. In all that time, even at his most negligent, he'd have been bound to notice if he was being followed, so no . . . he doesn't think there's any way they've tracked him down yet.

That will happen later this morning. Assuming they've been tipped off about his unexpected flight back to London, they'll put someone on his cottage in Wareham and shadow his every move once he turns up there. He hopes they do. He'll take them on the mother of all mystery tours, taking in a couple of solicitors, a local newspaper, Zelda's Bookshop, his bank in Wareham and, if he has time, maybe even throw in a visit to his ophthalmologist in Bournemouth, just to muddy the waters still further. He has appointments for none of these but that doesn't matter one bit as long as it's assumed he has a genuine reason for going there. Then, if everything goes according to plan, he'll take the hire car back to Heathrow in time to catch his return flight to Lisbon at 18.45 this evening. His itinerary ought to ensure Jimmy is intrigued as to what on earth he's up to. As long as it keeps his thoughts from straying anywhere near Adrian Lowe, it will be worth it.

In a taxi heading back to Waterloo, he replays his final conversation with Lowe, hoping he's done the right thing.

'You look to me like you need a break,' he said to him immediately before leaving.

'Tell me about it.'

'No,' he said, resting his hands on Lowe's shoulders . . . just heavily enough to make him feel uncomfortable. 'You're not listening. I'm telling you a holiday would be very much in your best interests.'

Lowe forced a grin and tried to pull away but Kavanagh was having none of it.

'You must have some place on your bucket list,' he persisted, giving Lowe's cheek a pat that was firm enough to make sure he had his attention. 'Take a few weeks out to drive across America. Try one of the Greek islands. What's the point of being the boss if you can't indulge yourself when the mood takes you?'

'Jon . . . I can't just drop everything and go swanning off on holiday. I've got a list as long as my arm—'

Kavanagh took a step forward, closing down the space, his face now inches from Lowe's.

'You seem to be missing the point. It's not a suggestion or request. If things go the way I think they will in the next week or so, all hell is about to break loose in the life of Jimmy Hayes and when that happens, you really don't want to be anywhere he can find you. More to the point, I can't afford for you to be here.'

Lowe tried to back off but found himself pressed up against a bookcase, with nowhere to go.

'Jesus,' he groaned, his expression a picture of wounded disbelief. 'You've got serious trust issues, you know that? I've just spent half the night talking it all through with you, helping you sort out this mess. You still don't think you can rely on me?'

'I did that once, if you remember,' said Kavanagh, jabbing Lowe in the chest to reinforce the message. 'This *mess*, as you call it, is all down to you. You told me yourself you're not a brave man – that if Jimmy's standing in front of you, telling you to do something, then that's what you do. *Nothing personal*, I think you said. If you'd crossed me like that twenty years ago, we wouldn't even be having this discussion.

'So the deal is this – the moment I leave, you're going to book a holiday online and you're going to be on the first flight out of here that you can get. Today if possible. Tomorrow at the latest. You tell no one where you're going, not even me. You don't ring anyone while you're away – you just leave a message at work before you go, telling them they're on their own for a fortnight. You've been ordered to take a complete break for health reasons. If the next couple of weeks go as I'm hoping, your situation is about to improve dramatically. If they don't, and I have any reason to suspect it's because of you, I'm going to tell Jimmy that I was here tonight and that you're the one who tipped me off about the fake dossier. You think *I've* got trust issues? Wait till Jimmy gets going.'

He stepped back and picked up the holdall he'd brought with him.

'My guess is the holiday's just started to look like the better option.'

It's a gamble, he tells himself now, as the taxi draws up outside the station. But it's not as if he's spoilt for choice when it comes to options. He's decided he's going to take down Jimmy. It's the only way. He's not going to be able to put up with this level of harassment and paranoia indefinitely. He's done everything he can think of to broker some sort of understanding between the two of them but clearly it's not going to work.

He has a plan and at present it has too many variables. There are four people he needs to talk to and what they have to say will almost certainly mean adjustments will be needed, but he'll just have to improvise. He's going to be doing this on a wing and a prayer.

He's also going to be doing it with one hand tied behind his back, because there's one thing on which he's not prepared to compromise. On the flight over here, he decided he's taken his last life. Whatever the outcome of this head-banging contest with Jimmy, his days as a killer are over. He's dealt with Lowe and will do the same with Anna and the Middleman. When the time comes, he'll deal with Jimmy too.

But he'll do it in a way he can live with.

If there's such a thing as redemption, he'll find it.

21

Later that evening
Heathrow to Lisbon

He's well into the return flight when it hits him.

Literally.

Having gone thirty-six hours without any sleep, he straps himself into his seat, puts his head back and goes out like a light. The pre-flight safety demonstration and take-off aren't even background noise – they don't register at all and for the next hour and a half he's completely out of it.

Until something fairly hefty strikes the top of his head and shoulder on its way to the floor.

He has no idea what's happening at first . . . or even where he is. His instincts, prompted by a gasp from someone nearby, are hinting at the possibility of some unspecified threat but it's no more than a reflex. Sleep-drugged he may be but he has enough about him to realise that danger doesn't come with profuse apologies, and the concern in the voice as a hand is placed on his shoulder is obviously genuine.

'I'm so sorry,' says a woman hovering over him. 'I was just trying to get at something in the overhead locker and this other case just . . . are you OK?'

She winces and he assumes it's because she's just noticed the scar.

'I'm fine,' he tells her.

'Are you sure? I didn't realise until too late and tried to grab it but it was too heavy. That must really hurt. Do you want me to fetch one of the cabin crew?'

He says that won't be necessary and thinks he's managed to reassure her until the passenger in the next seat helpfully points out that there's blood trickling down the side of his face. He dabs at it with a finger – comes up red.

'Dear God,' says the woman, inspecting the case that fell from the locker. 'Do you think that buckle caused it?' He's alert enough now to take in just how difficult it is for her to lift it. No wonder his head is sore.

Now the people sitting opposite are taking an interest. He explains it's nothing – scalp wounds always bleed profusely and look much worse than they are – but someone sends for a steward anyway. Much as he hates being the centre of attention, he has no choice but to sit still while they patch him up and fetch him a glass of water with a couple of paracetamol. The woman who set all this in motion is still in full self-flagellation mode and the crew are fretting about possible concussion. It's a good ten minutes before he finally manages to convince everyone that he's perfectly OK.

In actual fact, he's anything but. He's quite happy to take the paracetamol because he does indeed have a headache. He closes his eyes, hoping he'll be able to drift straight back off, but the moment he does so everything starts swaying back and forth behind his eyelids. He opens them again, picks out a spot on the back of the seat in front of his and focuses on it, hoping it might help to stabilise things a little. His eyes are too tired though and as soon as they begin to droop, the swimming sensation starts up again, bringing with it the first hint of nausea. He's also aware of pressure building inside his head, somewhere behind his eyes – or at least that's how it feels. It's not something he ever remembers experiencing before. He presses his fingers into both temples, rotating them slowly as if this circular motion might persuade whatever is causing the discomfort to break into tiny pieces and drift away.

Not daring to move his head, he reaches forward and gropes for a paper bag which he eventually manages to extricate from the webbed compartment in front of him, a gesture that doesn't escape the attention of the man next to him.

'Do you feel sick?' he asks tentatively.

Kavanagh waves away his concern.

'Just a precaution. Think I'll just . . .'

He gets to his feet, determined to make it as far as the toilet. Now that he's in full view, everyone is staring at him again. If he can just get away from all this fuss and attention he'll be in a better position to focus on exactly what is wrong with him. He needs a bit of privacy.

But even as he steps out into the aisle, he knows it's a mistake. The toilets might as well be several miles away.

And sleep comes at last as he hits one of the armrests on his way to the floor.

When he finally comes to, a Portuguese doctor, who happened to be among the passengers, is in the seat next to him. He speaks very little English so everything he says is filtered through the chief flight attendant. Her English is very good but she has difficulties with some of the more specialised vocabulary so Kavanagh is not altogether convinced he's getting the full picture. Certainly there are some exchanges in Portuguese which go on for much longer than the brief summary he receives in English.

From what he can gather, he was unconscious for a minute or two. The moment he came to, he was helped into a seat near the rear of the plane where he would be afforded a little more privacy. The doctor is adamant he has severe concussion and should be checked out the moment they land. He seems to regard this as non-negotiable. *Is danger,* he says repeatedly.

Kavanagh is no stranger to concussion. Until that fateful afternoon in Dunloughraine, he used to box for his battalion and took his fair share of blows to the head, so he is as aware as anyone of the need to take it seriously. But if there's one thing he is *not* going to do when the plane lands, it's spend several hours in a waiting room, only to be told he needs to be admitted for the night as a precaution. He doesn't have time to waste, neither does he want to run the risk of a scan complicating things still further by picking up on his little legacy from Dunloughraine. That could lead to even more questions, not to mention tests and scans that would delay his return to Praia D'El Rey so he is sticking to his guns . . . firmly but politely.

He insists he's fine, even though he suspects he may not be. Tells them he's a nervous flier at the best of times and that his usual state of anxiety has been exacerbated by lack of sleep and the shock of being dragged from it. If they'll just leave him alone and allow him to catch up for the remainder of the flight, he'll be right as rain by the time they land. Eventually the message gets through and he's allowed to sleep, but that doesn't mean the doctor is waving the white flag just yet.

When they finally land in Lisbon, he's woken by the flight attendant and asked to stay where he is. They've radioed ahead and a wheelchair is available to take him through customs to a medical unit where his condition can be more rigorously assessed. Kavanagh thanks them for their concern, gets to his feet and walks off the plane with everyone else instead.

The wait in Passport Control is interminable, the queues shuffling forward so slowly Kavanagh almost wishes he'd accepted the chance to be wheeled through before turning down their offer. It's hot and stuffy in here – if there's any air conditioning at all, it's making minimal impact. They need more gates open. *He* needs more gates open. If the paracetamol had any effect, it hasn't lasted long enough. He'll need to buy some more as soon as he's through the gate and out of this hellhole. It hasn't been four hours since he took the last tablets but he'll take his chances.

When he finally makes it through, he has a decision to make. To describe Praia D'El Rey as out of the way is a massive understatement and while he was still trapped in the queue he was all for finding the nearest hotel and booking a room for the night. But now that he's through and out in the open air again, he's having second thoughts. If he spends the night in Lisbon, the journey doesn't go away. It's just deferred until tomorrow morning and unless he leaves early he'll have lost the better part of the day by the time he's back at the villa. He decides instead to head back now and take a taxi the whole way. It's not going to be cheap but neither is a hotel room – at least he'll be able to sleep in the car.

He heads for the taxi rank in search of a driver who understands English. Unfortunately they all do and they're not slow in letting him know what they think of the prospect of travelling that far at ten o'clock at night. It's not until his fifth or sixth attempt that he finds someone prepared to take him. He suspects the quote he's eventually given includes a significant surcharge to make it worth the driver's while but by now he doesn't care. He's reached the stage where they can almost name their price and the relief that comes over him as he sinks into the rear seat and closes the door is almost indescribable. He tells the driver he'd rather do without the radio and asks him to wake him when they reach the outskirts of Praia D'El Rey and not before. Then he folds his jacket and uses it as a pillow against the window, presses his head against it and closes his eyes. This time there's no dizziness and he's asleep within minutes, haunted by strange dreams in which an army of nanoscopic metal fragments inch their way oh so slowly but inexorably across the landscape of his mind.

Mustering their forces for one final push.

It's anything but restful.

22

2nd July 2018
Praia D'El Rey

When he finally wakes, just after ten the following morning, his initial thought is there must be some mistake – he can't remember the last time this happened. He's sure he set the alarm for seven, thinking even that was a little self-indulgent. Then a vague memory surfaces . . . the alarm chirping merrily away until he groped for the phone and silenced it; lying there thinking *maybe just a few minutes longer*, as if that would make any real difference. He must have gone back off immediately and slept on for another three hours, which means he's already way behind schedule.

He throws back the sheet and stays still for a moment, making sure everything is OK.

Nausea – gone. He hasn't exactly got a raging appetite but at least he no longer feels as if he might throw up at any moment.

Headache – now no more than a pale imitation of last night's, which really was a work of art. Now all that's left is the same vague drowsiness which characterised those first few days after his operation in Musgrave Park. He feels sleep-drugged.

Vision – maybe a little on the blurry side but that's nothing unusual first thing in the morning. What matters more than anything else is that there's no suggestion of the room swimming before his eyes. That sensation though is still fresh in his memory, as if merely parked around the corner. If he doesn't want another surprise visit, he might need to accept that being fit doesn't make him invulnerable. He's pushed himself far too hard over the past couple of days and his limits are finding increasingly unsettling ways to make themselves known.

At least he was right about the concussion. The doctor's diagnosis was wide of the mark and the collective hysteria governing the response from the crew owed as much to damage limitation as anything else. If it was something other than sheer exhaustion that caused him to collapse the way he did, it seems to be taking a breather for the time being at least.

He feels human again and ready to face the day. It's the first time he's missed his early morning run since he arrived here but he doesn't feel inclined to make up for it now . . . and not just because of time constraints. The past thirty-six hours have been stressful and a run in humid conditions would be asking for trouble. Instead he'll make do with a swim in the sea. If the restorative powers of the Atlantic don't take care of any lingering after-effects from the flight, nothing will.

He makes himself breakfast and picks up his phone from the breakfast bar. As he turns on his notifications, two messages appear almost instantly, both from Anna. The first, which he must have slept through in the taxi, is just a quick check to determine whether he was back yet. She hopes that the urgent business that prompted his sudden decision to return to the UK has been successfully resolved.

The second was sent this morning, just a few minutes before he woke.

Noticed your curtains are closed so assume you're back.
Everything OK?

He hovers over the last two words. Genuine concern? Or has she been told to get in quickly and find out what he's been up to?

He taps out a quick reply.

Just walking down to the beach. Fancy a swim?

He finishes his slice of toast, drains the glass of juice and grabs a towel on his way out of the door.

Yesterday was phase one.

Time for phase two.

The cloudless skies and soaring temperatures have brought more people than usual to the beach this morning. Further south, the resorts on the Algarve will be heaving and space will be at a premium. Here on the west coast, things are less pressurised and Praia D'El Rey, being off the beaten track, is never exactly under siege. Even so, it looks to Kavanagh as if some of the golfers may have found the appeal of the beach too compelling to resist this morning.

He spreads his towel on a stretch of sand, away from most of the others. Then, stripping off his T-shirt, he wraps his phone inside it and weights it down with his beach shoes before setting off towards the water's edge.

The absence of any red flags is a welcome bonus. The lifeguards don't usually need much of an excuse to herd everyone inside the clearly defined safety zones and the sea is distinctly lively. The waves are constantly whipped up by the breeze and break with a force that frequently catches people unawares. As for the currents, they're deceptive enough – Kavanagh considers himself to be a strong swimmer but he's found himself being dragged further out than intended before now. He loves the physical challenge though, the raw elemental nature of the battle, and is keen to get in there before the lifeguards change their minds.

A few people are already in the water but not many have ventured any further than the shallows. The prospect of a refreshing dip in the sea may look very inviting to anyone roasting on a towel or sunbed, but those first few steps as the tide washes around the ankles are a pretty powerful disincentive. This is the Atlantic, not the Mediterranean. Having come this far, some choose to inch their way in, daring themselves to keep going until the water reaches their knees, maybe even their waist, at which point a decision has to be made. Either they dive into one of the crashing breakers or turn tail and run back to the shallows, which by this stage feel positively balmy in comparison.

Kavanagh knows only one way. He starts running before he even reaches the water, not least because the sand is threatening to burn the soles of his feet. When he reaches the shallows he doesn't stop to allow room for any doubts to creep in – he just keeps going until the first wave is suddenly there, rearing up in front of him. Then he dives into it and keeps swimming until he's well clear of the break zone.

He's panting heavily as he surfaces, stunned by the cold, even though he knew what to expect. Within seconds he can feel it getting to work on every extremity, numbing him by degrees if he stays still and treads water for too long. He eases into a steady crawl to keep his circulation moving, staying parallel to the shore and keeping an eye on any new arrivals.

He's been in the water no more than three or four minutes when he sees her. He's been picking out shapes away to his left where her apartment is situated, following them as best he can until they're near enough for him to rule them out. Instead she must have come down the cliff steps from behind the Marriott because he sees someone in what he – with his limited knowledge of women's fashion – wants to call a sarong but which is probably nothing of the sort. She's removed a large sunhat and is waving to him and in all honesty that's his only reason for supposing it's her. She can't be more than – what? – fifty yards away from him? He rubs his eyes to try to focus but the improvement is marginal at best.

The figure waves again before removing the outer garment which she folds and stores in her bag. Then she heads for the water, wearing a white bikini which shows off her tan. He watches with interest and some amusement, waiting for the gasp as she enters the water but there's nothing. She marches on, undeterred, stooping every few paces to scoop water into both hands and throw it over her unprotected skin. Then, as she reaches the first line of breakers, she dives into it exactly as he did earlier and stays under for a good five or six seconds before surfacing a few feet away from him.

'Hello again,' she gasps, sweeping several strands of hair from her face. 'How long have you been here?'

He assumes she means at the beach until she puts him right. He confirms that he arrived late last night but says nothing about the problems he encountered during the flight. He's surprised to realise that a small part of him would like to. He wonders what it must be like to speak freely, not feel you have to weigh every sentence in advance and dole out words like marked currency. But what is a lifelong recluse supposed to do for a sounding board?

Despite what he now knows, he can't help but feel drawn to Anna – not in any sleazy way but on a purely platonic and human level. He's lived most of his sixty-three years in self-imposed isolation, seen the distaste bordering on revulsion in the way others gawp at him and batted it away. *You think I need you?* It's only lately that he's found himself wondering whether letting someone else in, even just a friend, might not have its consolations. Would having for a while and losing be any worse than never having at all? Anna is a good and willing listener, albeit with questionable motives. It's ironic that right now she's probably the last person he can afford to open up to.

He's so lost in thought that he doesn't realise immediately that she's stopped talking. She's looking intently at him and, judging by the quiet smile, she's expecting an answer to a question he hasn't even heard. He apologises, tells her he was miles away.

'Trip go OK?'

'Yes.'

'That's good. You missed my version of "Summertime" the other night. I didn't see your message till after the set.'

'I'm sorry.'

'No worries. It went down well so I'll be using it again tonight.'

An elderly woman swims past them, slow deliberate strokes. Kavanagh wonders whether he ought to say something about the drift this far out but she looks as if she knows what she's doing. The depth of her tan suggests she's either local or has at least spent a lot of time out here.

'I wasn't sure when you'd be back,' Anna continues. 'I walked past your place last night around . . . I don't know, seven? Half seven? Then I saw the curtains were closed this morning so I knew you were back. Late flight?'

He nods.

'It was.'

She tilts her head to one side.

'You OK?' she asks. 'You seem a bit . . . I don't know. Distant, I suppose.'

'I'm fine. Tired.'

'Not surprised. Two flights – out one day, back the next. Bound to take a lot out of you.'

'Yes.'

Anna waits for him to elaborate, then sighs.

'I'm sorry, I'm talking too much again, I know. It's just . . . no offence but is there any way you could help me out a bit here? I don't think I've ever met anyone as uncomfortable as you are in conversation. You can be such hard work at times.'

By way of response, Kavanagh stretches his arms above his head and allows himself to slip below the surface of the water. It's deeper than he realised and it takes him a few seconds to touch the sea bed with his toes and push himself back up again. When he resurfaces, she's still there, waiting for an answer. She's not going to let this go.

'We spent the whole day together in Obidos,' she says, 'and I realised when I got back to the apartment that I still know next to nothing about you. I mean, are you like this with everyone, or just me? If you don't want company then just say so.'

The smile again. Despite everything, he'd swear it's genuine. He knows she's lied to him. Knows she's part of this crackpot scheme Jimmy has put together. But he's yet to determine the extent of her culpability and when she looks at him and smiles, he'd swear there's an innate sympathy there, an acceptance he's rarely found in anyone else. Miserable sod that he is, she actually seems at ease in his company ... as if all of a sudden he's more than just a scar on legs.

'Gone again,' she teases, cupping one hand and slapping the surface, sending a jet of water into his eyes. 'I swear I've never known anyone disappear in mid-conversation the way you do. What were you thinking just now? Go on, tell me. Let go just for once.'

Why not? he asks himself. It's not as if he can postpone this conversation indefinitely.

'You really want to know?'

She rolls her eyes in exasperation that is only partly feigned. 'Yes ... I want to know.'

'I was wondering,' he says, feeling his way into the sentence, '... just how much I can afford to trust you.'

She opts for an amused double-take.

'Excuse me?'

'I probably shouldn't. It's just ... I can't believe you'd be doing this if you felt you had any choice.'

The confusion is still there in her expression but now there's a touch of calculation added to the mix.

'Doing what?'

'I think you know. And you're right – there *are* things we need to talk about, but I don't think jet lag and song selection feature very high on the list.'

She doesn't say anything in reply but gives a tentative nod as if adjusting to the implications of what he's saying. Any trace of playfulness has quickly ebbed away.

'You're going to have to be a bit less cryptic than that.'

'OK,' says Kavanagh. 'Cards on the table. You want to know what I'm thinking? I'll tell you. I know why you're here. I know I'm being played. And I know who's behind it.'

He pauses briefly after each statement to allow the implications to sink in. She blinks rapidly but says nothing, so he presses ahead.

'I know the attack on you the other night was nothing of the sort. It was staged to suck me in. I should have realised right away but I don't seem to be as switched on as I used to be. The whole thing seems a bit over the top, even by Jimmy's standards, but I'm guessing he was worried I'd be suspicious if someone your age took a sudden interest in spending her free time with someone old enough to be her grandfather, so he came up with a situation that would make your interest in my company that little bit more plausible.'

He waits again in case there's anything she'd like to say to refute the accusations but she's not offering anything in the way of protest. *So who's not opening up now then, eh?*

'I don't know what they've told you about me or why I'm here,' he continues. 'I've even less idea how you managed to get yourself mixed up with someone like Jimmy in the first place, so I'm giving you the benefit of the doubt. I don't see you as someone who'd be happy about putting a stranger's life at risk unless someone's holding a gun to your head.'

Anna has gone white. He's not sure whether it's shock or concern for her own safety or maybe just the sharpness of the water starting to take effect. He keeps his eyes firmly fixed on hers, looking for any telltale signs.

'And I'm guessing that gun is possibly your sister.'

At the mention of Emmie, Anna opens her mouth and he thinks she's about to respond. Instead she turns suddenly and starts swimming back towards the shore. He's taken by surprise but there's nothing frantic about her stroke to suggest she's desperate to get away from him. He watches for a while, to make it quite clear that he's not pursuing, then swims after her. When she reaches the water's edge, instead of trekking across the sand to where she left her bag, she sits cross-legged in the shallows. He's so immersed in what she's doing that he loses track of the wave sequence and stands too early, taking the full force of a breaker in the small of his back. He stumbles forward for three or four paces to regain his balance, then wades through the water until he reaches her.

The tide has come in far enough to lap gently over a thin layer of small pebbles that break up the vast expanse of sand. Anna is picking up one stone after another, moving them around to fit a pattern that exists only in her head. Kavanagh doubts she's even aware of what she's doing. She's sitting hunched over, her hair keeping her face hidden. He sits and waits, happy for her to break the silence in her own good time.

'How long have you known?' she asks eventually.

'Not long.'

'Is that why you went back to England?'

'Yes.'

She nods, as if confirming something to herself.

'So what was it? Something I said? The Ches thing, right?'

'Right.'

He doesn't explain the other ways in which she slipped up. How he found out isn't important. There are far more pressing things to talk about.

'Where is your sister?' he asks.

Anna sits up straight, flicks the hair out of her face but seems unable to bring herself to look at him.

'Alaska,' she says, and this is just about the last thing he's expecting to hear. 'She's with a dance company on a cruise ship that left Vancouver four days ago. They're heading for some place called Seward, I think it is.'

He thinks about the photo he found in her room, the one with the handwritten message on the reverse side.

'And am I right? Are they holding her hostage somehow?'

She nods, then sniffs and rubs angrily at the corner of her eyes.

'In a way. They're using her to make sure I co-operate but she doesn't know the first thing about it. She still thinks she's landed this dream job on merit, rather than because she happens to be the only person I really care about. It's going to crush her if she ever finds out the whole thing was a set-up. Trust me . . . I know what that feels like.'

Kavanagh is playing catch-up and questions are forming a disorderly queue, each demanding a voice.

'So how does that work?' he asks. 'You're saying they're the ones who set up this cruise job for her? Why would they do that?'

And even as he's phrasing the question, the answer comes to him. On the ship, she's confined. They know exactly where she is and someone will be sticking to her like a limpet, keeping an eye on her every movement. If she's in London or at her dance college, keeping track of her 24/7 would be that much more difficult.

'There's this guy,' Anna is explaining. 'Every time Emmie rings me, he seems to be there. The other night, I got a bit anxious as she was about to ring off and urged her to be careful. He was there right next to her, telling her I wasn't to worry. He'd be sure to keep an eye on her. She obviously likes him and I'm probably being paranoid and worrying myself sick over nothing but . . .'

Her voice trails away. Kavanagh notices she's shivering. He tells her to wait there and walks over to collect his towel. He shakes the sand out of it, flinching as the breeze blows some of it back into his face, then carries it back to the water's edge and drapes it around her shoulders. She looks up and thanks him, her expression a mixture of remorse and anxiety.

He wants to know more about who issued the initial threat and how they first made contact. This time her shudder has nothing to do with the breeze.

'I didn't get a name. Rui, the manager at Cristi's – he called me in one evening after I'd done my set. He said there was someone important I needed to talk to. He left the two of us in his office but he didn't bother to introduce us.'

'What did he look like?'

'Old guy,' she says. 'Still looked after himself, though – he was in pretty good shape for his age. Shaved head. Very scary. He was just . . . *vile*. The things he said. I've never felt so intimidated.'

'How old?'

'Just old. I'm not very good at estimating once people get beyond a certain age.'

She looks up suddenly.

'I'm sorry – I didn't mean . . .'

'Any accent?'

'South,' she says. 'Essex. London. Like something out of *East Enders*.'

'And you say he came out here to threaten you in person?'

'Yes.'

Not good, thinks Kavanagh. Vic is the poster boy for xenophobia. Hates travelling abroad. Hates foreigners. Can't stand the food. Jimmy will know this so if he's sent him to put the fear of God into Anna, it's a clear indication of just how serious he is about this scheme of his. And *very scary* is almost certainly not an exaggeration. In all the time he worked with Vic, he never knew him to tone things down for anyone, irrespective of gender, age or even disability. He's a one-act play and a very convincing one at that. It angers him that Anna and her sister have been dragged into this. Like Conor and his family, they should never come within a hundred miles of someone like Vic Abraham. This is his doing – he feels he's tainted them.

'And this was before I got here, presumably?'

Safe assumption – any earlier and the risk of their paths crossing would have been too great.

'About a week after I started so . . . three weeks ago?'

'Have you heard from him since?' he asks.

She shakes her head.

'Not him personally. He told me if I had anything to report, I should do it through Robbie.'

'Robbie? Ah . . . your pet stalker.'

She sketches an unconvincing attempt at a smile.

'Robbie's OK, honestly. You scared the hell out of him the other night. You weren't supposed to get anywhere near him. He was meant to make a grab for me, then leg it the moment you showed up, but I hit him harder than we'd agreed. I think the nosebleed distracted him and you were all over him before he knew what was happening.'

Kavanagh brings her back to Vic's visit and, more specifically, the reason for it.

'He said I was only here because of him. He was the one who set it up, not Ches, and he'd got a little job for me. I said I already had a job thank you and that's when he started bringing Emmie into the conversation to get my attention. He said she's not in danger and doesn't need to know about what he called *our little arrangement* as long as I do what he says. It's only for a couple of months – once it's over and done with, Emmie and I can go back to the same boring little lives we were leading before. As long as I keep my mouth shut and do as I'm told, we'll both be OK. If I start getting ideas though, try to tip her off, they're monitoring her calls and they'll know. If I go to the authorities or tell anyone else what's going on, same thing . . . they will know. If I love my sister, I'll do exactly as I'm told.'

She looks at the pebble she's holding, as if mystified as to how it got there. Then she hurls it into the water.

'I've looked after Emmie all my life,' she says, staring out to sea. 'I'm really sorry but I don't honestly see what else I could have done.'

There are some things Anna doesn't need to know right now, it occurs to Kavanagh. One of them is that Jimmy is in blinkered pursuit of the endgame and if he gets his way, Kavanagh won't be the only casualty. Anna can do everything that's asked of her and it will make no difference. Both sisters will be seen as loose ends and if anyone understands what that means to the Syndicate, it's Kavanagh. It's the block on which he put his own neck nearly twenty years ago and even after all this time they're hellbent on finding an axe sharp enough to do the job.

Anna and Emmie's only chance of coming through unscathed lies with him. It's a binary outcome – he takes down Jimmy or they all lose.

'So why do they want you to get close to me?' he says. 'You say you have to report back to them through this Robbie character. What do they want exactly?'

'Whatever I can tell them. The old guy warned me you're naturally suspicious and prefer to keep yourself to yourself, so it wouldn't be easy to get close to you. He suggested I use my imagination. Do whatever it takes.'

Kavanagh doesn't need the sudden flush of colour to her cheeks to know she's dealing in euphemisms. Vic will have been anything but subtle.

'He wants to know what you're doing on a day-to-day basis, where you go, whether you meet with anyone in particular. If I get a chance he wants me to go through any papers you've got – he's interested in legal documents, your phone messages and contacts, any memory sticks . . . that sort of thing. He said I need to be really careful, though – you're dangerous. And he wants regular reports on anything relating to your health for some reason.'

'My health?'

'Right. He seemed a bit obsessed with it. If you have to have a check-up, go to the hospital, or anything along those lines, I'm to let him know the moment it happens.'

Kavanagh thinks back to that evening in The Quay Inn. What was it Jimmy said? *You're not the safe bet you used to be.* He seems haunted by the possibility that Kavanagh might keel over unexpectedly before he can disable the automatic release of whatever evidence it is he's holding. And when Jimmy was arguing against the idea of allowing him until September to get everything ready, he asked, *how do I know you're not going to be pulling some stroke the moment my back's turned?* That should have been the clearest possible indication that he wasn't to be trusted. He was never going to keep his distance, whatever he'd promised.

'Did you tell them I flew home yesterday?'

She nods her head and apologises.

He waves it away. There's no damage done there. If they took the opportunity to search his villa while he was away, there's nothing there that will be of any use to them.

The fog around Jimmy's intentions is gradually starting to lift. Kavanagh realises now that he's been looking at this the wrong way. He's been wondering what was so special about Portugal. The answer is, nothing ... unless you count the fact that the Syndicate probably has some stake in Cristi's and the manager is presumably on board. Otherwise it could have been anywhere ... as long as it wasn't London. She'd have been in different clubs every night, all over the city. If some big guy with a scar shows up night after night, she's going to notice – he's not exactly inconspicuous. And even if she doesn't think *stalker,* she's certainly going to be wary at the very least and no way is she going to be seeking opportunities to spend time in his company. Jimmy may hate him with a vengeance but he's never taken him for an idiot. He knows he'd see through it. Anna might as well have the word *bait* tattooed across her forehead.

In somewhere like Praia D'El Rey though, the same principle applies as with Emmie on the boat. It's a contained situation. Two people there for the summer, both on their own. One venue. Throw in the chance to prove he's one of the good guys and what could be more natural than that they should spend a bit of time together?

'I'm so sorry,' she says, as they walk back up the beach to collect the rest of their things. 'You must hate me.'

'I don't.'

'I didn't know what else to do. It's not like I asked to be involved in any of this. This isn't me. I'm not someone who allows herself to be pushed around as a rule but this man ... he really put the fear of God into me. And just hearing him mention Emmie's name ...'

She breaks off and he thinks for one awful moment that she's going to cry. He hasn't the faintest idea how to respond if she does. What's the accepted protocol nowadays? Does he put his arm round her? Pat her on the shoulder? He's sure that whatever he does, even if it's nothing, it will be wrong.

'You did the right thing,' he says, hoping to make it clear that he understands the dilemma she's been facing. 'You had no choice. And he's a dangerous man.'

'He said the same about you,' she says, returning his towel. She picks up her own and starts frantically rubbing her hair. Whether intentionally or not, it serves to keep her face hidden for a few moments.

'What did he say exactly?'

She stops rubbing, allows the towel to slide from her face.

'It doesn't matter.'

'It does to me.'

She turns away, unable to meet his gaze, and fusses around in her bag for her sarong-thing.

'He said you're a psychopath. That you're a killer.'

She leaves a significant pause for him to leap in and tell her that's preposterous.

'I believed him at the time,' she says in the absence of any reply. 'I mean, why wouldn't I? I hadn't even met you. That's why Robbie nearly wet himself when you had your arm around his throat. But that was before . . .'

She's looking at him now, waiting for him to say that Vic is lying. It's clear she needs something to cling to. The temptation to lie and make himself more acceptable in her eyes is almost overwhelming. He could give her as much context as it would take for her to understand . . . tell her about his parents and Katy, how he was lucky to escape with his life not just that night but in the bomb blast at Dunloughraine as well, how Maurice stepped in as a surrogate father, then cruelly used what had happened to his family to manipulate him into going after Leon Murphy. But what will that serve if he can't even excuse himself? Anna may be able to empathise with the nine-year-old boy in Bristol and even admire the soldier rushing to the aid of a wounded comrade but none of that will offer any mitigation for how he spent the eight years he was with the Syndicate. He won't lie to her.

'I haven't been that person for twenty years,' he says, choosing his words carefully. 'Almost as long as you've been alive.'

She takes half a step away from him. It's the slightest of movements and might have been caused by a loss of balance in the sand but he's never going to miss it.

'It's not who I am now,' he continues. 'I walked away and that's why all this madness is happening. No one does that, you see. They want to make an example of me.'

She's still appraising him and he can see the uncertainty in her eyes. She wants to believe him and maybe that's the best he can hope for right now. Even more than he deserves perhaps. But he's not sure she can separate him from the chaos that's been brought into her life and that of her sister.

'He also said you were looking for a girl . . . someone called Jessica Murphy. She's about my age and I'm expected to do anything I can to make you think I might have been her until I was supposedly adopted as a kid. That's why you'd be desperate to seek me out. If you started asking me questions about when I was very young, I was to tell you I don't remember anything before the age of four. I told him that would be easy because the earliest memory I've got is a trip to the zoo for my fifth birthday and that was the closest he came to a smile in all the time he was there. He said I'd do just fine.'

She gathers up her things and waits for him to pull on his T-shirt and beach shoes rather than walk off. He draws encouragement from this. It feels like a minor step in the right direction.

'So who is this Jessica anyway?' she asks. 'Did you think I was her?'

'Yes. For a while.'

'She must be important to you.'

'She is.'

Anna risks a sideways glance.

'I know I don't have any right to ask,' she says, 'but am I allowed to know why?'

She doesn't think he's going to answer at first. Then he clears his throat.

'I owe her. From way back.'

Anna says nothing. She wants to know but suspects from the pained expression on his face that she won't get an answer.

'This Robbie,' he says, as if grabbing at an opportunity to move on, 'what's the set-up there? Do you meet at agreed times or just when there's something worth reporting?'

'I phone him. Why?'

Kavanagh thinks it through.

Comes to a decision.

'Would it be in any way suspicious for you to arrange to see him after you've finished at Cristi's tonight? It wouldn't be too late?'

She shakes her head.

'Not at all. I've done it before. Why?'

'I want you to call him this afternoon. Tell him I got back last night and that you've spent most of the day with me playing catch-up.'

'Do I tell him you know about him?'

'No. I don't want to risk him contacting others until I've spoken with him. Set up a meeting – eleven o'clock tonight. You've found out something they're going to want to know in London but you can't talk about it over the phone. Make it that abandoned place on the clifftop where you met the other night.'

She turns to face him, raising one hand to shade her eyes from the sun.

'You know about that?'

'Eleven o'clock – remember.'

'You're not going to hurt him, are you?' she asks anxiously. 'He's OK. He's just a big kid who's got himself mixed up in something that's way too much for him to handle ... pretty much the same way I did. He's as unhappy as I am about what we've been doing but he's scared and doesn't know how to get out of it.'

And there it is.

Don't hurt him.

Confirmation, if needed, that these same assumptions will follow him wherever he goes for the rest of his life. He's persuaded himself that if anyone is ever going to see beyond the scar, surely it will be Anna ... but unless he finds a way to break through this crippling wall of mistrust that separates him from everyone else, this is how it will always be. He's viewed it until now as some sort of security, a barrier to shield him from the rejection of people who can never come close to understanding what he's been through and how it's coloured his view of the world. He thought it was there to keep others out. It's never felt more like a prison than it does now.

And if he doesn't set about dismantling it in the next few minutes, he's not sure he'll ever be free of it.

'You want to know why she's important?' he asks. 'Jessica Murphy?'

Anna nods.

Deep breath.

Swallow.

'I killed her father.'

And there it is – the whole thing reduced to four simple words. He watches Anna closely, checking her expression for something, although he's not sure what to expect. Fear, maybe? Outrage? Disgust?

Instead there's a frown, a gentle incline of the head which almost feels like an invitation to continue. Explain.

'She was three years old. I didn't know she was in bed upstairs at the time.'

And now he's started talking, all of a sudden it feels more like a dam than a wall that's coming apart, because the words that once refused to flow now surge forward as if there's no way they'll ever stop. They're picked up by the same breeze that, only seconds earlier, was whipping the waves into a frenzy and causing them to crash on the shore just yards from where they'd been sitting.

And still she's listening, as he tells her about Katy, the fire that destroyed his family, dredging up memories and feelings of guilt he's never even wanted to confront, let alone share. She's still there.

Listening.

And this, he thinks, must be what it's like not to be alone.

Just after midday his phone pings – an email. With an attachment. Bizarre sender's address that could only ever be a temporary one for expediency. No signature. Just a simple message.

Wish you were here.

Not.

Figured I owe you this . . . if only for all the jelly babies over the years.

Am hoping you consider grovelling sufficient and debts repaid in full.

Be lucky.

He opens the attachment and a photo appears on the screen. Underneath is the name Jessica Elgar along with date of birth and current contact details. No dossier – Lowe won't have had time to compile anything like the bogus file based on Anna Hill's life. He probably had these details all along and held them back yesterday in case he needed a bargaining chip. It's hard to be angry with him though. He didn't have to send this.

Kavanagh googles her and she's relatively easy to find. She has quite a presence across a range of social media and describes herself as a chilled stay at home parent. Happily married to Steve. Loving mum to Lily. A number of photos show her smiling happily at the camera. In some of these, she's with a bearded man in his late twenties and a small girl.

Who must be about three years old.

Now he has more emails to send and calls to make and is really pushed for time if he's going to have everything in place to take on Jimmy with any realistic prospect of success.

Even so, he finds himself drawn back to the photos now and again.

Touching the screen every so often with his index finger.

The expression on the little girl's face sweeps away the intervening years like so much confetti.

Kavanagh is here half an hour early, inside the larger of the two abandoned houses. He's stationed himself at one of the openings in the wall, encouraged by the absence of any windows or doors in the entire building, because that should make it easier to hear anyone approaching. Having followed Anna three nights ago, he knows he can't possibly be seen from the footpath on the other side of the golf course. At the same time, Robbie will have to cross the fairway to reach the house and the moon will light him up like a Christmas tree the moment he does so. He's in prime position, all bases covered. All he has to do is stay alert. And wait patiently.

He tries to ignore the scurrying sounds that break the silence every now and then. His grandparents were plagued by a rat infestation in one of their outhouses when he was young and he's felt uncomfortable around them ever since, but he tells himself that whatever form of wildlife has made its home here, it's almost certainly more intimidated than he is.

He's having trouble keeping track of the time. His phone is off as a precaution and it's too dark in here to read the dial on his wristwatch. He has a flashback to when this sort of situation was routine for him, practically an everyday occurrence. Night manoeuvres in the army. Surveillance for the Syndicate. Hours of patient concentration. He doesn't remember suffering any physical discomfort back then. Boredom, yes; mind-numbing monotony that stretched minutes into hours and tested his commitment in ways that the eventual confrontation never could. But now he has a catalogue of aches and pains to contend with, just from standing in the same place for half an hour. He wants to get up from his crouched position and get the blood circulating again in his legs, flex his back muscles. His body, it seems to him, is finding ever more inventive ways to remind him he's not getting any younger.

Time continues to drag its heels. He picks at holes in the wall with his fingers. Counts off in batches of thirty seconds. Pictures Robbie parking his car where he left it three nights ago and follows his progress from there in his imagination. Still nothing. Doubts are just beginning to creep in when he finally senses movement out on the fairway. Sure enough, a wiry figure saunters casually across the course, heading with no apparent urgency in his direction. He's wearing a baseball cap, the peak tugged down to hide most of his face, but there's no mistaking Robbie's swagger. Kavanagh edges closer to the entrance, careful not to disturb any of the loose stones and debris that would give away his presence. He presses his back against the wall and waits.

And waits.

Nothing.

He hears the sound of a match being struck outside, some metres away at a guess, but it's hard to be sure. Seconds later he's still alone inside the building. He's annoyed with himself. It hasn't occurred to him that Robbie might wait outside and it should have. Why wouldn't he? He thinks he's meeting Anna and from where he is now he'll be able to see her when she crosses the golf course. It's late and the air has a distinctly fresh feel to it but it's still pleasant enough. Why would anyone turn down a sky full of stars for the chance to share a dank, crumbling space with the local rodent population unless he had to?

Kavanagh takes stock. If Robbie stays outside, he's going to have to make the first move and without the element of surprise in his favour the situation won't be easily contained. He may be just the other side of this wall – equally he could be several yards away. He's not going to be lit up by the moon any longer. It's black as sin over here and by the time Kavanagh's stepped out into the open and worked out exactly where the boy is, he'll have taken off like a bat out of hell. With the benefit of a decent head start, he could turn what should be a routine interception into a shitstorm.

He's still pondering this dilemma when he hears footsteps coming closer and, to his relief, a shape finally steps through the entrance. Seizing his chance, he steps swiftly in behind Robbie and wraps his forearm around his throat, dislodging the baseball cap and dragging him backwards so that he can't get any real purchase with his feet. Just in case he's harbouring any silly ideas about using it as a weapon, he slaps the cigarette to the floor with his other hand, which he then clamps over Robbie's mouth. He's squirming, using both hands to tug at the arm across his throat, so Kavanagh tightens the grip to get his attention.

'Stay very, very still,' he says, almost whispering into his ear. 'I know you're scared but the more you struggle, the more pressure I have to apply. I don't want to hurt you but I do need you to do exactly as I say. Nod your head if you understand.'

He slackens his grip just a fraction to make it easier for Robbie to comply. He nods, lowering his hands to show willing.

'OK. In a few moments, I'm going to take my hand away from your mouth to make it easier for you to breathe. I'm trusting you to behave. If that turns out to be a mistake, it will be yours, not mine. You know what a choke hold is?'

Another nod.

'You'll be unconscious in seconds. The problem is, I haven't needed to resort to anything like that in nearly twenty years so I may be a bit rusty. Any number of things could go wrong. Are we quite clear on this?'

A muffled sound escapes from Robbie's throat which Kavanagh takes as assent. Keeping the headlock in place, he moves his other hand a few inches from the boy's mouth, ready to slam it back in place at the first suggestion that he's about to shout for help. When it's clear that's not going to happen, he reaches into his pocket and takes out a set of handcuffs which he gives to Robbie.

'Right wrist only,' he tells him.

'Can I just say something?' gasps Robbie. If he's trying to keep the tremor out of his voice, it hasn't worked.

'Right wrist. *Now*.'

Robbie holds both hands up in front of his face so that he can see over the powerful forearm that is blocking his view. When Kavanagh hears the restraint click into place, he releases him from the head lock and grabs the other end of the handcuffs, swiftly fastening it around his own left wrist. Then he sits amidst the rubble and tries not to think about the noises he heard earlier. He yanks on the cuffs and Robbie, who looks equally dubious about the idea, follows suit.

'OK,' says Kavanagh. 'This is what's going to happen. You and I are going to have a little talk. I don't know you at all. Anna tells me the obnoxious little toerag from the other night was all an act. According to her, you're a nice enough kid who's in way over his head and would like to find a way out. It would be nice to think I could trust her judgement, but the two of you don't have much of a track record for honesty so far and I've got a lot riding on this. If I'm going to be putting my life in someone else's hands I'm going to take a lot of convincing, you understand? So the next fifteen minutes or so are going to be crucial if you want to get out of this in one piece. You're going to listen to what I have to say, give an honest answer to every question I put to you and do everything you can think of to persuade me I'm not making the biggest mistake of my life.'

'Can I just ask something?' says Robbie.

'I haven't finished.'

'Please? I'm not going to cause any trouble. I promise I'll answer any questions you ask, but there's something I need to know first.'

This is a very different Robbie from the arrogant, self-preening yob of a few nights ago. Kavanagh isn't ready yet to draw any hard and fast conclusions from it.

'What is it?' he asks.

Robbie has the stricken look of someone who hardly dares to ask.

'Is Anna OK?'

And if nothing else, Kavanagh decides, that is a big step in the right direction.

23

3rd July 2018
London and Praia D'El Rey

It's getting on for one in the morning when the call comes through. Jimmy checks his phone and sees Vic's name pop up on the screen. He rejects it and slumps back in the seat, gazing out at the London backdrop as it flashes past his window. Lights. Action. Places, everybody.

He's always been fascinated by this whole other world out there that most people never get to see, a shadow economy getting ready to crank itself into gear, generated by a population whose hours mean they rarely get to see the light of day. A service industry dedicated to the dark. He loves London – its diversity, its immediacy. It's an impact city – you can love it or hate it but indifference isn't an option. He himself can't imagine living anywhere else.

It's been a perfect evening all round – a bit of business, a bit of pleasure. He's put in an appearance at a drinks reception on the Thames Embankment, a chance to press the flesh with a totally compromised junior minister, whose sexual indiscretions have left him very much in the pocket of the Syndicate, and a few other dignitaries who are partial to a little grease from time to time. That's led to at least one interesting land deal proposal he's going to have to investigate in the next few days. He'll get the whizz kids to go in behind the figures before he goes any further with it. They'll let him know where the catch is – and there *will* be one. There always is.

From there he's moved on to The Tin Tack Club in Soho and splashed the cash on a couple of models who must have stumbled in by mistake or they'd never have gone anywhere near the place without minders and a course of penicillin. A few drinks with them have led to him spending the last couple of hours at a flat in Notting Hill. Lihua doesn't need to know anything about that. She might get the right idea.

His mobile starts up again and he mutters under his breath. Vic knows the drill. He wouldn't ring back straightaway unless it was urgent. He nods to Lars who's looking questioningly at him in the rear-view mirror. The partition duly slides up to afford Jimmy a bit of privacy as he answers the call.

'This is a bit late for you, isn't it?' he says. 'Not worried about your beauty sleep?'

'Where are you?'

Vic's manner is brusque and businesslike at the best of times but he sounds grumpier than usual. Urgent enough, then.

'Home . . . as good as. Lars is just dropping me off.'

'I'll be there in ten.'

No way, he thinks.

'Think again. I'm dead on my feet. I need the sleep, even if you don't.'

'Sleep can wait, Jimmy. We've got a problem.'

'No, *you've* got a problem. Deal with it and bring me up to speed in the morning. Show a bit of initiative – it's what I pay you for.'

'It'll be too late by then – trust me. I'm sending you a text . . . hang on a minute. Came in an hour ago from the burner the kid's been using.'

'What kid?'

'The kid in Pray-a whatever the fuck it's called.'

'And?'

'And the text didn't come from him.'

'I thought you just said it did.'

'I said it came from the burner he's been using. He's not the one who sent it.'

Robbie Something, Jimmy thinks. One of Rui Monteiro's bar staff at the club in Praia D'El Rey. Drama student on a gap year. Rui vouched for him personally. Much cheaper option than sending someone out there specially. What the fuck's he done now?

'How do you know he didn't send it?'

'See for yourself. Ah . . . these fucking fingers.'

Vic is still in the Stone Age when it comes to technology. Still struggling with the most basic tasks. The text takes forever to come through.

Tell the organ grinder he has until 2 a.m. to ring me on this number. One second late and you've got a shitstorm coming your way.

Jimmy frowns at the screen.

'What the fuck is that supposed to mean?'

'It means it's Kavanagh,' says Vic. 'And if he's got the kid's burner, you realise what this means, right?'

'No, Vic. I'm some sort of retard all of a sudden. What's all this shit about organ grinders?'

'I'll explain when I get there. Five minutes.'

'Make it two.'

Jimmy snaps the phone shut and throws it onto the seat next to him.

Shit.

His perfect evening has just developed an irritating kink.

'Where the hell are you phoning from? You know what time it is here?'

Kavanagh has the phone on speaker and Jimmy is coming through loud and clear. So too does his mood. There is nothing conciliatory or vaguely apologetic about his tone of voice.

'Really? Are you sure that's how you want to play this?'

'I don't need lectures from you, old man. I get a call from Vic telling me to ring this number immediately and I've done just that. Whatever it is you want to say, get on with it, will you? I could do with a decent night's sleep for a change.'

'Did you read the text I sent?'

'Yeah, I read it . . . and you're through to the organ grinder so tell me what's so special about 2 a.m. and why I should worry about some shitstorm coming my way cos I haven't got the first fucking idea what you're on about.'

Kavanagh has to work hard to keep his own irritation under control. The nuclear deterrent analogy he's always attached to the understanding he had with Maurice needs to stay right at the forefront of his thinking now. At least one person with a finger on the button has to keep his composure. The moment both sides are out of control, there *is* no deterrent worthy of the name. Just a pissing contest fuelled by ego.

'OK,' he says, keeping his tone as neutral as possible. 'You can drop the innocent act for a start. One – you know exactly where I am. You planted the girl there. Two – you know whose phone I'm using otherwise you wouldn't have been in such a hurry to call me back. Three – the fact that I now have it should tell you all you need to know about the wisdom of sending a kid to do a man's job. Ready to talk sensibly?'

'You wouldn't be recording this, would you?' says Jimmy after a noticeable pause.

'Why would I do that?'

'Now who's playing dumb? I seem to remember the old man thought he could trust you and look where that got him.'

Kavanagh is not prepared to concede one inch of the moral high ground.

'Well, that worked both ways. I trusted him too. It didn't occur to me for one moment that he was capable of using what happened to my parents and my baby sister as a motivational tool.'

There's a pause before Jimmy's voice comes back, sounding slightly puzzled.

'I don't know anything about that. I was a kid when you left, remember?'

It sounds plausible enough. Jimmy will know he was orphaned because the first thing he'll have done when seeking to settle this dispute between the two of them is look for any vulnerable areas to exploit. One of his great frustrations will have been that Kavanagh is difficult to get at. He has no dependents at all now that his grandparents are both dead as well. No wife, no significant other . . . not even anyone you'd call a close friend, which is why Jimmy has been reduced to issuing vague threats against the life he's managed to carve out for himself in Wareham. Would Maurice or Vic have told him about Leon Murphy? About the fake arson story they fed to him to make sure he was well and truly motivated? On balance, he thinks it's unlikely.

'Anyway, the answer is no,' he says eventually. 'I'm not taping this. I don't need to, not now I have taped testimony from the two kids you sent out here. Thank you for that. The boy was able to tell me quite a few interesting things about your man Rui Monteiro and the set-up here at Cristi's. As for the girl, the conversation she had with Vic made quite an impression on her. I'm not going to pretend anything they've given me is strong enough on its own to put you away but when you add it to everything I already have, it sort of paints a picture, if you see what I mean. It'll keep those lawyers of yours busy and cramp your style for a fair bit.'

'I'm glad they were so helpful,' says Jimmy. It's not clear whether the yawn in his voice is genuine or for show. 'I'll be sure to make my feelings clear when I next see them.'

'Well, unfortunately that's not going to happen.'

'No?'

'No. I'm afraid Cristi's is going to need another member of the bar staff and a different star attraction for the summer. You might like to tell Ches Headley to update the list of clients on his website while you're at it.'

There's a pause while Jimmy digests this.

'Bullshit,' he says eventually, the mocking laugh designed to make it clear he's not fooled for one minute. 'Nice try, old man, but I'd keep well away from the poker tables if I were you. No way have you offed either of them, especially the girl. You haven't got it in you anymore. That's why you left, remember? You went soft all of a sudden. Didn't want to live among the savages anymore. Too good for the likes of us.'

'I've played back their tapes a few times,' Kavanagh continues, ignoring the cheap jibe, 'and what leaps out is just how frightened they were. Vic did his usual thorough job of spelling out what would happen if they didn't do exactly as he said and they were well and truly convinced their lives were under threat. Once they go missing and those tapes come to light – which, I promise you, will happen if you leave me with no choice – I reckon you'll have the National Crime Agency all over you and I don't think you want that.'

'Again ... you're embarrassing yourself. Is this the best you can do? Jesus, tell me you were better than this back in the day!'

'I'm glad you're so amused. Have you tried contacting either of them in the past few hours? My guess is no.'

'So you've turned them and squirrelled them away somewhere,' Jimmy says with a verbal shrug. 'You think I give a shit where they are? I'll tell you what, go ahead. Do it. Off the pair of them. Save me the trouble. Fucking amateurs. You think you can threaten me?'

'It's not a threat, Jimmy. It's just how things are. You asked what it is I want – I'll tell you. I want you to fly out here.'

'Why?'

'We need to sit down again. Face to face.'

'No way – are you kidding me? We've done that already.'

'And things have changed.'

'How?' Jimmy asks, his exasperation showing through. 'What's changed, for fuck's sake?'

'Not over the phone. I'll explain when you're here. There's a return ticket in your name for this Friday waiting for you at the flight desk – say the word and I'll send you the details. Just the one ticket. If you bring anyone else, they can buy their own. And if they're coming to do anything other than hold your hand, tell them not to bother with a return.'

'Forget it. You think I'm flying all the way out there to meet you one-to-one? It's not your *eyes* that need testing.'

'What's the matter, Jimmy? You think this soft old man presents a threat?'

'I think he's a total fucking nutjob, is what I think.'

Kavanagh sits back in his chair. If Jimmy's still on the phone, it's for a reason. The hook is in. Time to reel him in.

'Two reasons why you don't need to worry about your safety here. One – we both know you'll bring back-up even though I've asked for it to be just the two of us. And two – if I wanted to kill you, I'd choose London every time rather than some golf resort in Portugal. It's a matter of practicalities. Ask Vic – I'm sure he's listening in. London would be a walk in the park. Any number of ways I could get near to you without anyone knowing I was there. Out here? I can't afford to try anything like that, even if I wanted to. I stand out like a sore thumb.'

He pauses to allow Jimmy to test the logistics of this for himself.

'Let's keep this real,' he continues. 'I don't want to kill you, Jimmy. You know full well I was in London two days ago. I could have taken you out any time I wanted. I told you ... I want to talk.'

'We already did that, remember? That's an hour of my life I'm never going to get back. Why should I put myself through that again?'

It's Kavanagh's turn to take a moment. 'Things have moved on since then. My own circumstances have . . . let's say, they've changed. I have a very different perspective on things from when we met in Wareham. I'm not going into any detail over the phone but I need to explain a few things to you. And there's something I need to give you.'

'Like what?'

'I'll be here Friday evening. If you haven't shown by Saturday morning, I'll know you're not coming but you need to know this. If that happens, you'll leave me no choice. I'll activate the release of all the documents and I'll be out of here. You'll never find me, I can promise you that – I've had plenty of time to plan this properly. And you'll spend the rest of your life wondering whether today's the day when I'll find *you*. Friday evening – we can put this all to bed. Tell me it's not the better option.'

Kavanagh falls silent and holds his breath. There is a lot riding on the next few seconds and even though he's presented the argument as logically and clearly as he can, he's not confident logic or clarity hold much sway against wounded ego and the lure of payback. This could still go either way.

'I'll get back to you,' mutters Jimmy and hangs up immediately . . . and Kavanagh knows that's a yes, however Jimmy wants to dress it up.

He'll be here Friday.

The final piece is slotting into place.

Even if Kavanagh may have just signed his own death warrant.

He taps the burner against his front teeth, taking time to compose himself. Then he turns round and faces Anna and Robbie who are sitting next to each other on the two-seater sofa. The expression on their faces tells the story of the gamut of emotions they've run in the past few minutes. Not shocked – they believed Kavanagh when he explained to them beforehand what they might expect to hear. Drained though. And definitely frightened.

'I'm sorry,' he tells them. 'That can't have been easy. But you had to know what you're up against.'

Robbie in particular looks ashen.

'He said he didn't give a shit whether we were dead or not.'

'I know this will sound ridiculous but try not to take it personally.'

'He thinks you've saved him the trouble.'

Kavanagh drops the burner to the floor and stamps on it three times.

'People like Jimmy Hayes don't even see other people as individuals. They're just figures on a spreadsheet, pieces on a chess board. You know the phrase *collateral damage*?'

Robbie nods and says he thinks so, in a way that actually suggests the exact opposite.

'He's not targeting you specifically. He just hates loose ends, things that might trip him up later. I had to make sure you understand what you're dealing with because there's always a moment – usually if things don't go quite as you're hoping – when you find yourself thinking maybe you made the wrong decision. Picked the wrong side. You'll start asking yourself whether maybe I was exaggerating things. Was the situation really that bad? Would he really have been so dangerous? You need a convincing reason to put as much distance between yourself and his kind as possible. Well, now you have it.'

Anna hasn't taken her eyes off him since he turned to face them. She's staring at him now with her head tilted in that quirky way of hers when she's trying to work through a jumble of thoughts.

'Are you OK?' she asks.

Kavanagh nods.

'There's something you're not telling us, isn't there?'

'There's plenty I'm not telling you, but nothing that affects you in any way.'

She shakes her head.

'I don't understand,' she says. 'You said you had an agreement and he broke it. What's to stop him doing the same again this time?'

Kavanagh wonders how best to phrase this. The two of them need to leave now. Robbie is dropping her off in Lisbon, then driving to Albufeira where friends of his are working as lifeguards. He can hide himself away there for a few days, by which time the situation should be a lot clearer. Anna will have a much longer and tougher journey, fraught with possible pitfalls. They both need to be thinking about themselves, not worrying about what might or might not happen on Friday between himself and Jimmy.

'He won't,' he says, with all the confidence he can muster. 'He can't afford to.'

He wishes that were true.

Knows that it isn't.

Suspects it's not going to make a blind bit of difference either way.

24

6th July 2018
Praia D'El Rey

The downpour doesn't last long. The strong breezes that brought the clouds racing in are just as quick to sweep them away again, but for those ten to fifteen minutes during which they hold dominion over the skies, the rain is rampant. Unrelenting. Driven by a forceful wind, it batters the windows of the villa and skitters down the road, kicking up tiny explosions off the tarmac.

Momentarily dragged away from his book, Kavanagh suddenly remembers a T-shirt he draped over a poolside chair earlier and a pair of trainers he left out to air. He opens the back door and scuttles outside to retrieve them. As if embracing the inevitable, he stands in the open, throws his arms wide and head back, and offers himself up to the elements. Only when running over Durdle Door has he felt so at one with nature. So alive.

An hour later, when he next looks up from the book, the blue skies are back, and his wet clothing – glaring reproachfully at him from a corner of the room – is the only reminder of the deluge that swept through earlier. He checks his watch and decides maybe he ought to grab something to eat. Making himself a sandwich, he tries to avoid all mental references to last suppers. He wonders what Jesus would have made of Diet Sprite.

He takes the food back to his chair by the window and immerses himself again in his book. By the time he's finished it, the light is already bleeding out of the sky. He's been reading solidly for just over four hours and his eyes are tired. He understands that straining them in this way may not be the smartest of moves, but he's been on a mission, determined to finish it before Jimmy gets here. He prefers not to look too closely at why that might be.

Running the cold tap in the bathroom, he cups his hands and splashes water over his face. He soaks a flannel and dabs at each eye in turn, his vision much improved from earlier when he was seriously worried that another episode might be on its way. If there was such a thing as the ultimate example of bad timing, that would have been it for sure. He blinks and looks at himself in the mirror. If things go wrong tonight, it's not going to be because his eyes have let him down.

He stands at the window and looks out at the encroaching darkness. Tries to convince himself that Anna and Robbie are safe. He heard from both yesterday. Robbie's sudden disappearance from the area will have been noted at Cristi's and presumably reported back to London, which can only be a good thing. The longer Robbie's whereabouts remain a mystery, the more likely it is that uncertainty will creep into Jimmy's mind as to exactly what's happened here. Kavanagh suspects keeping a low profile is entirely alien to the lad but the events of the past few days have clearly shaken him. If he's canny enough and keeps his head down, he has a realistic chance of slipping through the net in the chaos that is going to swamp Jimmy in the coming weeks and months. He's going to have much more pressing matters to deal with.

Hopefully.

Anna flew out two days ago. Three flights, twenty hours in total, changing at Boston and Minneapolis. She swears she and Emmie will reimburse him first chance they get but mentally he's written it off. What exactly has he been saving for all these years if not an opportunity such as this?

She sent a cryptic text yesterday – short and to the point, in case it somehow made its way into the wrong hands.

Arrived safely in A

A for Anchorage – ahead of her, a connecting trip by rail or bus, whichever will get her to Seward the earlier. The cruise ship is due into port today – should actually be docking around now, he realises – but disembarkation is bound to be a lengthy process. In the absence of any further news, he's doing his best to stay positive. Now that the huge distance separating her from her sister is taken out of the equation, someone as resourceful and determined as Anna has every chance of pulling this off, especially with the element of surprise so overwhelmingly in her favour. It would be reassuring though to have another update confirming it.

Alone at the window, he watches a couple as they head down the hill towards the car park. They're arm in arm, laughing, apparently without a care in the world. He wonders what Jessica Murphy is doing this very minute. *Jessica Elgar*, he corrects himself. He imagines her in another life – so much kinder than the one he's known – walking down this same hill, one arm around her husband, the other holding her daughter's hand. And pictures himself, climbing in the opposite direction. Steve nods, Jessica smiles. Not even a glance at the scar, let alone a flinch – it's his fantasy so it can take whatever shape he chooses. They say *good evening* to each other, laugh about the downpour earlier. *Have you ever seen anything like it?* Talk for a minute or two before going their separate ways.

Small talk.

Again he feels that tug, not a longing as such but certainly an awareness that he has missed out on something, pushed it to the margins of his life. Almost as if he knows that's where it will always be anyway, whatever he does. The mantra to which he's clung all his life is that you can't miss what you've never had. It's a lifebelt in serious danger of losing any buoyancy it's ever possessed.

He watches now as the couple continue down the hill, passing a figure coming the other way. Instantly there's something familiar about this man but it's only as he turns into the short driveway leading to his villa that he can see clearly who it is.

Jimmy's early.

Kavanagh throws open the door and steps to one side to allow him to enter. Jimmy stays where he is and indicates that he wants to frisk him first.

'Unless you have an objection for some reason,' he says.

'Seriously?' Kavanagh takes a step forward and lifts both arms.

'Can't be too careful,' says Jimmy. He pats him down, then assumes the position to extend the same courtesy to Kavanagh, who shakes his head and leads the way into the living room. He leaves the sofa for his visitor and squeezes into the small armchair, which he's positioned closer to the sofa than usual. He doesn't think Jimmy's likely to try anything but he doesn't want too much distance between them if he's wrong.

'Very trusting of you,' Jimmy says. 'I thought you old pros never left anything to chance.'

Kavanagh shrugs his shoulders.

'If you're here to kill me, you're not going to be carrying. You'll leave that to whoever you brought with you. As for you frisking me, like I told you the other night – if I wanted to take you out, this is the last place I'd choose.'

'Isn't that what you'd be saying if you *were* planning to kill me?'

Kavanagh screws up his face. Fair point.

'You want a drink?' he asks.

Jimmy's expression is less than enthusiastic.

'Not if all you've got is that gut rot you usually pour down your throat.'

Kavanagh rises silently and walks over to the window and picks up a carrier bag. He takes a bottle of Médoc from it and offers it to his visitor.

'You kidding me?' says Jimmy, examining the label and looking up in disbelief.

'Bought it specially for the occasion. It's what you were drinking that night in Wareham.'

He hands a glass to Jimmy and fetches a soft drink from the fridge for himself. He takes his time, allowing his mind to sift through the implications of Jimmy's early arrival.

'Earlier flight?' he says, resuming his seat. 'You didn't use the ticket I left at the desk then?'

Jimmy has already poured his first glass and is swirling it round in front of his face.

'Wasn't convenient. After you called the other night, it dawned on me. If I was going to have to travel all the way out here, I might as well make the most of it. I've got friends with a villa just outside Seville so I flew there two days ago. Felipe lent me his car to drive up here. Took me the best part of five hours and I'm knackered, so this had better be worth it.'

'You're not driving back tonight then.'

'Mmm, this is half decent, by the way,' he says, holding the glass up to the light. 'Driving back? Not to Seville, no. I'm heading off to the Algarve once we're done. Brought my clubs with me. There's some cracking courses in that area. Felipe's booked us into a hotel in Albufeira.'

Kavanagh doesn't blink. Any conversation with Jimmy is like a jigsaw puzzle. The pieces with the straight edges rarely present much of a problem. It's when you try to move into the middle that the real challenge comes. Some of the pieces look so odd, you wonder whether they've put the right picture on the box. Some look OK when you first fit them but when examined more closely they turn out to belong to another part of the puzzle altogether. And some will inevitably be missing, usually crucial pieces. All you can do is keep moving around the ones you have until some semblance of the picture emerges.

The rogue pieces this time:

The villa just outside Seville.

So convenient. And so much easier to visit Praia D'El Rey from there without leaving a paper trail than flying from Heathrow to Lisbon.

Felipe let me use his car to drive up here.

According to Adrian Lowe, Jimmy never drives anywhere if he can help it. Sees being driven as one of the essential trappings of power. He certainly wouldn't take on a five-hour drive in a foreign country and then set out for the Algarve the same evening – that's another three hours minimum. If Jimmy came by car, he hasn't come alone. And where is the car? Come to that, where is the driver?

Albufeira.

Coincidence? Or is Jimmy messing with his head? Kavanagh decides he can't bring himself to believe the latter. If it's true and the Syndicate has already managed to track Robbie down, the boy's not the only one who's in a lot of trouble. Has to be a coincidence, surely. You think Algarve, Albufeira's not going to be far from your lips. It's not such a stretch.

Jimmy takes a sip from his glass and puts it on the floor next to him.

'OK. You're the one who asked for this sit-down. I'm here. Like I said, this had better be good.'

By way of response, Kavanagh walks over to the table and picks up a folder stuffed with documents of one sort or another. On top of it is an old VHS video cassette. He brings them over to Jimmy and hands them to him without saying a word. Jimmy looks up at him with a slightly bemused expression on his face and holds up the video.

'Haven't seen one of these in a while. Do people still use them?'

'If they have the right machine.'

'Have you got one?'

'At home. Not here.'

'Well, I sure as hell haven't. What is it?'

'It's a recording of a meeting between Maurice, Vic and a building contractor who was getting a lot of grief from a competitor. This was back in the late 90s and they were exploring ways of persuading this competitor to back off. Couple of months later, the same guy was a victim of an apparent hit and run. A man named Leon Murphy got hold of this copy somehow and thought he could use it to blackmail Vic and your father into letting him walk away from the Syndicate. He was wrong.'

'Leon Murphy,' Jimmy says, trawling through the memory banks. 'Sounds familiar. Isn't he the guy—?'

'Yes.'

Jimmy nods and takes the video out of its box. He turns it over several times, scrutinising it with the fascination of someone unexpectedly reunited with a childhood toy.

'You've seen it, I presume?'

'Yes.'

'So how incriminating is it?'

'Enough.'

'And how come you have a copy?'

'Your father sent me to Murphy's house to deal with him for his supposed involvement in an arson attack that wiped out an entire family. He told me to make sure I got hold of the video before I dealt with him. Stressed how important that was. I was supposed to burn it before I left, but I got sidetracked.'

By a sneeze.

By a little girl at the top of the stairs.

'And these papers,' Jimmy says, tugging until they come away from the folder, 'I take it these are the evidence you've been threatening us with all these years.'

'Yes.'

Jimmy gives a low chuckle.

'I thought you were bluffing,' he says, shaking his head as he moves from one document to the next. 'Fuck me ... all these years, I never really believed you had anything that could hurt us. I'd have bet my life on it.'

'Nothing's worth betting your life on,' says Kavanagh, although he's uncomfortably aware that's a pretty fair description of what he's doing right now.

'And I suppose this is where you tell me these are all copies and you still have the originals tucked away safely, right?'

Kavanagh shakes his head.

'No. They're the originals. There are no copies.'

'Sure. As if you're going to say anything else.'

'I understand why you'd think that but I've been going over what you said when we met that evening in Wareham.'

Jimmy's eyes have narrowed to slits. He's definitely intrigued now.

'Which was?'

'You said I've been looking at it the wrong way all this time, believing that the package is the only thing that's kept you at bay. The way you see it, far from protecting me, it's been the only thing that puts me at risk because it keeps me relevant. Without these papers and the video, I'm just some nobody running a bookshop in the back end of beyond and you've got far more important things to worry about in London. You wouldn't even give me a moment's thought otherwise. Seems to me there might be more than a grain of truth in that so I'm handing it all over to you – just like I agreed, only ahead of schedule. So you tell me – if I'm going to do that, what would be the point of making copies and keeping them? I'd just be perpetuating the situation we're in now. How is that going to solve anything?'

'So what you're saying,' says Jimmy, scratching his head, 'is that you're now accepting the agreement I put forward two months ago. You couldn't have done that back then and saved me the fucking schlepp all the way out here?'

'Things have changed since then. I've got a different perspective on it now.'

'So you said on the phone. You going to explain what that's all about? I mean, I don't see how what you're doing here is any different from putting a gun in my hand and trusting me not to shoot you. You could have done that any time in the last twenty years. Why now?'

'You're right,' says Kavanagh, momentarily distracted. 'Everything's going to come down to trust. If that's the case, maybe it would be better if you asked your friend to join us. I'm finding it difficult to concentrate with him the other side of that door.'

Jimmy stares for a moment . . . then breaks into a smile.

'What makes you think I've got a friend in the hallway?'

'That does,' says Kavanagh, pointing to a small yellow light on a device that's plugged into a wall socket at ground level. 'It tells me the circuit was broken a couple of minutes ago.'

Jimmy seems more amused than embarrassed. He gets to his feet and opens the door, then nods and walks back to his seat. He may not be at all disconcerted but the expression on Vic's face as he enters the room suggests he doesn't see anything humorous about the situation. He follows Jimmy and joins him on the sofa.

Kavanagh nods as he passes in front of him.

'Nice to see you, Vic.'

'Fuck you too.'

'Should I check you for weapons?'

By way of response, Vic pulls something from his jacket pocket and rests it on the arm of the sofa. A 9 mm automatic with fitted suppressor. Kavanagh suspects his hand is not going to stray far from it. Not good. Still . . . better in here where he can see him.

'You were saying,' says Jimmy, bringing the conversation back to where they left off. 'There's something you wanted to explain.'

Kavanagh's mouth is dry all of a sudden. He takes another sip and draws on the mental draft he prepared earlier. Prepared and re-drafted, polishing it until it sounded convincing.

'When we talked in Wareham, you mentioned my appointments with an ophthalmologist,' he says, waving his hand at a moth which seems confused by all the lights in the room. 'How much do you know about the problems I've been having?'

Jimmy picks up the bottle and pours himself another glass.

'Assume I know nothing,' he says, settling back into the sofa and crossing one leg over his knee. Sitting next to him, Vic hasn't moved an inch, eyes still locked on his nemesis.

Kavanagh explains about the recent deterioration in his vision. The *episodes*, as he calls them. He includes in his narrative the fall while running above Durdle Door and the momentary loss of vision. He tells Jimmy about Judith Weimann's take on things and her insistence that he needs to subject himself to a series of tests as soon as possible.

'So what are you doing here then?' asks Jimmy. 'Not that I give a shit, but if it was me, I'd get myself checked out right away instead of chasing ghosts from the past.'

Not now, thinks Kavanagh. If he has his way, they'll certainly be addressing at some stage the cruel hoax which put Anna here in harm's way through no fault of her own and led him further than ever from the person he was actually seeking, but that will have to wait for now. He can't allow himself to be distracted from the point he needs to make.

'I've got more important things to do,' he says. 'Any referrals and operations are going to have to wait.'

He asks how much they know about the injuries he sustained in the bomb blast at Dunloughraine. He'd shared with Maurice what really happened that afternoon and assumes there's been a gradual trickle down over the years because that's the way these things usually work. Jimmy, it turns out, knows some of it but the tiny fragments of shrapnel, too close to the optic nerve for safe removal, seem to come as something of a surprise.

'I've always known roughly where they are,' Kavanagh explains. 'I can't explain how. I just sense them from time to time. I suffer from severe migraines every now and then – have done ever since the blast. The pain is very much localised, like these fragments are reminding me they're there, creeping ever closer to the nerve. I was told by the surgeons right at the outset that there was a significant risk of losing my sight at some stage in the future. I've had years of thinking I might get away with it but these episodes are coming more frequently now and I can't afford to ignore them.'

He pauses, watching the other two to gauge their reaction. Vic is *whatever* – the personal tragedies of other people have never been of interest to him and empathy is not a concept he's ever come close to embracing. Jimmy is listening, soaking it all up. For his own peace of mind, he needs to understand what has brought about Kavanagh's change of heart since their last meeting and if this explanation is going to be passed off as a contributory factor, he will want to subject its authenticity to the tightest scrutiny.

'If the worst comes to the worst, I'm not sure how well I'll be able to adjust when the time comes. I know people lose their sight all the time and manage to adapt and lead productive and happy lives but I'm not sure I can do that. I lead a very simple and solitary life. I run to keep fit. I read for several hours every day. Take those pleasures away from me and you might as well take everything else.'

There's a hiss as the moth hits the light bulb overhead and drifts slowly to the floor like a sycamore seed.

'You want to know what's prompted the change of heart?' he continues. 'Simple – if you take away what makes life special, the thought of dying loses some of its sting. Puts the risk into some sort of perspective. Don't get me wrong – I still have things I want to do in the time I have left and you know that finding Leon Murphy's daughter is right up there. But I want to be able to focus my attention on these things, not feel obliged to look over my shoulder every five seconds. I've sunk a substantial proportion of my life savings into tracking her down and following her out here and it's all for nothing because you've fed me the wrong girl and I've been too eager to bite. All of that's happened because of this . . . *impasse* that's been there for too long. So that's why I've given you the files. That's why I've backed down and given you everything you asked for. You say it's been a millstone around my neck? Let's put it to the test.'

Vic snorts.

'Not now, Vic.' Jimmy's eyes are on Kavanagh – they haven't left him since he started talking.

'Do we really have to sit here and listen to—'

'I said *not now*.'

Vic shakes his head and flicks at the dead moth with his foot. Jimmy leans forward, fingers steepled in front of his mouth.

'I'm sorry to hear about your problems,' he says. 'I don't expect you to believe me but I really am. Have you given any thought as to how it will affect your ability to work?'

Kavanagh frowns.

'Work's the last thing on my mind at the moment. I'm sixty-three so I'll be retired soon. The bookshop is in good hands so it's not going to fall apart if I take a backseat. I've effectively been doing that for a while now.'

'You're talking about Dorset. What about London? What are you going to be able to do there?'

Kavanagh doesn't see it at first. He takes it as a genuine, if confusing, question.

'I don't understand. What's London got to do with anything?'

'Well, I sort of assumed you'd be moving back. It's a helluva commute.'

And now he knows. The quiet smile playing at the corner of Jimmy's mouth is matched by the smirk of the man sitting next to him. And it almost comes as a relief to Kavanagh in a strange way. He's been working hard to keep the tension out of his voice, to act as if this is just a simple business meeting, but it's been there all right. There's something almost liberating about being able to let go. About recognising the endgame for what it is. He notices that Vic's fingers are now resting loosely on top of the gun. If he makes a move – which he is obviously itching to do – Kavanagh won't get near him in time. Not from here.

He decides to play stupid in the hope that he can drag it out long enough for an opportunity, however unlikely, to present itself.

'Who said anything about moving back to London?'

'Well . . . how else is this going to work?'

Kavanagh continues to plug away.

'The agreement was I'd hand over everything I have and you'd leave me alone to live my life as I choose.'

'Not how I remember it,' says Jimmy. 'What I said was handing over the documents would get your friends off the hook. We'd stay away from Wareham and no one there would ever find out what their highly respected bookseller used to do for a living. I never said anything about you staying there.'

'You can't be serious.'

Kavanagh sits further forward on his chair, hoping to cut the distance. Vic is watching him and responds by slipping his index finger through the trigger guard.

'Be reasonable,' says Jimmy, spreading his arms. 'It's like everything else in business. Perception is everything. There are people who think you managed to give us the finger and walk away from us without any sort of repercussions. Not only that but blackmailed us into the bargain. That's what it's always been about as far as I'm concerned. Try looking at it from our point of view for once. How do you think that looks?'

Kavanagh shakes his head.

'Are you seriously trying to tell me it's made that much difference to the way you're perceived by everyone else? You make it sound like it's opened the door for everyone else to pour through. How many people exactly have done what I did and walked away in the last twenty years?'

'None,' admits Jimmy. 'But the problem lies in the question itself. It shouldn't be twenty years. Twenty years is an embarrassment. It should be *how many have ever left and got away with it?* And the answer needs to be *none.*'

'I'm not going back to London,' says Kavanagh, digging in. There's a line here that needs to be made as clear as possible.

'Of course you are,' says Jimmy, as if brushing the fanciful notion aside. 'If it's accommodation you're worried about, forget it. I'm sure we can find a bedsit for you somewhere. As for what work you'll do, we'll have to give a bit of thought to that. To be honest I hadn't expected you to fold quite as quickly as you have done but I'll put my mind to it when we get back. Obviously you can't go back into the same line of work as before. It's not just because you can't cut it anymore. There's also the message that would give to everyone else. Perception again.'

'It's not happening, Jimmy.'

Stand-off.

Jimmy stares at Kavanagh, waiting for him to blink.

Kavanagh stares right back.

Five seconds tick by. Ten.

'Jimmy?' asks Vic.

'OK.'

Vic picks up the gun and fires.

A suppressor – contrary to most people's expectations from film and TV – does not reduce the noise level to a soft *pffft*. It does make an appreciable difference so that from next door it might easily be confused with more innocent everyday activity but in a confined space it's still loud enough. Kavanagh flinches at the noise but forces himself to keep his eyes fixed on Jimmy. If Vic has missed from six feet away, it's for a reason.

'Is that supposed to impress me?' he asks. 'Is this where I fall apart and promise to do whatever you want?'

'Dunno,' says Jimmy. 'How stupid are you?'

'I'm not going back to the Syndicate, Jimmy.'

Jimmy purses his lips. Nods.

Vic fires again. And this time Kavanagh doubles over as his right knee explodes.

The pain is excruciating, literally breathtaking. In the immediate aftermath of the bomb blast at Dunloughraine, when he came to in the recovery ward, his thoughts were a swirling mass of confused, morphine-induced impressions. Of the pain itself he remembers very little. Fear, yes. Confusion, undoubtedly. But the physical pain was controlled, compared to the emotional trauma he had to confront. This, though – this is something else. There's no morphine here. What he's experiencing is a combination of intense burning and a deep, penetrating ache that seems to be burrowing deeper with every passing second.

Instinctively he reaches behind him and grabs the T-shirt he brought in earlier. He presses it against his kneecap and is relieved to note that the blood loss is less severe than might have been expected. He doesn't think an artery has been hit and does his best not to think of the damage that has been done to bone, cartilage, muscle and nerve as the bullet scythed its way through. His first thought is that it's going to be a long time before he runs again. Then the reality of the situation strikes home and he finds himself laughing through gritted teeth at the absurdity of it all – that even with his own death staring him in the face, he should be calculating the damage done to his prospects of getting back to full fitness.

He's vaguely aware of Jimmy's voice in the background,
almost drowned out by a series of guttural, drawn-out groans.
It's a moment or two before he realises they're coming from him.

'I'm so pleased you said no,' Jimmy says, pouring a third glass
of wine. 'I was sort of banking on the fact you'd turn it down. I'll
be totally honest with you now – I don't know what I'd have done
if you'd accepted. I'm not sure we had a plan B, did we, Vic?'

Either Vic has decided it's a rhetorical question or he's so
focused on Kavanagh, and the move he's hoping he'll make, that
he hasn't heard it. His face is a picture of total concentration.

'Does that hurt?' Jimmy asks with just a trace of mock
concern. 'Just wondering, that's all. I'd imagine it must do. You
know, most people would assume Vic was just a lousy shot, hitting your knee from about six feet away, but you know better,
don't you? You know that's precisely where he was aiming. Just
like you know his next one is going to take the other knee out.
What I'm saying is, he could finish you off anytime he wanted
to but that's not how this is going to work. Perception again,
right? When word gets back, and I promise you it will, yours
will be what they call a cautionary tale. They'll know you suffered long and hard before the lights went out ... just in case
anyone else starts getting ideas above his station. You could say
you're unlucky to keep falling foul of our need for clarity. On
the other hand, you could ask yourself whose fault it is you're
on the receiving end in the first place.'

Kavanagh, shirt still pressed tightly against the wounded
knee, says something but it's slurred. Mumbled. Jimmy has to
ask him to repeat it.

'I said,' gasps Kavanagh, forcing himself to sit upright and look his tormentor in the eye, 'this has nothing to do with deterrents.'

Jimmy is amused by this.

'Really? So what's your theory, Einstein?'

Kavanagh takes a deep breath. When the words come out, they do so with a hiss, caused by the occasional sudden intake of breath.

'It's about revenge. You're insecure, Jimmy. Always were. You've been handed a level of responsibility that's way . . . *way* beyond your capabilities. A real leader needs gravitas. Maurice had it. You can't even spell it. Maurice could always see the bigger picture . . . you can never see further than the end of your nose. You live in the here and now – everything's about instant gratification. Always has been. You're not fit for purpose. Never were and everyone knows it. And deep down, you know it too. You're . . . Jesus . . . you're still the kid who pissed his pants when I threw him out of The Grosvenor.'

Jimmy's smile is still in place but it's a pale, sickly imitation of what was there a few moments ago. It looks as if it might shatter any minute.

'Vic?' he says.

Vic raises the gun and Kavanagh's other knee is blown away by the impact. If the first was painful, this is just about unbear-able. Almost immediately the blood starts to pour out and he immediately transfers the shirt to the other leg, trying to staunch the flow. It looks bad, as if maybe an artery has been nicked. If it has, he knows what that will mean.

He can feel himself drifting mentally, as if someone has slapped a cloth over his face and soaked it in chloroform. To counteract the soporific effect of the body's insistence on shut-ting down, he presses harder on the knee and growls.

Somewhere he can hear a phone ping. It's an incoming message. His phone's on the table but it might as well be in the cottage in Wareham because he has no chance of reaching it from here. The only way he's going to see this last message is to ask either Jimmy or Vic to pass it to him and that's not going to happen. He won't give them the satisfaction.

Jimmy is chuntering away in the background. Agitated. That last volley of home truths has got to him, scythed through any remaining semblance of civility. He's muttering now. *Who's pathetic now, eh? Big man on his knees. Who's laughing now?*

Kavanagh makes one last effort to make himself understood.

'You think this is all your own work? Don't flatter yourself. You haven't killed me. Sean did that a long, long time ago. If he wasn't such a useless piece of shit . . .'

'You leave my brother out of this.'

'The only reason the truck was able to get close enough was because Sean was playing silly buggers as usual instead of doing his job. Froze like a total amateur when he realised what was happening. If anyone's killed me, it was your big brother.'

And as he watches an enraged Jimmy take the gun from Vic's hands, he tells himself it doesn't matter now. He doesn't need to see the text. It's his last message and it can say whatever he wants it to say. In his mind, he's reaching for it and he can see the letters arranged on the screen before him more clearly than anything he's seen for weeks. No blur. No fuzzy edges.

Got her.
Thank you.
You're a good man.

Something like that. And even before he hears the next explosion, the screen goes blank.

Jimmy and Vic ransack the place before leaving. If there's anything left here that ties Kavanagh to them, they need to get rid of it. Vic works, grim-faced, still brooding over Jimmy's refusal to take his advice and simply torch the place. They discussed it during the journey here, Vic keen to stock up on accelerants that will take care of the problem in a flash. Jimmy wouldn't budge, wanting to make sure they were well clear of the area and, with a bit of luck, this fucking awful country, before someone stumbled on Kavanagh. They'd tried to come up with a way of removing him from the villa altogether and dumping him somewhere else but the risk of someone looking out of the window at the wrong moment was not one Jimmy was prepared to take. Similarly a fire would bring people running and who could say whether someone might remember the two guys heading for the car park in the opposite direction?

Vic slams the lid on the laptop and yanks it off the desk, leaving the plug still jammed in the wall socket. Jimmy picks up Kavanagh's phone and smashes it against the table, then thinks better of it and slips it into his pocket. They work their way methodically through the villa, grabbing anything that looks vaguely like a document and dropping it into a suitcase they've found in Kavanagh's bedroom. They're not remotely concerned about the possibility of being interrupted. There's been no loud disturbance to speak of – the suppressor having done its job effectively – and there's no sign of activity or interest from any of the neighbouring villas.

When they've completed the search, they leave by the back door and use an access road to avoid being seen leaving the area. It's not too late for people to be returning from the clubhouse or Cristi's but the sky is black as sin and there's no shortage of last-minute detours they can make if they hear someone coming. Their walk back to the car park is unhurried, uneventful. As soon as they reach it, Vic zaps the car from some distance away and already they can hear the muffled sound of a phone ringing.

'Did you leave the burner in the car?' asks Jimmy.

Vic shrugs his shoulders. Throws the suitcase into the boot.

Jimmy ducks into the back seat and Vic takes the phone out from under the dashboard. It's fallen silent now so he checks it.

'Oscar,' he announces with a resigned shake of the head. He doesn't have a lot of time for the so-called whizz kids in the techie brigade.

Jimmy clicks his fingers and the phone is passed back to him. The screen tells him he has four missed calls and four voicemail messages.

He listens to the first, a short non-specific call, asking him to ring back ASAP. There's an urgency about it that doesn't bode well. The second message confirms this.

'Mr Hayes – we've picked up on a live feed that was activated earlier this evening. I really need to speak with you.'

By the time he makes the third call, Oscar's tone is bordering on the desperate.

'Mr Hayes – I'm worried you're being set up. Please call me ASAP.'

He doesn't need to listen to the other. Knows what it will say. *Shit.*

His mind shuts down for a moment. Time stands still. Banshees are screaming in his head. Kavanagh promised him a shitstorm but he never thought for one moment it would come to this. Not in a million years. Vic hasn't heard the message but can tell something has gone wrong and is asking, 'What is it? What's happened?' and Jimmy wonders how many different ways there are to ask the same fucking question. He needs to think and Vic needs to *SHUT THE FUCK UP*.

He tells him to drive – get the hell out of Praia D'El Rey. All he can think right now is if they can put some distance between themselves and here, maybe make it down to Albufeira, this can still be salvaged. Felipe will rustle up any number of people who will swear he and Vic were there with them all evening. A lot will depend on the sound and picture quality of the live feed, but if there's the slightest room for ambiguity, the legal boys will drive a bus through any charges levelled against them. Let them earn their money for once – God knows, they charge him enough. There might be a way out of this yet, he tells himself.

And that's when he first hears the sirens in the distance and sees flashing lights coming toward them, still half a mile away as they drive past Cristi's on the long, straight road leading out of Praia D'El Rey. He yells at Vic to stop the car and within seconds he's out, running across the scrubland, heading for the distant woods. No idea what lies beyond them. No long- or even short-term plan now. Just escape. Anywhere. Escape and regroup. *Get to Albufeira.* That's all that matters.

He's already fallen twice, tripping in the dark over the rough, uneven ground, when he hears the first of the vehicles skid across the gravel at the side of the road and come to a halt. There are shouts as car doors are flung open and in the headlights he can see Vic, standing with his hands on the bonnet of the car. Jimmy has this wild moment of hope that maybe he can use Vic as a distraction . . . as long as they were too far away to see him slip out of the car and head out across the unlit scrubland, he still has a chance. Vic will find a way to stall them, throw them off the scent. He may be well and truly fucked but he's not the sort to crumble at the first hint of a crisis. He's old school. The Syndicate runs through his veins. No way will he give him up. No way. And if there's any wriggle room at all with the images that came through from the live feed, there may just be a way for him to get clear of this mess despite everything. But he can't be found here. That's the one non-negotiable in all this. It's Albufeira or he's fucked.

Then he hears the dogs.

And knows they're coming in his direction.

Responding less to logic than some desperate survival instinct, he sprints through the all-enveloping darkness, refusing to accept the laws of nature . . . as if convinced that somewhere out there in this desolate scrubland, maybe in the distant woods, there's a refuge waiting for him, urging him on for one final effort. But the treacherous, uneven ground brings him to his knees yet again . . . and as the barking comes closer and closer he hauls himself to his feet one final time, chest heaving.

Turns to face his pursuers.

And they're all around him before he knows it.

He thinks, on balance, he may have misjudged this.

Epilogue

6th April 2019
Tyneham, Dorset

She slides into a pew, leans forward with hands clasped in her lap and blocks out the handful of people dotted around the building. They're scrutinising the exhibit boards, probably too engrossed to wonder why a young woman might want to offer up a prayer in a church that was deconsecrated long before she was born. Not that it's a prayer anyway, she corrects herself. More a moment of reflection. An attempt at making a connection somehow with a shadow.

She's here in Tyneham in search of Jon Kavanagh, determined to come away with at least some understanding as to who this man was and what it is that connects the two of them. She left Edgbaston at five this morning to allow herself as much time as possible to question neighbours, friends, work colleagues . . . anyone who might be able to provide some substance to fill the blurred outline she has of him at the moment. She's come away with next to nothing so far. There's just one more meeting lined up – if that doesn't shed more light on things, this is going to feel like a wasted journey. She's not sure what other avenues are open to her.

The only person able to talk with any semblance of authority about him so far has been Conor, the new owner of Zelda's Bookshop. He was her first port of call this morning and he was happy to sit and talk to her for an hour or so while he took an early lunch break. He worked with Kavanagh for years and even he had to admit there was little he could tell her.

'Jon was the most fiercely private person I've ever met,' he told her. 'I know next to nothing about his life before he came to Wareham. I don't know if he would have been prepared to open up if I'd pushed him but somehow I doubt it. I think part of the reason we were able to work together so effectively for so long was because he trusted me to know where the line was drawn and respect it.'

According to Conor, the only time their conversation ever strayed beyond the mundane and transactional was when it came to books. That was their shared passion, the one context in which Kavanagh was happy to lower the drawbridge. Even then his preference had been to keep his cards close to his chest. It must have five years before he let slip the reason for the name of the shop, Zelda having been the wife of F. Scott Fitzgerald. Only in the world of literature, it seemed, had he made room for a touch of sentimentality.

Conor was unable to shed any light on why she will be inheriting Kavanagh's cottage once the solicitors stop dragging their heels and probate is cleared. Similarly he knows nothing about the box that was delivered to her soon after she'd been traced and her identity confirmed. There has to be a story attached to Barney the dinosaur. She vaguely remembers watching him on children's TV, even though she can't have been much more than a toddler back then and is pretty sure she used to have a stuffed toy of her own at one time. Her memories of specifics during those early years however are shrouded in mists and quite where Jon Kavanagh comes into all this is a mystery.

It was Conor who suggested Tyneham as an appropriate place for the two of them to meet.

'I think Jon felt more at peace there than anywhere else,' he said. 'He used to go there most weekends. He enjoyed watching the cars arrive and the visitors come and go, liked the fact that Tyneham is being kept alive somehow. And there's an atmosphere about the place – it's hard to put it into words. If you want to know Jon Kavanagh, that's as good a place as any to start looking.'

And he was right. There *is* something about this village. She was struck by it the moment she got here, ridiculously ahead of schedule, and started her tour of the ruins – houses, lives, dreams. An air of desolation hangs over the place, a deep, deep sadness that swirls like wisps of fog, in and out of the shattered buildings. She had no trouble finding the bench Conor had referred to and sat there for a while, trying to slip into Kavanagh's shoes and understand what it was he was searching for. At one point her phone had started chirping, the Pharrell Williams ringtone incongruously loud and chipper in such a sombre setting as this. Instinctively she'd switched it off without even looking to see who was calling. The modern world had no business intruding here.

She didn't enter the church with any intention other than to read more about the lives of the villagers who lost everything, but the moment she saw the pews she felt drawn to them. She's not a religious person but there has always been something about stained glass windows and a cool, dark interior that awakens in her an instinct to sit and reflect. To take time out. She knew as soon as she entered the building that the exhibition was going to be of secondary importance.

Now, still leaning forward in the pew, her moment of reflection is disturbed briefly by a small girl who walks in front of her, holding a teddy bear in one hand. She stands there with one finger in her mouth and waves the bear in front of Jess's face. Her mortified mother hurries over and ushers her away, rolling her eyes as she mouths the word *sorry*. Jess smiles and closes her eyes again . . . and this time she does offer up a prayer. For Jon Kavanagh, whoever he might have been. Man of mystery and shadows. A man who – whether she and Steve sell the cottage or place it with a letting agency – will have made a material difference to the quality of their lives. She would have welcomed the opportunity to thank him in person but this will have to do instead.

God bless.

She feels something brush past her, the lightest of featherlike touches, and assumes someone has moved into the pew behind her. She sneaks a look over her shoulder, then stands and turns around, surprised to find no one there. At the same moment a burst of sunlight pours through the stained-glass windows like liquid honey and picks out a figure in the doorway. The woman pauses briefly before making her way hesitantly towards her. There's a smile, a curious tilt of the head, then an arm reaches out towards her and pulls her into an affectionate embrace.

'Hi,' says Anna, slipping into the pew next to her. 'I'm sorry I'm a bit late. I'm guessing you must be Jessica.'

Acknowledgements

The Syndicate is set in several locations and has taken me to a number of places I would definitely recommend to readers. The three I'd like to highlight in particular are:

- Praia D'El Rey, Portugal. It really does exist, although I've played fast and loose with a few details. There is, for instance, no *Cristi's* on the road leading out of the resort, and I feel obliged to make it quite clear that I have no reason to suspect any links to criminal organisations in London. It is a fantastic place to stay, irrespective of whether or not you enjoy a round of golf, and the beach and sea are scenic beyond belief.
- Durdle Door, Dorset. This is such a popular area of outstanding natural beauty that many will probably already have discovered it for themselves. It was here that I first came up with the character of Jon Kavanagh, and I was quick to seize an excuse to go back there and make sure the geographical details were as I'd remembered them. Fantastic clifftop walks ... if you have the energy to get up there!
- Tyneham Village. This place had as profound an effect on me as it did on Kavanagh and simply wouldn't let go. If you've already visited it, I suspect you know what I mean. It's only a short drive from Lulworth Cove, Durdle Door and Wareham, so it's possible to take in all three on a day trip.

Unlike its two immediate predecessors, *The Syndicate* has been three years in the making and has undergone a number of makeovers in that time. A lot of people have played their part in bringing it to publication, and it feels invidious somehow to single out some at the expense of others. With that in mind, please forgive me for resorting to my favourite ploy of thanking everyone who has contributed, in however minor a capacity. Your support is always appreciated.

Having said that, I'd like to offer a few special thanks to:

- My initial reading team of Sue, Carrie, Gemma and Elaine for the cheerleading and constant encouragement.
- Katherine Sunderland and Ellie Piddington for workshopping sessions of the highest calibre. I'm sure my editors at Bonnier will be eternally grateful to you for sharing the load.
- Mike Jack for checking the authenticity of Maurice's voice and accent.
- Chris Whitaker and Caroline Carver for an ever available shoulder to cry on whenever it was needed.
- Lisa Moylett and Zoe Apostolides at CMM for stepping in at such short notice and guiding me through the final stages with such skill and sympathy. I am so fortunate to have found you guys.
- All at Bonnier Zaffre, but especially Katherine, Jennie and Ciara for believing in the project and constantly challenging lazy assumptions.
- Elaine. As ever.